## THE PHOTON TORPEDO STRUCK THE KLINGON FLAGSHIP WITH DAZZLING, WHITE-HOT FORCE.

"We have fired on the chancellor's ship," Spock stated heavily.

Kirk wheeled, his expression stunned. "Uhura, monitor! Chekov, find out what's going on down in Weapons!"

A second torpedo flared in the bottom corner of the main viewscreen.

"*Who's doing that?*" Kirk cried as it hurtled at the battle cruiser.

"The Klingon ship's hull has been breached," Spock reported. "They have lost gravity and are slowly losing life support. Damage to the vessel is severe." He straightened and faced his captain. "Jim, they never even raised their shields."

# Look for STAR TREK Fiction from Pocket Books

## Star Trek: The Original Series

## Star Trek: The Next Generation

Most Pocket Books are available at special quantity discounts for bulk purchases for sales promotions, premiums or fund raising. Special books or book excerpts can also be created to fit specific needs.

For details write the office of the Vice President of Special Markets, Pocket Books, 1230 Avenue of the Americas, New York, New York 10020.

# STAR TREK VI

## THE UNDISCOVERED COUNTRY

### A NOVEL BY J.M. DILLARD
### SCREENPLAY BY
### NICHOLAS MEYER & DENNY MARTIN FLINN
### STORY BY LEONARD NIMOY AND
### NICHOLAS MEYER & DENNY MARTIN FLINN

**POCKET BOOKS**

New York   London   Toronto   Sydney   Tokyo   Singapore

This book is a work of fiction. Names, characters, places and incidents are either products of the author's imagination or are used fictitiously. Any resemblance to actual events or locales or persons, living or dead, is entirely coincidental.

An *Original* Publication of POCKET BOOKS

POCKET BOOKS, a division of Simon & Schuster Inc.
1230 Avenue of the Americas, New York, NY 10020

Copyright © 1992 by Paramount Pictures. All Rights Reserved.

STAR TREK is a Registered Trademark of
Paramount Pictures.

This book is published by Pocket Books, a division of
Simon & Schuster Inc., under exclusive license from
Paramount Pictures.

All rights reserved, including the right to reproduce
this book or portions thereof in any form whatsoever.
For information address Pocket Books, 1230 Avenue
of the Americas, New York, NY 10020

ISBN: 0-671-75883-7

First Pocket Books printing January 1992

10  9  8  7  6  5  4  3  2  1

POCKET and colophon are registered trademarks of
Simon & Schuster Inc.

Printed in the U.S.A.

To "Star Trek" fans everywhere,
who keep the dream alive

*Very special thanks to:*

Ralph Winter
Denny Martin Flinn
The ETs: Dave and Kevin
Mike Okuda
Michael Kochman
My BC, George

But that the dread of something after death,
The undiscovered country from whose bourn
No traveler returns, puzzles the will,
And makes us rather bear those ills we have
Than fly to others that we know not of?
Thus conscience does make cowards of us all;
And thus the native hue of resolution
Is sicklied o'er with the pale cast of thought,
And enterprises of great pith and moment
With this regard their currents turn awry,
And lose the name of action.

*Hamlet*, Act III, Scene 1

# THE UNDISCOVERED COUNTRY

# Prologue

"CAPTAIN KIRK?" The slight, anxious woman waiting at the door to Carol Marcus's hospital room did not smile. "I'm Kwan-mei Suarez, the mathematician on the Themis project."

Kirk stepped forward and clasped both her hands. Kwan-mei's grip was firm, her tone calm, but there was faint agony in her eyes. The sight steadied Kirk, allowed him to focus on pain other than his own.

The past twenty-four hours—hearing the news about Carol, enduring the eternity-long shuttle ride to Starbase Twenty-three—had been a hellish exercise in control. He had not allowed himself to think, to indulge his imagination in what life would be like if Carol died before he arrived.

He'd tried not to think that he had been on

Earth, on shore leave, the first leave in six years that they had not spent together. Driven as always, she'd insisted on going to Themis to oversee setup of the research facility there. Jim had protested mildly, but Carol had insisted. It was safe, for gods' sake— it was light-years from Kudao and the Klingon Neutral Zone, and besides, it was near a well-protected starbase. Lightning wouldn't strike twice.

He had made noises about going, as if his mere presence might protect her, but it hadn't made sense; she would have been terrifically busy, and he would have spent his entire leave shuttling to and from. Besides, in a few months he'd be returning permanently to her.

Yet he could not shake the vague superstition that, because he had broken the pattern, he was somehow responsible.

Jim touched Kwan-mei's arm briefly, wanting to give comfort, needing it himself. "It's Jim, please. Carol spoke of you. I know you're good friends."

"I don't mean to intrude," Kwan-mei said. She glanced uncertainly at the door. Jim got the impression she was normally reserved, a person who took a long time to get to know—but circumstances were forcing her to get to know Jim very quickly. "You probably want to see her alone," she said, "but I was there when it happened. I'll be outside if you have any questions, if you want to know—"

"Is she awake?"

Kwan-mei shook her head, swinging straight, chin-length hair, black streaked with auburn.

2

"She's still in a coma. Did they tell you about her condition? Do you know—"

"Unless there's been a change in the past twenty-four hours, I know." Jim paused and, when she offered nothing further, said, "I'll be back out in just a moment." He meant to say it easily, but it came out tightly coiled.

She nodded as if understanding.

The tiny room was dimly lit, but the window overlooked the starbase's sprawling botanical garden, bright with artificial sunlight. Carol lay on the bed, lips parted, chest rising and falling in time with the respirator. As he approached, in profile she appeared unreally beautiful and bloodless, a polished ivory carving, golden hair spread on the pillow; then, as he bent to kiss her, he saw the scars mottling the left side of her face—covered with bright pink skin synthetic, already healing in little more than a day.

She was on the respirator because of damage to the brain stem. The doctors were trying injections of cloned cells in conjunction with drugs to stimulate the area to repair itself, but they had warned Jim that it would be days before they would know whether Carol would respond to the treatment.

Jim sat in the chair beside the bed and took her hand; her touch was cool and dry. He had steeled himself for a far more horrifying sight; during the sleepless hours aboard the shuttle, he had pictured Carol mutilated almost beyond recognition.

It was harder this way. Jim smoothed the hair

away from the unmarred skin on her forehead, half believing his touch might wake her, as it always had.

Over the years he had spent every available moment of leave with her. It had become clear that when he returned from his last mission, they would be together. She had her research, which was expanding rapidly; he had deep-space experience. When he retired, Carol said, Marcuslabs could use his help, his skills, his diplomacy. He had begun to take comfort in the notion that, when the *Enterprise* was no longer his, Carol would be waiting.

They had quit blaming each other for being so much alike, so fiercely independent; they had quit blaming each other for a number of things, including the loss of their son.

David's death should have driven them further apart; instead, it had brought them together.

A decade earlier Jim Kirk had stood in the corridor outside Carol Marcus's town house in suburban Virginia and allowed himself only an instant's hesitation before pressing the buzzer.

Almost a year had passed since David's death. During that year Jim had tried repeatedly to contact Carol. He had wanted to be the first to tell her, but circumstance made that impossible. Now he simply wanted to speak to her about it, to tell what he knew, to offer what comfort he could.

And to understand the reason for her silence. He could only interpret it as an accusation. And he had felt indirectly responsible for his son's death, though the months had brought some small amount of perspective and a lessening of guilt.

Carol had not answered the signal those times he had attempted to contact her when the *Enterprise* was within communication range of Earth. Jim was determined to speak to her, even if it meant waiting until he was on leave and could track her down in person.

He had not decided what he would do if she refused to answer her door.

The viewscreen beside the buzzer lit up, indicating that Kirk was being scrutinized by the town house's tenant.

Carol's face flickered on the screen, then vanished before he could judge her expression. No word of greeting . . . yet she had shown him her face. Jim did not know whether this was a bad or good sign.

The door swung open. He drew in a breath and stepped inside. A vacant foyer led to a generous living room where Carol stood beside stacks of boxes with antigrav handles. Most of the furniture had been pushed to one side, against bare walls. She seemed wan, tired, as stripped and empty as the room. Jim felt frightened for her.

"Come in," she said. The invitation was not warm but weary, the surrender of a defeated opponent. "I suppose we should get this over with. You know, if you'd come a day later, you would have missed me."

Jim tried to smile. "I'm in luck."

"I don't think so. Sit." She waved him toward the

only chair that wasn't cluttered with boxes or debris.

Jim shook his head. "I'll stand. But you look as if you could use a seat."

"Suit yourself." She sagged, exhausted, into the chair.

Jim stood, awkward. He wanted to touch her—embrace her, console her—but this was not the Carol he had loved as a young man, the Carol Marcus he had known later as friend and mother of his son during the Genesis mission. This woman was older, thinner, shrouded in anger and grief. He kept his distance.

"I tried to contact you after David died," Jim said.

She looked beyond him at the stark white walls. "When I first got the news, I stayed on Delta for a while. By the time I returned to Earth, you had galloped off on another mission."

"But later I left messages—"

"I got them. I couldn't deal with them at the time. I'm not sure I can now, even after all this time."

Jim just looked at her. He'd spent that time planning all he wanted to tell her; now his carefully chosen words deserted him.

"Carol," he began, his voice barely above a whisper. "When David was killed, I wanted to be the one to tell you."

"Why?" Flat, angry. An accusation.

"Because he was *our* son. And because I know how he died—"

"Klingons killed him. That's enough, isn't it?"

Jim didn't answer.

"You know, you sound so concerned about me. But if you really are, then why hasn't it occurred to you that I obviously don't care to see you again? What do you want from me after all this time, Jim? Forgiveness? Absolution?"

"That's not what I came here for."

"Then tell me what you want."

"I wanted to tell you how David died," Jim said, fighting to keep his own anger and grief from showing in his voice. "I thought it might comfort you. I wanted to be sure, when I didn't hear from you in all this time, that you were all right."

"All right?" Carol jerked to her feet and gave a short laugh, humorless and bitter. "David's gone, and you want me to tell you everything's just swell. You come back into my life, and suddenly Genesis is destroyed and my four dearest friends are killed, murdered by a madman seeking revenge on you. Maybe Khan wasn't your fault. But then I lost David, and something in me broke. . . .

"Maybe it's not fair to blame you, but I was always afraid I'd lose him if he found out you were his father. And I was right. Except that I thought I'd lose him to a starship, the way I did you. I never thought I'd lose him the way I did, that he would die such a horrible death—"

"He died protecting someone else," Jim said quickly. "Lieutenant Saavik. She told me he died bravely, trying to save her life. It happened very quickly."

Carol's face crumpled; she sank back into the chair and seemed to shrink, to be swallowed up by it. Jim went over to her and put a hand on her arm. She did not respond, but she did not draw away.

"You'd think," she managed at last in a low voice, "that with time I'd get over David's death, that I could accept the way it happened, that I'd realize you weren't to blame. But I can't help you resolve whatever guilt or pain you still feel over David's death. Hell, I can't even resolve my own." Her voice dropped to a whisper. "I'm so *angry*. . . . I want to hurt someone—the Klingon who killed David, but he's not here, so I find the nearest substitute." She began to cry. "They're animals; they have no respect for life. They murdered my son for the sheer sport of it, without a second's thought—"

Jim gathered her into his arms; she held him fiercely and wept.

"I'm angry, too," Jim murmured. He patted her back, slowly, as one would comfort a child.

"Why?" Carol moaned against his shoulder. "Why would they kill David? Why?"

He stayed with Carol for an hour, then let Kwan-mei Suarez lead him to a quiet alcove where they sat down.

"You were there?" Jim asked. Suarez bore no visible signs of injury, except for a very slight irregular line at her neck where the darker skin synthetic had almost healed.

"I was there," she said, in a voice dulled by guilt.

8

"Hardly a scratch on me, except for a few cuts and bruises. I wasn't even knocked out—luckily for the others, I suppose; I was able to radio for help in time to save Carol. Unbelievable, isn't it? The walls collapse on us, and I'm a little shaken, that's all. Jackson—Jackson Dahl, our biologist"—the way she said the name familiarly, then added the gloss let Kirk know the two were lovers—"broke his spine, but he'll be all right. Carol was hurt worst. And Sohlar was killed."

"Sohlar?" Jim asked, trying to remember whether Carol had mentioned a Vulcan on the project.

Kwan-mei tried to smile and couldn't. Her eyes, beautiful beneath a shining film of tears, were brown flecked with forest green. "Maybe you can understand how we feel about losing him. Carol said your first officer is a Vulcan. Sohlar was an engineer with incredible talent. No sense of humor whatsoever—at least, he pretended not to have one—but we were all very fond of him." Her expression hardened. "His leg was crushed. It severed the artery in his thigh. He bled to death while I was talking to him. He knew it, of course, and was so matter-of-fact, so calm, about it . . . He kept trying to comfort *me. . . .*" Her voice trailed off.

After a moment Jim asked, "Did you see anything during the attack? Or was there just the explosion?"

"When they first fired on us, we thought it was an earthquake. We knew about Kudao, of course, but to think that they would dare attempt an attack so far inside Federation space just seemed so insane . . ." She shook her head. "I ran to the window to see what was happening. Before the building went down, I could see the phaserfire coming right out of the sky."

"Did you get a good look at the ships?"

"I couldn't see them. As I said, the phaserfire came out of nowhere."

"The vessels were outside the atmosphere, then."

"No." Firm shake of the head. "It was so strange; Sohlar saw it with me and remarked on it. We could see the phaserfire very clearly. It seemed to originate *below* the clouds, as if the ship were simply invisible, as if the fire came out of nowhere."

Jim nodded sympathetically while believing none of it. What Kwan-mei was suggesting was entirely impossible; the Klingons did not possess a ship capable of firing while cloaked—and for that matter, neither did the Federation or the Romulans. After what she had been through, Jim could hardly fault her for an unreliable memory of the event.

"Captain Kirk?"

He turned to see a uniformed Starfleet medic standing over them. "There's an Admiral Cartwright trying to track you down, sir," she said. "If you'll follow me . . ."

She left him in a vacant doctor's office, where Cartwright's dark-skinned features waited on the comm screen.

"Jim," Cartwright said, catching sight of Kirk on

his side of the channel. "I heard about Carol Marcus. I'm sorry. How is she?"

"Unchanged," Jim said expressionlessly. "They won't know for several days."

"I'm sorry," Cartwright repeated, and from the change in his tone Jim knew he wasn't speaking this time of Carol. "We need you back at headquarters. I wouldn't ask for you at a time like this, Jim, but Rear Admiral Smillie himself gave the order. Something's up, something very big."

"The Klingons," Kirk said. "First Kudao, now Themis. This has to do with them, doesn't it?"

"Still classified, Jim. I don't know myself. But between you and me, I wouldn't be surprised."

*Are they insane? What are they trying to do?* Jim almost asked, echoing Kwan-mei, but that would have been pointless. The message from the Klingons was all too clear.

Three weeks before, the Klingons had orchestrated a bloody massacre of human settlers on Kudao, located well inside Federation space. The outcry had been massive, especially since a visiting news correspondent had managed to escape with pictures of grisly torture scenes that were soon splashed all over the Federation media. Kudao's and Earth's governments were quick to claim that the depredation was directly linked to the Organians' recent disappearance, that the Klingons clearly wished to provoke a war.

The Empire denied the charge, claiming that the Kudao massacre was carried out by renegades, pirates, not sanctioned by the government. Not *formally* sanctioned, Kirk believed; but like most in Starfleet, he did not doubt the Empire's surreptitious involvement. He had seen the grisly pictures of human victims and their Klingon tormentors and had found himself superimposing on them the face of Kruge, the Klingon commander who had given the order to kill David.

It had become difficult not to hate.

*You Klingon bastard, you killed my son. . . .*

He knew that Carol had seen the same pictures, experienced the same renewal of grief, though they pointedly avoided the subject in their communications.

On the screen, Cartwright sighed. "Look, we've got a shuttle for you, leaving in the next hour. They'll find you at the hospital. I'm sorry. If there's anything I can do . . ."

Jim rose. "No. Nothing."

The admiral nodded. The screen faded to black.

Kwan-mei Suarez was still waiting for him in the little alcove. Before Kirk could take his seat, she asked, "You have to leave, don't you?"

Jim nodded, fighting guilt. "I don't want to. It's an emergency."

"At Starfleet Headquarters." A statement, not a question. Kwan-mei folded her small hands and looked beyond Jim, at the wall. "I know. There's going to be a war, isn't there?"

Kirk almost did not reply, and then he answered truthfully: "I don't know."

"Why?" Kwan-mei whispered, her face suddenly

twisted with anger. "Why do the Klingons want to kill us all? Why do they want war?"

Jim looked away.

She recovered herself, smiled apologetically, touched his hand. "If Carol wakes up while you're gone, I'll tell her you were here."

# Chapter One

ABOARD THE USS *Excelsior,* Captain Hikaru Sulu lifted his teacup from the console arm of the command chair and took a leisurely sip as he surveyed the bridge. Nearby, his science officer, Lieutenant Commander Valtane, absently smoothed his dark mustache with thumb and forefinger as he studied the report that had just come up from the Science Department.

Sulu had not seen the report, but he suspected it said that *Excelsior*'s three-year mission in the Reydovan sector was complete. Sulu allowed himself to feel a measure of pride in his ship and his crew—both had performed admirably over the past three years—and to remember that there had been a time, more than a decade past, when he had despaired of ever having this ship, this crew to command.

Yet Sulu did not believe in regrets. He had none about helping Kirk and the *Enterprise* bridge crew rescue Spock from Genesis, although it meant that *Excelsior* was given instead to Styles, while Sulu accepted a temporary reduction in rank in order to serve under Kirk. More than a year had passed before Styles received a sideways promotion to Starfleet Headquarters and Sulu was given the assignment promised him almost two years before.

The captain smiled faintly as he remembered the ribbing Scott had given him about *Excelsior*. "A bucket of bolts," the engineer had called her. *Excelsior* had long since proved herself to be far more than that. He would have liked to give Scotty a tour of her now.

Valtane harrumphed softly to himself; the rate of mustache-stroking increased. Sulu's smile widened for only an instant, then disappeared before Valtane saw it. Sulu had originally requested a Vulcan science officer, but none had been available at the time. He was glad now to have Masoud Valtane, a Rigellian native descended from Earth stock—and most unabashedly human. Valtane fit the stereotype of the absentminded research scientist perfectly, though he was absentminded only in terms of his social interaction with the crew, never in terms of his duties: indeed, his concentration on his research was so intense that he had once reported to sickbay with a broken nose. When asked how the injury occurred, the science officer sheepishly reported that he had run into a bulkhead while reading a report.

And Valtane had no sense of humor whatsoever, so far as Sulu could tell. He took comments as literally as a Vulcan, which reminded his captain fondly on more than one occasion of another science officer.

The *Excelsior* and her crew had spent the last three years charting the Reydovan sector, which was relatively lifeless and of little interest to anyone except xenogeologists such as Valtane. Other than the unusual composition of many of the planets' atmospheres, there was little of note about the Reydovan sector—except for the fact that some areas of it bordered Klingon space.

Under normal conditions that fact would have prompted nothing more than an increase in alertness. But relations between the Klingon Empire and the Federation were far from normal. In light of the Kudao massacre and the Organians' disappearance, Sulu ordered yellow alert each time *Excelsior* skirted the neutral area separating Klingon and Federation space. Both events had occurred well after *Excelsior*'s assignment to the sector. Privately, Sulu felt that had a ship less well defended than *Excelsior* been assigned, the mission would have been scrubbed.

For the past several weeks, since the ship had entered Beta quadrant, nearest the Klingon border, the tension level on board had escalated. Federation-Klingon relations had deteriorated to the level of twenty years before, when Sulu had served as a lieutenant aboard the *Enterprise,* called

17

to protect a planet called Organia. War had seemed inevitable then.

It was beginning to look inevitable now. One more attack should do it. And without the Organians, Sulu wondered, what deus ex machina would stop it from happening this time?

*Excelsior,* at least, had been spared a confrontation with the Klingons thus far. And it seemed none would occur. Over the last duty shift, the crew had begun to relax. The sense of relief on the bridge was palpable; in many respects it had been an easy mission, but it had also been one of sustained tension, without incident or action to break the unrelenting monotony—in other words, nerve-rackingly dull.

Three years without incident. Without adventure. They had been lucky, Sulu argued to himself, but he could not avoid the comparison to his life on the *Enterprise,* could not help but wonder whether this particular mission aboard *Excelsior* would make any difference in the universal scheme.

He had almost begun to hope that something would happen. Just to break the tension on the bridge, of course.

Behind him, Valtane sighed wistfully; Sulu repressed a small smile. He had come to know the science officer well, and though they were not friends, they respected each other. The entire crew, Sulu included, was glad to see the mission end—all except Valtane. He had seemed blithely ignorant of the Klingon threat, genuinely excited by the data collected in Reydovan. The ship had been too far from any starbase or habitable planet for genuine shore leave; Sulu doubted Valtane noticed. Sulu had always thought it was because Spock was Vulcan that he never required shore leave; now he wondered if it didn't have more to do with the position of science officer.

Valtane moved to the side of the conn and proffered the captain his datapad. Sulu took it and glanced at the contents. His guess was confirmed. Readouts indicated they had done a thorough scan of the sector, had missed no atmosphere-clad planets. *Excelsior*'s state-of-the-art scanners had provided an amazingly detailed analysis while operating from a far greater distance than did their standard starship counterparts.

Pleased with the performance of his ship and crew, Sulu glanced up at Valtane. "According to this, we've completed our exploration of the entire sector."

Valtane nodded, the wistfulness now hidden, his eyes reflecting only the same pride Sulu felt. "Fifty-four planets—and their gaseous atmospheric anomalies. Our sensing and analytic equipment worked very well."

"Time we were heading home," Sulu began. "Three years is—"

He stopped, distracted by a faint high-pitched clatter. Valtane heard it, too, and frowned.

Sulu looked down to see the teacup trembling in its saucer a split second before he became aware that the entire ship was vibrating. He glanced up at Valtane, who hurried to his station.

The vibration increased to teeth-chattering intensity as the ship tried to shake herself apart. The teacup shattered; scalding liquid splashed onto the console, onto Sulu's arm.

Valtane shouted from the science console over the growing rumble. "I have an energy wave from two-four-zero degrees mark six port—"

"Visual!" Sulu ordered.

The bridge viewscreen flared brightly as an enormous shock front approached, carrying with it roiling superheated gases and flaming chunks of debris.

"My God," Sulu breathed. Then, louder: *"Shields."* The bridge lights flickered, then pulsed blood-red as ship's sensors detected the danger.

*Excelsior* reeled and lurched to starboard. Sulu braced himself in his chair and watched the riotous ballet, a tumble of limbs in crimson shadow, sail by as Valtane and others reached vainly for support and fell.

The ship slowly rolled back to center and righted herself. Sulu straightened and extended a hand to his science officer while he scanned the bridge. No serious injuries, although Janice Rand sat at the comm board gingerly touching her nose as if to make sure it remained in its proper place. The other personnel were already struggling to their feet amid the chatter of damage reports and the Klaxon's insistent whine.

"What the hell is going on?"

Sulu had barely spoken when the ship pitched again, buffeted by the wave.

One arm gripping the navigation console, the Halkan, Lojur, called, "Captain, helm is not responding."

"Starboard thrusters. Turn her into the wave!"

"Captain Sulu!" A faint voice emanated from the comm grid on the arm of his chair. Sulu could hear the hiss of cracked coolant seals in the background. "Engine room. What's going on up—"

The channel sputtered and failed as *Excelsior* heaved. Clutching the arms of his chair, Sulu cried, "Quarter impulse power!"

The strategy worked. The ship bucked one final time, then righted herself.

The Klaxon ceased; the scarlet glow faded, replaced by normal lighting. For one instant the bridge fell resoundingly still. Not daring to draw breath, Sulu waited with his crew.

The ship remained stable. Abruptly, comm chatter resumed.

"Damage report," Sulu said, finding it odd to speak in a normal tone.

"Seem to be in one piece, Captain," Rand reported behind him from Communications. "We're checking all systems."

Sulu turned to Valtane, who was already back on his feet and peering down at his console. "Don't tell me that was any asteroid shower."

"Negative." Valtane's tone carried a question. "The subspace shock wave originated at bearing three-two-three, mark seven-five, the location of"

—he turned to face his captain, dark brows lifted in puzzlement—"Praxis. A Klingon moon. Barren of indigenous life-forms, but—"

"Essential as a resource," Sulu finished. "Praxis is their key energy-production facility." He paused, remembering his desire for something, anything, to happen to ease the monotony. What was that Old Earth saying? Be careful what you wish for . . .

He turned to Rand. "Send to Klingon High Command: 'This is *Excelsior,* a Federation starship traveling through Beta quadrant of the Reydovan sector. We have monitored a large explosion in your sector. *Do you require assistance?'*"

Rand did her best to remain deadpan as she replied, "Aye, sir."

He swiveled to find Valtane looking at him with an expression of mild surprise. "Mr. Valtane, any more data?"

The science officer leaned over his station and studied the readout. "I have confirmed the location, sir, but . . ." His voice trailed off as he blinked, then frowned at the screen.

"What is it?" Sulu demanded.

Valtane straightened and faced his captain. "I cannot confirm the existence of Praxis."

Sulu trusted his science officer completely. Nevertheless, he rose, strode over to Valtane's station, and looked at the readout.

"My scanners are focused on the Amrita solar system, on the correct coordinates," Valtane stated behind the captain's right shoulder. Sulu stared for

22

an instant at the display, then checked the coordinates himself. Valtane was, as always, correct.

Sulu stared into empty space.

"Magnify," he ordered. Valtane complied. The image wavered, then was enlarged to reveal a chunk of dead rock, no longer a sphere. Sulu doubted a quarter of the moon's original mass remained.

"Praxis?" he asked in disbelief, though he knew the answer.

"What's left of it." Valtane's voice was hushed.

"Captain," Rand called, "I'm getting a recorded response from Klingon High Command."

Sulu moved to the conn and settled on the edge of his chair. "On screen."

The main viewer brightened abruptly, but the grainy, slightly out-of-focus image jerked as if on the verge of scrolling vertically—or so Sulu thought until he realized the ground beneath the figure was heaving.

A wild-eyed, disheveled Klingon officer—Sulu could not make out his rank—stared unseeing at the *Excelsior* crew as he fought to keep his balance. His face contorted suddenly with an emotion Sulu had never seen on a Klingon face: fear.

"This is an emergency!" he rasped, though he could barely be heard over the growing background roar. "We have suffered—"

The screen flickered, then went ominously dark.

A different Klingon face, in focus this time, appeared. "This is Brigadier Kerla, speaking for the High Command." Kerla's dark hair flowed onto broad, powerful shoulders. To Sulu he seemed young to have achieved such rank, but his tone was confident and controlled, that of one long accustomed to power. "There has been an incident on Praxis. However, everything is under control."

*Right,* Sulu wanted to say. *So under control it rattled the stuffing out of my ship.*

"We have no need for assistance. Obey treaty stipulations and remain outside the Neutral Zone." The Klingon paused. "Transmission ends now."

Brigadier Kerla's leonine visage wavered, then disappeared. Sulu stared at the blank viewscreen, unable to believe three-quarters of what he'd just heard. "An *incident!*"

Yet he realized this "incident" was exactly the sort of thing that could serve to bring peace . . . or war. Here was an opportunity to make this mission count in the universal scheme after all—and Sulu was determined to use it.

Rand interrupted his train of thought. "Do we report this, sir?"

Sulu swiveled his chair to face her. "Are you kidding? Send the following message to Starfleet Command. . . ."

At Starfleet Headquarters in San Francisco, Dr. Leonard H. McCoy, more than a little disgruntled for a good many reasons, entered the briefing room. One: his shore leave had been cut a full day short, when he'd been having a marvelous time spoiling the bejesus out of his daughter Joanna's kids. Two:

24

he'd had to pass four security checks just to get to this damnable meeting. And three: these emergency briefings always boded ill. This particular summons to HQ had an especially ominous ring to it, and judging from the number of bemedaled brass in the room—including Admiral Cartwright, who sat near the empty lectern—McCoy guessed they were in serious trouble indeed. Three months to retirement, and Starfleet was still hell-bent on getting them all killed.

He was hardly surprised to see Scott, Uhura, and Chekov, already seated, with two places saved.

"I hope one of those is for me," McCoy stage-whispered to Uhura. She smiled—rather anxiously, the doctor thought—and nodded as she patted the chair beside her. "Anybody have any idea what this is all about?"

Scott, his broad, ruddy face set in a scowl, leaned over to whisper, "Haven't ye paid any attention to the news lately, man? There's only one thing this could mean."

McCoy shrugged. "I avoid it whenever I can. All they want to harp about these days is the Kudao tragedy."

"I think that's what he's referring to, Doctor," Chekov offered, his expression as grim as that of everyone else in the room.

Scott motioned for McCoy to lean closer, then said in his ear: "War. That's what it means."

"No." The doctor drew away swiftly, unwilling to hear; he did not want to think of war, not on this day he had spent teaching his three-year-old granddaughter how to swim. "Scotty, it's not gonna come to that. We've been close to war with the Klingons before—"

"Dinna ye hear about the attack on Themis?"

"Themis?" McCoy blinked. "I've been a little too busy with my grandkids to keep up with the news. You mean the Klingons—"

"Attacked another planet," Chekov finished, beating Scott to the punch. "This one sparsely populated—mostly just scientists, in research facilities, but farther from the border. The news was released only a few hours ago, though it happened two days before."

"Another attack," the doctor whispered, and closed his eyes. "Was anyone killed?"

"Aye," Scott said darkly. "Some of the researchers. The projects were mostly agricultural, not even classified—no reason for the bloody Klingons to damn near blow the entire planet to bits."

"My God, that's horrible. Are they sure the Klingon government—"

"No, they're not sure," Uhura interjected, leaning forward suddenly with more than a tinge of irritation. "Some of the survivors say they saw Klingon ships, but there's no hard evidence—"

"What more evidence do ye need?" Scott countered. "The fact is, the Klingons want war. Kudao made that clear enough. And with the Organians gone—"

"Stop it, Scotty," Uhura scolded him. "If Smillie

comes out and announces we're at war, then we'll be at war. Until then, I'm technically still on leave—and I've heard enough about Kudao and the Klingons, thank you."

Scott sat back with a harrumph.

"Well, where's Spock?" McCoy asked, with a feeble attempt at cheerfulness. The Vulcan had left the *Enterprise* a full six weeks before, when everyone else had been given only two weeks' leave. It was totally out of character for Spock to request extended shore leave, and McCoy was curious to know why.

Chekov shook his head. "No one has seen him. I don't believe he is coming."

"Really?" McCoy arched a brow in surprise, then lowered it as he caught sight of Jim Kirk coming through the door. "Jim! Over here!"

Kirk came in, looking as though someone had just died. He and Cartwright exchanged a look McCoy could not fathom, then Jim took his seat with a curt nod to everyone. Clearly, he had a lot more on his mind than this briefing. McCoy knew that the Kudao incident had stirred up painful memories of David's death, for both Jim and Carol Marcus. And now this business on Themis. No wonder Jim looked as though he were at a funeral.

*Or maybe,* McCoy thought with a sudden thrill of horror, *Scotty was right about war, and Jim already knows it.*

"What's up?" Jim asked, though he sounded uninterested in hearing the answer.

"Maybe they're throwing us a retirement party," McCoy said lightly.

The others must have sensed the captain's mood; even Scotty joined the effort to cheer Jim up. "That suits me," he confided. "I just bought a boat."

Uhura sighed. "Well, this better be good. I'm supposed to be chairing a seminar at the Academy."

*Maybe that's* your *idea of a vacation,* McCoy was about to quip, but Chekov leaned forward to ask seriously: "Captain, isn't this just for top brass?"

Kirk glanced around the room and nodded. "And us, apparently."

"And if we're all here," McCoy said, "where's Sulu?" He half meant it as a joke; Sulu had left the *Enterprise* more than ten years before to captain the *Excelsior,* but McCoy still found it hard to think of the *Enterprise* crew without him.

As he looked around, Kirk murmured, "Captain Sulu's on assignment. Anyone seen Spock?"

Chekov opened his mouth to answer, but shut it again when a young Starfleet aide-de-camp—*Children,* McCoy thought disgustedly, *children are running the universe*—her demeanor austere and impressive, gaveled the meeting to order.

"This briefing is classified," she said. "There will be no recording devices. Gentlepersons, the C-in-C."

Starfleet's commander in chief, his manner far more casual than that of his aide, entered. Rear Admiral William Smillie, the youngest individual ever to achieve the position of C-in-C, did not require formalities to impress others; he allowed his stellar record to speak for itself. McCoy liked Admiral Smillie more than his predecessor for one good reason: Smillie kept things brief and to the point.

True to form, Smillie said, "As you were. I'll make this as simple as possible. The Klingon Empire has roughly fifty years of life left to it."

The collective gasp of surprise was so loud that McCoy would have smiled if he hadn't been so taken aback himself. He tried to catch Scotty's eye to give him a "see, I told you" look, but the engineer was still staring owlishly at Smillie.

"For full details," the admiral continued, "I am turning this briefing over to our special Federation envoy."

There was no collective gasp this time when Spock walked to the lectern, but McCoy heard Jim Kirk's sharp intake of breath beside him.

"Good morning," Spock said—almost pleasantly, McCoy thought. The experience of sharing minds when McCoy served as the vessel for Spock's *katra*, his spirit, had done the Vulcan some good. "Two months ago a Federation starship monitored an explosion on the Klingon moon Praxis. We believe it was caused by overmining and insufficient safety precautions. A reactor exploded, contaminating the Klingon homeworld's atmosphere and causing an instability in their orbit. Unless the planet's orbit is corrected, the resultant change in weather patterns will eventually destroy their agriculture.

"The moon's decimation means an almost eighty percent loss of available energy—Praxis was one of their largest and most convenient sources of dilithium—and a deadly pollution of their ozone. They will have depleted their supply of oxygen in less than fifty Earth years. Due to their enormous military budget, the Klingon economy does not have the resources with which to combat this catastrophe.

"Last month, at the behest of the . . . Vulcan ambassador, I opened a dialogue with Gorkon, chancellor of the Klingon High Council. He proposes to commence negotiations at once."

"Negotiations for what?" someone asked.

Spock glanced to his left and met the gaze of his questioner: Admiral Cartwright.

"The dismantling of our space stations and starbases along the Klingon Neutral Zone," the Vulcan replied. "An end to seventy years of unremitting hostility the Klingons can no longer afford."

"So we're totally discounting the Organians?" someone in the back asked.

Spock nodded. "In light of the recent attacks on Kudao and Themis as well as those on relatively unprotected border worlds, it seems wise. All attempts on the Federation's behalf to contact the Organians concerning Klingon violation of treaty have failed. Indications are that they are unwilling or unable to further intervene to prevent a war."

A murmur traveled through the crowd at this; it quickly stilled as Spock continued.

"If the Klingons sue for peace, we could accumulate savings in defense expenditures, leaving the Federation economy free to grapple with urgent social problems . . ."

"Bill," a captain McCoy didn't recognize, his tone one of alarm, addressed Smillie, "are we talking about mothballing the Fleet?"

McCoy studied the young captain and wondered whether he belonged to the small but vocal group chafing to turn Starfleet into a military rather than an exploratory arm of the Federation. A pacifist to the core, McCoy had been amazed when he first learned such a movement existed; he still found it difficult to believe that such a barbaric concept lingered in a theoretically civilized age.

To his credit, Admiral Smillie answered sternly, "I'm sure our exploration and science programs would not be affected, but the facts speak for themselves, Captain."

Admiral Cartwright rose angrily. "I must protest. To offer the Klingons a safe haven within Federation space is suicide! Klingons would become the alien underclass of the galaxy. And if we dismantled the Fleet, we'd be defenseless before an aggressive species with a foothold on our territory, led by an unprincipled tyrant. The opportunity *here* is to embargo trading, force them to run through their own resources faster, and bring them to their knees. Perhaps even find a way to get the Romulans to cooperate in this, since the Klingons rely heavily on trade with them. Then we'll be in a far better position to dictate terms."

Sounds of approval issued from a few in the audience; most listened in silence, as did McCoy. On one level, he agreed with Cartwright. He had seen the results of the Klingons' treachery firsthand enough times not to trust them—and for God's sake, look at what had happened to David Marcus. But he did not like Cartwright's *tone,* the clear undercurrent of hate in the admiral's words.

At the thought of David Marcus, McCoy glanced over at Jim. The captain's expression was impassive, but he was staring at Spock with an intensity that could have melted transparent aluminum.

Smillie spoke as Cartwright sat down. "Starfleet is under civilian control, Admiral Cartwright. The decision is a political, not a military, one—and it's been made."

"Sir," Kirk said urgently.

Smillie turned. "Captain Kirk?"

"Sir, I'm no diplomat, but the Klingons have never been trustworthy. I'm forced to agree with Admiral Cartwright. This is"—Kirk groped for the words—"a terrible, a terrifying, idea . . ."

The aide leaned over to whisper something into Admiral Smillie's ear. The C-in-C's expression softened slightly; he looked back at Kirk. "Your son was killed by a Klingon, wasn't he, Captain?" he asked in a sympathetic tone.

The question drew an angry gasp from McCoy. He'd thought Smillie was a straight shooter, but to bring up such a painful subject for Jim, especially *now,* of all times, and in front of *this* group, just to discredit Jim's opinion . . .

No matter that the doctor agreed with only the first half of it while part of him agreed wholeheartedly with Spock. He glared at Smillie, then turned protectively toward Jim, who was still poker-faced, but ashen.

"Yes, sir," Jim replied stiffly.

"I'm sorry," Smillie continued, in the same tone of sympathy. "But Captain Spock has persuaded the Federation that this situation is too promising to ignore."

Spock nodded. "It is imperative that we act *now* to support the Gorkon initiative, lest more conservative elements persuade his Empire that it would be better to attempt a military solution and die fighting." The Vulcan didn't say as much, but McCoy guessed the implication: *And before the same thing happens to us* . . . Spock's words were reasoned, logical, but the doctor fancied he saw concern for Jim in the Vulcan's dark eyes. "We must strive to remember that not all Klingons subscribe to the militaristic ethics of the warrior class. Granted, the warriors constitute a strong, vocal minority, which has maintained power for centuries. But Gorkon represents a different group, with a different viewpoint. After a long struggle, this previously silent majority has come to power, with Gorkon as their spokesperson. He—and the Federation—cannot afford to pass up the opportunity for peace Praxis affords. Even the powerful military has been forced to consider a treaty."

The C-in-C smiled. "Captain Kirk, you are to be our first olive branch."

"Me?" Kirk gaped at Smillie in disbelief. Whispers rustled through the audience.

"We have volunteered to rendezvous with the Klingon ship that is bringing Chancellor Gorkon here," Spock said, "and to escort him safely through Federation space."

Kirk stared, too thunderstruck to reply.

Smillie nodded, pleased. "As it happens, Kirk, the chancellor specifically requested you and your officers."

"Me and my—" Kirk broke off. Scott muttered an oath under his breath; Chekov and Uhura merely gaped, and McCoy joined them, unable to do otherwise.

Kirk found his voice. *"Why,* in God's name?"

Smillie was unperturbed by the reactions. "There are some Klingons who feel the same about a peace treaty—a *real* one, not one forced on us by the Organians—as yourself and Admiral Cartwright. They'll think twice about attacking the *Enterprise* under your command."

"I have personally vouched for you in this matter, Captain," Spock added.

"You have personally—" Kirk began, and stopped, too furious to finish.

*What in the devil's name is Spock trying to do to Jim?* McCoy thought, in a burst of anger. *He could have asked for a different starship. Why not* Excelsior? *The Klingons wouldn't dare attack her.*

And then he wondered: Was this Spock's way of trying to force them to deal with the hatred that had been growing in Jim, in them all, nurtured by the media coverage of the slaughter on Kudao?

"You will accord Chancellor Gorkon full diplomatic courtesy, Captain Kirk," Admiral Smillie was saying, all traces of sympathy gone from his voice.

"Surely," Jim countered, straining to be reasonable, to keep the anger under control, "a full ambassador would be better equipped to—"

Smillie cut him off. "If there's no further business, I wish you and your crew godspeed. Thank you all."

The officers in the room rose as their commander dismissed them with a quick nod. Smillie left, followed by his aide. The others filed out quietly, which surprised McCoy. He had expected some rather lively arguments, given the controversial order Smillie had just issued. Even Scotty, normally outspoken when it came to the topic of Klingons, said nothing, merely shook his head and glanced in the captain's direction. McCoy wanted to say something to him—after all, they should at least be relieved there wasn't going to be a war—but the sight of Jim's face stopped him.

The captain still sat, stunned and furious, staring at Spock, who remained by the lectern. McCoy understood: they were waiting to speak to each other, and Jim's expression prompted the doctor to decide he would just as soon miss out on the upcoming discussion. He sighed and turned to follow Chekov and Uhura, who were moving silently toward the door. Admiral Cartwright blocked his path.

His expression one of concern, Cartwright leaned over to address the seated captain. "I don't know whether to congratulate you or not, Jim."

Kirk met his eyes but did not reply.

"I wouldn't," McCoy said softly, and left, still wondering why he did not feel relieved there would not be a war.

Kirk sat in the empty briefing room and stared at his first officer.

Spock could not have known, of course, when he volunteered the *Enterprise,* that Carol Marcus would be among the wounded on Themis. The incident had not yet occurred when Spock was making diplomatic overtures to the Klingons.

But Jim did not doubt that Spock had known how his captain would feel about this particular assignment, even before Themis; he did not doubt that Spock had decided to volunteer him despite that knowledge—first, because it was logical; second, because Spock obviously thought it would help Jim completely recover from his grief over David, from his . . .

He balked mentally at the word "hate."

Why shouldn't he hate? After all the Klingons had done to him, why shouldn't he?

The thought that Spock might be doing this for

Kirk's own good made him all the more furious. Before Themis, perhaps, Jim could have dealt with it graciously, but now . . .

Spock studied him from the lectern, waiting patiently for the captain to break the silence.

Jim turned his face away and did not speak for some time. When he did, the depth of his anger startled them both.

*"We* volunteered?" he asked bitterly. He was Spock's commanding officer, regardless of whatever status Spock might have held as special envoy. The Vulcan seemed to have forgotten who was supposed to be giving the orders.

"Why does it have to be me? Why can't it be Sulu? The Klingons have more reason to be afraid of *Excelsior*—"

"There is an old Vulcan proverb," Spock said, his tone as rational and soothing as Kirk's was heated. " 'Only Nixon could go to China.' "

"What the hell is that supposed to mean?"

"The Klingons have good reason to fear the *Excelsior,* particularly under Captain Sulu's command. But they are more afraid of you. You have become a legend among them. You have earned their fear and, more importantly, their respect. That is vital to the success of this mission."

"Had I known what you were up to," Kirk said, fighting to keep his voice from shaking with rage, "I would never have granted your request for extended leave."

Spock merely looked at him.

"How could you vouch for me? That's"—Kirk broke off, too incensed to find the words— "arrogant presumption."

"Jim," Spock said earnestly, "I was asked by my father to open neg—"

Kirk didn't let him finish. "I know your father's the Vulcan ambassador, for God's sake, but you know how I feel about this." His voice dropped as anger and grief welled within him—over the loss of his son, over the near loss of Carol. "You're talking about the people who killed David. Who slaughtered all those innocents on Kudao." He faltered, glanced away. "Who injured Carol. The doctors don't know if she'll live."

Spock stiffened, and after a beat of startled silence said, "My sincerest condolences, Captain. I did not know."

*And would it have made any difference if you had?* Jim wondered.

"I assume she was wounded on Themis?"

Jim nodded, remembering Kwan-mei and her grief over Sohlar. "I spoke with one of the Themis survivors. She said they had no time to react, never even saw the ship that attacked them; the phaserfire seemed to come out of nowhere." He jerked his head in Spock's direction. "Unarmed scientists, and the Klingons never gave them a chance. How can you deal with killers—"

"All Klingons did not kill David, Captain. All Klingons did not murder the Kudao settlers, or those on Themis. You are blaming an entire race for the acts of a few individuals."

38

"Spock, the entire Klingon race is made up of cold-blooded murderers like Kruge! Killing is their way of life, all they understand." Carol and Kwan-mei's voices echoed in his mind. "They're *animals . . .*"

A stranger might have said the Vulcan did not react, but Kirk knew him all too well. Spock's eyes narrowed slightly; his lips parted only a few millimeters. Kirk saw the disapproval in that infinitesimal change of expression.

The disapproval wavered, then vanished and was replaced by concern. "You are upset, but when you have recovered, you will agree. Jim, there is an historic opportunity here—"

*"Don't trust them. Don't believe them,"* Kirk said, thinking of Kruge, remembering the voice of Saavik: *Captain, David is dead. . . .*

"They're dying," Spock said softly.

*"Let them die."*

Jim repressed a shudder of horror at the realization that the words were his own. Yet, gripped by pain that had been buried for the past eleven years, he could not deny he meant them. Nor did he back down from Spock's silent, reproachful gaze.

He felt infinitely tired. The journey to Themis had drained him, left him without the strength to deal with his growing hatred. It was unfair of Spock to force him to confront it now.

Spock looked away for a time, then gazed thoughtfully at Kirk.

"I grieve with you over the death of your son, Captain, and the injuries to Carol Marcus. I know

39

you well enough to know you are not yourself and do not mean all you have said.

"We have been given a choice: peace or war. As a Vulcan, I am bound to choose peace."

"I don't want war, either, Spock," Kirk answered wearily. "But why does it have to be me? Let someone younger go."

"Chancellor Gorkon requested you. And Admiral Smillie has made his decision."

"In other words, I have no choice in the matter. You've forced me into it." The thought rekindled his anger. "Has it occurred to you that this crew is due for retirement in three months? We've done our bit for king and country!"

They locked gazes—Kirk's furious, Spock's patient. For a moment neither spoke.

"I may not be myself," Kirk said at last, "but you shouldn't have forced this. And you're a fool if you think the Klingons intend to negotiate in good faith. At some point, you'll realize you should have listened to me."

He left to report to the *Enterprise*, feeling at once ashamed at the depth of his own hatred and far too angry to care.

# Chapter Two

REPORTING TO THE *Enterprise* early the next morning, McCoy stepped onto the turbolift and found himself alone with Jim Kirk. The captain appeared to have slept little—McCoy himself had found a good night's rest impossible, considering the political import of the mission—but seemed far less angry, far more approachable, than he had the day before. Even so, Jim was trying to mask the fact that something was troubling him.

McCoy could hardly blame him. During his bout with insomnia last night, the doctor had decided that both Jim and Spock were right, each in his own way. Peace with the Klingons made sense, at least theoretically, and Gorkon *had* requested the *Enterprise.* It would have been very bad politics to refuse.

But at the same time, McCoy felt angry at Spock, at Starfleet, for refusing to consider Jim's feelings in all of this. Kudao had painfully reminded them all of David's death. No matter that it had all happened a long time ago . . .

Funny, he'd never noticed until that moment how much silver had crept into Jim's hair over the past few years. The traumatic events of the past decade had aged them. With a slow trickle of sadness, McCoy realized that he would stand beside Jim on this lift, on the bridge, only a few times more.

Kirk nodded at the doctor and touched the control; the lift began to ascend. After so many years, words were unneeded: each knew where the other was headed.

With a sense of urgency, McCoy decided the timing and circumstances were good, and launched right into it.

"Lift, stop." He faced Jim as the turbolift decelerated and came to a smooth halt. "Jim, this mission's eating at you. Do you feel up to talking about it?"

Kirk stared straight ahead at the seam in the lift doors and released a slow breath, then glanced at McCoy. "I thought . . . I suppose no one told you. Carol was on Themis during the attack."

"My God," McCoy whispered, stunned. "I had no idea—"

"I suppose Command doesn't want the information released in view of . . . my involvement in this mission."

"Is she all right?"

Kirk looked away. "The building collapsed on

them; Carol had severe head injuries. Damage to the brain stem. She's on life support now. They should know in a week whether the implants will take."

The doctor put a hand on Jim's shoulder. "Jim, I'm so sorry. How can they—the sons of bitches—how can they even *ask* you to be here? Smillie could have asked someone else. He could have asked Sulu."

"Maybe." Jim straightened, met McCoy's gaze once again. "I can't buck orders, Bones. Even if I could have stayed with Carol, I keep telling myself —what good could I do, being with her now? Looking at it selfishly, at least this way I can stay busy until I know something. This mission won't take a week. A few days at most. And then I'll be with her again."

*If she doesn't die in the meantime,* McCoy thought. He knew Jim thought it, too, but neither of them dared voice it.

Jim shook his head gently. "But this particular . . . assignment isn't making things easier."

"Of course it isn't," McCoy said. "I can't believe they have the nerve—"

"I couldn't believe it when I heard myself with Spock yesterday." He twisted his lips grimly, something less than a smile. "I really shocked him. I told him we should let all the Klingons die. That they were animals."

Half jokingly, half bitterly, McCoy replied, "I've known a couple in my day that were."

"I don't want war, Bones."

43

"None of us do," the doctor soothed.

"I just don't want Klingons on my ship." Kirk lowered his voice. "Not now. It's more than just what they did to Carol. I don't know why, after all these years, David's death is haunting me again—both of us, though we didn't talk about it. Kudao, I suppose . . ."

"That's probably part of it. But when David was killed, you didn't have time to grieve for him. You were too busy trying to save the lives of your crew. You've always been the captain—always so busy taking responsibility for everyone else's life that you don't have time for your own.

"Don't you realize, Jim, you're having to give up the *Enterprise* again? Maybe your conscious mind hasn't wanted to face up to it, but your subconscious remembers. We're all retiring in three months. And when we do, you won't be James T. Kirk, captain, always living up to impossibly high ideals. Instead, you'll be forced to deal with Jim Kirk, human being." McCoy's tone softened. "Maybe the human being has never been able to forgive the Klingons for the death of his son. Kruge stole the only family you had, stole the chance you had to get to know David. He won't be waiting for you when you retire."

*And now maybe neither will Carol. . . .*

Jim stood quietly, without meeting the doctor's gaze, for such a long time that McCoy feared he had overstepped his bounds. And then the captain touched the controls, and the lift started smoothly upward again.

When the doors finally snapped open, he turned to McCoy. "Maybe you're right, Doctor. But Spock is wrong to trust the Klingons. I still think the treaty is a mistake."

McCoy sighed. "You wanna know something? Deep down, so do I. So do I. . . ."

By midday all hands had reported to their stations and the *Enterprise* was ready for departure.

Kirk had had some time to reflect on his conversation with McCoy. Despite his grief, he had resolved two things: one, that he would in no way allow his personal feelings to jeopardize the success of this last mission; and two, that he would in no way trust the Klingons. That he would leave to Spock, as diplomat; Kirk's concern was his crew— and the Federation's best interests.

And there remained the fact that he had no choice. His orders were to transport Klingons and treat them as honored guests aboard his vessel. Therefore he would do so.

By the time he and Spock headed for the bridge in the turbolift, Jim felt able to broach the subject calmly.

"Spock . . . I'm still not happy about your manipulating me into this. But I know I said a lot of angry things yesterday. I just want you to know that I don't want a war any more than you do. Despite what happened on Themis, I'll afford the Klingons every courtesy."

Spock lifted a brow in mild surprise. "I had no doubt whatsoever of that, Captain. I regret the most unfortunate timing. Is there any further word on Dr. Marcus's condition?"

Kirk shook his head. "I don't think either of us needs to apologize, Spock. You couldn't have known what was going to happen; you just did what you felt you had to do. Now we both have a job to do, and we're going to get it done."

Spock nodded. "Perhaps it is just as well that we do not entirely agree on the Klingon issue. My acquaintance with Dr. McCoy has taught me the value of a devil's advocate."

Jim actually smiled. "In other words, you're admitting that McCoy has been right on more than one occasion."

The Vulcan frowned. "I do not believe I said exactly that, Cap—"

He broke off as the lift doors opened onto the bridge.

The last time, Jim thought, as he stepped out and moved toward the conn, where McCoy was already standing, while Spock crossed to his station. Could this really be the last time they'd be taking her out of spacedock?

He stopped and did a slight double take as the conn swung around and a young Vulcan female vacated the chair.

"Captain on the bridge," she said, rising. Her straight black hair, short and severe, framed fragilely beautiful features.

The bridge crew stood to attention.

"As you were," Kirk said. He frowned, puzzled. "Have we met, Lieutenant . . . ?"

"Valeris, sir. We were told you would need a helmsman"—as she spoke, she caught sight of Spock, and her gaze became one of recognition—"so I volunteered." She regarded Spock with an expression of such ardent respect and devotion that Kirk raised his eyebrows and directed a curious half smile at his first officer.

Spock gave a slight nod. "Lieutenant, it is agreeable to see you again." He explained to Kirk. "The lieutenant recently graduated at the top of her class from Starfleet Academy. I was her sponsor."

"Ah," Kirk said. Certainly Valeris's behavior toward Spock was Vulcanly correct, but some well-sharpened instinct told him that her feelings for him were more than platonic. Impossible to tell, however, whether Spock returned those feelings—or was even aware of them. "Congratulations, Lieutenant. You must be very proud."

She lifted a brow in such a credible impersonation of Spock that Kirk almost grinned. "I don't believe so, sir."

"She's a Vulcan all right," McCoy quipped beside him.

Valeris assumed her station at the helm.

"All right, let's get this over with," Kirk said. "Departure stations." He pressed a control on the console arm. "Scotty?"

"Aye, sir."

"Stand by. Get me Spacedock Control, Uhura."

"Control, reading, sir," Uhura said behind him.

"Control," Kirk said, his senses sharpened by the realization that this was the last time he would

47

command this vessel out of spacedock, "this is *Enterprise,* requesting permission to depart."

Uhura put the dockmaster through on audio. "This is Control," a male voice droned. *"Enterprise,* you are granted permission to depart. Thirty seconds for port gates."

"Clear all moorings," Valeris intoned from the helm.

"Awaiting port gates from this mark." Kirk glanced surreptitiously at Spock, realizing that this was indeed his last chance to get even for a little joke the Vulcan had played on him years before, in this very situation, albeit with a different protégé.

He'd damn near scared Jim to death.

"Moorings cleared," the dockmaster confirmed.

"Aft thrust—" Valeris began, but the captain interrupted.

"Thank you," he said loudly to Control, drowning out the young Vulcan's voice. "Lieutenant Valeris, one-quarter impulse power."

Valeris turned to face him with less than perfect Vulcan control. Perhaps, Kirk thought, Spock had made it his mission in life to help others gain emotional mastery. This one certainly could use some practice.

"Captain," Valeris said, "may I remind you that regulations specify thrusters only while in spacedock?"

"Uh, Jim," McCoy said nervously, from where he stood to the left of the helm.

But the rest of the crew seemed to catch on

immediately—including Uhura, who murmured softly, "Here we go again."

And Spock, who remained absolutely poker-faced.

"You heard the order, Lieutenant," Kirk told Valeris.

Her expression unreadable, she swiveled back to the helm and complied.

Jim smiled and settled into his chair as the *Enterprise* screamed out of dock and exited through the just-opening bay doors into the freedom of space.

"Lieutenant," he said at length.

Valeris faced him, her expression impassive.

"I don't care if I'm senile. If I sit in this chair and give the word, you jump."

"Aye, sir," she said.

"Plot a course for Kronos, Lieutenant."

"Kronos, sir?" Her tone conveyed faint surprise. Only the senior bridge crew had attended the classified briefing and knew of the switch in assignment.

"I'm still in the chair," Kirk reminded her pleasantly.

"Aye, sir."

Captain's personal log, Stardate 9522.6:
   They say you can't teach an old dog new tricks—and maybe they're right. It seems to me our mission to escort the chancellor of the Klingon High Council is problematic at best.
   I have never trusted Klingons and never will. And I'm

beginning to think McCoy is right: I've never been able to forgive them for the death of my son. As a Starfleet officer, I am duty bound to follow orders, and I will do so. The Klingons will be extended every diplomatic courtesy. Yet I remain convinced that any attempts at dialogue with them will be futile; our cultures are simply too different, and too much hatred has been stirred up within the Federation over the massacres on Kudao and now Themis. The Klingons have left behind a trail of embittered survivors within the Federation. Spock says this could be an historic moment and I'd like to believe him—but how can history get past people like me?

Several hours after the spacedock maneuver, Kirk paused in the dictation of his personal log and his unpacking to set a portrait of David on his desk, a gift from Carol some birthdays ago. The holo captured David in a rare smiling moment, allowing Jim to forget, if he chose, the anger that had driven the young man.

He had once asked Carol about David's anger; she had remarked dryly that Jim needed only to look as far as his own early years.

Ridiculous, of course. He had never been full of free-floating hostility—at least, not to the same degree as David. Carol had remained skeptical.

A delicate cough made him start. He wheeled about to face Lieutenant Valeris, standing in the open cabin doorway. Behind her, the corridor lighting was dimmed in deference to the ship's night.

He felt a flare of irritation at the intrusion as well as embarrassment at the thought that he might have been overheard dictating his log, and made a mental note to remind Spock to have a little discussion with his protégée about courtesy and human customs.

"Come on, Valeris, you *could* knock."

The greenish hue of her complexion deepened, but she kept her composure as she said, "We are almost at the rendezvous, Captain. I thought you would want to know."

"Right." Kirk found his jacket and slipped into it as she watched intently. He got the impression she wanted to say more but had not yet found the words.

"Valeris," he said. "That's not a Vulcan name, is it? It sounds almost . . . Klingon." Impossible, of course; she showed no trace of Klingon heritage. To all outward appearances, she looked to be a full Vulcan.

Her color deepened; she shook her head once, quickly, and Kirk found himself thinking of Spock's other protégée, Saavik. He wondered whether this woman had the same background. It would certainly explain her occasional slip in terms of Vulcan control.

"Permission to speak freely, sir?" Valeris asked.

He gazed expectantly at her. She correctly interpreted his expression and silence as giving permission, and continued awkwardly.

"I gather you are not enthusiastic about the assignment. I do not think many on board are. Sir."

Kirk stared hard at her, unable to fathom what she was getting at. As a Vulcan, and particularly as Spock's protégée, she no doubt supported all efforts to establish peaceful relations with the Klingon Empire and was disturbed by the strong anti-Klingon sentiment she perceived in the ship's crew —and now in its captain.

He was in no mood to hear a lecture about humans and Klingons and prejudice—especially from this wet-behind-the-pointed-ears Academy grad.

"You piloted well out of spacedock, Lieutenant," Kirk began evenly.

She almost smiled. "I have always wanted to try that."

He stepped past her. "Only don't try putting words in my mouth."

Valeris paused at the door to Spock's quarters.

She debated whether she had exercised poor judgment in contacting the captain in person. She could easily have communicated with him from the bridge, but she had wanted to explain to him that she understood how difficult this particular mission was for him, that she knew of Carol Marcus's injuries and of the death of his son, not from third parties, but from the one who had witnessed it.

And she had had other errands to perform on this deck, as well as another personal reason: she wanted to speak privately with Spock.

Even now she had not found the words to adequately express herself to him. She feared she would sound emotional, self-serving—certainly her attempt to speak openly to the captain had backfired—and she did not want Spock to think his investment in her had been in vain.

She had learned of his availability as a sponsor quite by chance, at the government office in ShanaiKahr where she'd applied for Vulcan citizenship. There had been a Vulcan in a Starfleet uniform waiting in the queue. Valeris had wanted to join Starfleet since she was a child; she asked the officer questions and learned of Spock's patronage.

She and Lieutenant Saavik had since become friends.

She felt a kinship with Saavik, though Saavik was half Vulcan and half Romulan and Valeris was a full-blooded Vulcan. Despite the differences in their background, they shared an experience: neither had been raised in the Vulcan tradition; both had chosen it later in life. And neither had a proper Vulcan name.

She had meant to make legal application in ShanaiKahr to change her name to one more appropriate for a Vulcan, until Saavik had said, *Spock told me that, because of my mixed heritage, I am unique and must therefore find my own path. You are a full-blooded Vulcan, but your past makes you unique. You would do yourself a disservice to forget it.*

Both had worked hard to make up the gaps in their education, and Valeris had studied privately with a Vulcan tutor to acquire the emotional control most Vulcans learned as children.

Even now, though, she experienced difficulty. Some outworlders believed Vulcans lacked feelings entirely, that their emotional mastery was effortless. Valeris knew it was acquired only after years of study and great difficulty.

For that reason she admired Spock greatly. She felt a kinship with him as well; both of them had worked to overcome what some Vulcans might consider an unfortunate parentage. She also feared proving a disappointment to him: he, half human, displayed a control far superior to hers.

She had, at times, seen him show the merest hint of emotion. But she suspected even those displays were the result of a deliberate decision.

She wanted to prove worthy of him.

She pressed the door buzzer, and heard his voice. "Enter."

The door opened, then closed behind her as she stepped into Spock's quarters.

She was intrigued. He had visited her only twice at the Academy, and she had never seen his personal effects before. The cabin was functional but not cold, reflecting the mixed heritage of its occupant. She noted the flickering statue and the polished meditation stone as well as a number of Earth antiques, including a Chagall hung on the wall.

Dressed in his meditation robe, Spock reached out to light a votive candle.

"I have come to tell you," Valeris said, "that we have arrived at the rendezvous point."

He nodded, but did not hurry anxiously as the

captain had. Their presence on the bridge would not be required until the Klingon vessel arrived.

He turned to study her, and seemed to sense that there was more she wished to say. "You have done well, Valeris. As your sponsor at the Academy I have followed your career with . . . satisfaction. And, as a Vulcan, you have surpassed my expectations."

So. Perhaps he had also sensed her concern. His words evoked deep gratitude and, most illogically, embarrassment in her. Valeris struggled to keep from flushing and did not entirely succeed. She had learned biocontrol late in life and still found it the most challenging of her studies. She turned away and began inspecting the Chagall. It belonged to an Old Earth style of painting that she found incomprehensible.

"You wished to see me?" Spock asked, as she continued to scrutinize the painting. He gestured at the low divan.

She drew a breath and sat. There were many things she wished to discuss with him; she began with the least important one. "I meant no disrespect to the captain today—"

"It was in no way disrespectful. You had an obligation to remind him. It is illogical to blindly obey authority."

"If I am not mistaken, Captain Kirk demanded my blind obedience."

"He demanded your trust. That is quite a different thing."

She frowned. "I do not see how."

"He correctly judged that the bay doors would open sufficiently for the *Enterprise* to pass through safely. He was attempting to demonstrate that, although he is scheduled for retirement in the near future, his skills as a commanding officer are undiminished." Spock's expression warmed subtly, as if from an inward smile. "And he was exacting . . . revenge on another member of the bridge crew. I believe the expression is 'turning the tables.'"

Valeris did not understand, but she did not pursue the matter.

"I feel certain the captain was pleased with your performance," Spock continued. "You navigated most ably and demonstrated your knowledge of docking maneuvers." He paused, clearly thinking that their conversation was now finished and she would excuse herself.

Valeris continued examining the Chagall, wondering how to broach the next subject she wished to discuss.

"Do you like the painting, Lieutenant?"

"I do not understand this representation," she admitted.

"It is a depiction from ancient Earth mythology. The expulsion from Paradise."

She frowned. "Why keep it in your quarters?"

A moment passed before Spock answered—and when he spoke, there was an odd quality to his voice.

"It is a reminder to me that all things must end."

"Sir," she said, standing. "It is of endings I wish to speak. I address you as a kindred intellect. Do you not recognize that a turning point has been reached in the affairs of the Federation?"

"History is filled with turning points," Spock said, unruffled by her intensity. At her puzzled reaction, he added: "You must have faith."

"Faith . . . ?"

"That the universe will unfold as it should."

"Is that logical?" Valeris asked, confused by her mentor's advice. She had met with him only a handful of times, but had thought she had come to know him well. In her mind, he had come to represent the epitome of logic, of all that she strove to achieve. She had admired his intelligence, his control, but now she felt she was speaking, not with the Vulcan, but with the human. "Surely we must—"

"Klingon battle cruiser off the port bow," a voice blared through the bulkhead comm grid. "All hands on deck. Repeat . . ."

With swift, practiced skill, Spock slipped his meditation robe off and his uniform jacket on.

"Logic is the beginning of wisdom, Lieutenant, not the end," he said, as the two of them started for the door. Before it opened, he stopped and faced her. "This will be my last voyage aboard this ship as a member of her crew. A Vulcan of your demonstrated ability should have no difficulty rising to the occasion. As you are aware, nature abhors a vacuum. I intend you to replace me."

Valeris fought back a rush of very un-Vulcan emotion. "I could only succeed you, sir. Never replace you."

They headed for the bridge in silence. She had not communicated all that she wished, but considered that perhaps such things were best left unsaid.

Kirk stepped onto the bridge seconds before Spock and Valeris followed. The sight on the main viewscreen stopped all three.

A Klingon battle cruiser loomed to port at alarmingly close range. Crew members were doing their best to appear nonchalant about the fact, but there was tension in Chekov's voice as he asked, "Captain, shall we raise our shields?"

Valeris crossed the bridge and took her place beside Chekov at the helm.

Kirk glanced at his first officer and saw the message in Spock's expression: *Trust me.*

Spock he trusted; Klingons were another matter altogether. He scowled, knowing that raising the shields would be the worst possible diplomatic move—and wanting to anyway.

He did not give the order.

From the corner of his eye he saw Chekov catch his expression, realize no order was forthcoming, and turn back toward the dread-inspiring sight on the screen.

"Never been this close," Kirk murmured. He'd had Klingons on board the *Enterprise*, to be sure—most recently, Captain Klaa and the crew of the Klingon vessel *Okrona*. But even then, Klaa had

had the grace to maintain a respectable distance between his ship and the *Enterprise.*

And Klaa's ship had been tiny compared to the monstrous vessel that hovered before them now.

Certainly the Federation and the Klingon Empire had never been this close to real peace. There had been the treaty forced on both parties by the Organians—an uneasy truce, at best. *With the Organians gone,* Kirk wondered, *would the Klingons come to us now if it hadn't been for Praxis?*

"The chancellor is undoubtedly awaiting our signal," Spock said gently beside him.

Kirk drew in a breath and gave the Vulcan an "I hope you know what you're doing" look before taking the conn. "Uhura, hailing frequencies. Helm, right standard rudder. Bring us alongside."

"Right standard rudder," Lieutenant Valeris replied. "Z plus five degrees."

"Channel open, Captain," Uhura reported.

Kirk collected himself. "This is the Federation starship *Enterprise,* Captain James T. Kirk commanding."

As he spoke, the image of the battle cruiser wavered and vanished, replaced by the lordly countenance of a Klingon dressed in the red and black vestments of his culture's aristocracy. His neatly trimmed beard was streaked with silver.

"This is *Kronos One,"* he said. "I am Chancellor Gorkon." His speech seemed more cultivated, less rasping, than that of other Klingons.

Kirk managed to nod politely, but found it difficult not to think of Carol and David and the pictures of Kudao as he said, "Chancellor. We have been ordered to escort you through Federation space to your meeting on Earth."

Gorkon's tone was disarmingly gracious. "Thank you, Captain."

"Would you and your party care to dine this evening aboard the *Enterprise* with my officers, as guests of the United Federation of Planets?"

Kirk sensed rather than saw the surprised glances from his crew.

If the Klingon chancellor caught them, he gave no sign. "We'd be delighted to accept your gracious invitation," Gorkon said pleasantly.

Kirk tried to smile. "We'll make arrangements to have you beamed aboard at nineteen-thirty hours."

Gorkon gave a formal nod. "I shall look forward to it."

The screen darkened abruptly.

Kirk turned to Spock and said softly, "I hope you're happy."

"Captain." Valeris rose from the helm.

Kirk turned, half expecting to hear that *Kronos*'s shields had gone up and she had armed herself.

But the lieutenant stepped over to the conn and lowered her voice discreetly so that the others would not hear. "There is a supply of Romulan ale aboard. Perhaps it might make the evening pass more . . . smoothly?"

Kirk stared at her in amazement, then allowed himself a faint grin. Lieutenant Valeris was clearly far from a typical Vulcan; there was a boldness about her that Kirk liked, and she actually had something of a sense of humor. He vowed silently to ask Spock about her later. "Officer thinking, Lieutenant."

Yet as he turned and headed with Spock and McCoy for the lift, he could not shake the conviction that allowing Klingons aboard the *Enterprise* would lead to disaster.

# Chapter Three

THE CAPTAIN PAUSED at the lift entrance to survey his officers. "I'll expect the senior bridge crew to be present at the dinner," he said, then stepped inside with Mr. Spock and the doctor.

"Aye, sir," Uhura answered softly as the doors closed over them, and released a slow breath. The atmosphere on the bridge fairly crackled with an odd, unpleasant tension—in part, she decided, because for many of the senior crew, this voyage would be the last. Kirk, McCoy, and Scott were officially retiring; so was Spock, who, though his Vulcan blood caused him to age far more slowly, was leaving out of loyalty to the captain, Uhura felt. Chekov planned to transfer off *Enterprise* and was toying with the notion of leaving the Fleet. As for Uhura, she planned to go back to teaching at the

Academy, to give back some of what she had gotten out of Starfleet.

But at least some of the uneasiness on the bridge had to do with the assignment. Uhura had noted the captain's sharp downturn in mood and the tension between him and Spock since yesterday's briefing. She sympathized with Kirk; his son's death and the loss of the original *Enterprise* no doubt made all of this very difficult for him.

Still, he had entertained Klingons once before on the *Enterprise,* in honor of Captain Klaa. He had seemed completely recovered from his grief then; at least, Uhura had not sensed the same depth of anger in him.

Something had happened to awaken his pain and hate. Kudao, which had stirred the hatred sleeping in them all. Klingons had attacked and killed hundreds of innocent settlers on that world. In the months since the Organians' disappearance, there had been many smaller raids such as the one on Themis—all of them, according to the official word of the Klingon High Council, committed by pirates, unsanctioned by the government.

Uhura was enough of a skeptic to realize that the attacks probably *weren't* officially sanctioned and had been committed by a small faction within the military, but the Klingon government would do nothing to stop them. The Klingons would sit back and let the Federation be provoked to the point of war, while they wooed the Romulans and debated among themselves whether they possessed sufficient weaponry to emerge as victors.

Klingon culture glorified war. For a Klingon, there was no greater honor than to be permitted to die a warrior's death.

Was it really possible that there were those within the Empire who had grown weary of fighting, who saw a better way?

Uhura believed it was, and that Praxis had provided the impetus for change within the Empire. Chancellor Gorkon had managed to convince the High Council, but would he be able to win over those in the Federation?

She admired and respected Mr. Spock for his diplomatic efforts, and she fervently believed he was right. A peace treaty was the only sane course. But the attack on Kudao would make that difficult, if not impossible. The Klingons had been portrayed as villains in the media to the extent that political cartoons portrayed them with horns sprouting from their ridged foreheads.

The Praxis explosion might have come too late to do the galaxy any good.

Uhura glanced up to see Chekov, relieved of duty, heading for the lift. He stopped at the communications console and leaned over to whisper: "Guess who's coming to dinner?" There was irony in his tone.

Uhura felt a flash of indignation. Diplomatic relations with the Klingons were delicate, mercurial, at best. Everything Spock was trying to achieve could be all too easily destroyed. "Chekov, an attitude like that isn't going to help."

Chekov drew back in mild surprise. "What attitude? How are we *supposed* to feel about Klingons coming aboard this ship, after what they've done to the captain?"

"I don't want to hear about that," she said firmly. "I've heard it enough times from Mr. Scott. He seems to have forgotten the time *Okrona*'s crew came on board and we all saw him drinking scotch with General Korrd. Everyone except Spock seems to have forgotten that General Korrd helped save the captain's life."

Chekov's lip twisted skeptically. "General Korrd was under duress. Spock had to . . . persuade him."

"He could have refused." She sighed. "It's difficult enough, with the captain feeling the way he does . . . and everyone talking about nothing but Kudao. David Marcus died more than a decade ago. There's no excuse for the amount of hatred I've seen."

"No excuse?" Chekov's brown eyes narrowed with disbelief. "They kill the captain's son, almost kill Carol Marcus, and you say—"

"Carol Marcus?" Uhura caught her breath with a jolt of sickening surprise, not wanting to understand and yet understanding instantly. She sank back into her chair. "Chekov, no . . ."

"She was on Themis," Chekov said heavily, in a voice too low to be heard by the others on the bridge. "No one is supposed to know, but I heard Dr. McCoy speaking to his nurse in sickbay this morning when I reported for my physical. Carol is in a coma; the doctors aren't even sure she will live."

Uhura closed her eyes.

"Do you still think Mr. Scott is wrong to be angry?" Chekov asked. "Do you still want to have a pleasant dinner with the Klingons and pretend like everything is all right?"

Uhura shook her head. "No. But I will." She lifted her face toward him. "Don't you see, Pavel? *These* Klingons want peace. They want to stop the killing."

His lips thinned to a grim line. "Do they? I don't trust them."

"I don't want to myself, but what other choice do we have?"

Chekov did not answer, but the look in his eyes—which said that he might actually consider that second, unspeakable option—frightened her.

"If that's the way everyone feels," Uhura said softly, "then gods help us. We'll be lucky if we're not at war by the time dessert is served."

In the *Enterprise* transporter room, Kirk forced himself not to finger the collar of his dress uniform for the thousandth time. Beside him, McCoy and Spock waited—the doctor fidgeting, Spock motionless—as Scotty worked the transporter controls.

Jim's discomfort at the thought of Klingons aboard the *Enterprise* again had nearly been overwhelmed by the realization that this was an unparalleled moment in history. For the first time, Klingons and Federation members were willingly attempting to forge peace.

Could this have been what the Organians intended all along? Kirk wondered. Were they remaining silent in order to prod both parties into seeking peace voluntarily, a peace that would not be threatened the instant the galactic referees were out of the picture?

"Maybe if their particles just got a wee bit mixed," Scott muttered as he pressed a control.

Kirk shot him a reproving look; Scott hastily directed his attention to his console. Despite his personal feelings, the captain had made it clear to his crew that the Klingon guests were to be treated with the utmost courtesy.

Now if he could just follow his own order . . .

A light flickered on Scott's board, indicating that the chancellor's party had assembled and were waiting on *Kronos One*'s transporter pad. "Energize," Kirk said, feeling his pulse quicken.

Scott's fingers played the board with virtuoso skill, so familiar with their task that the engineer did not look down at the controls, but watched with the others as five vague forms shimmered, then began to coalesce on the pads.

Amid the transporter's shrill whine, three male figures, dressed in solid military black—two security guards and a high-ranking young officer who looked familiar—materialized on the back pads, followed by Gorkon, a female, and an older officer on the front.

The others waited respectfully while Gorkon stepped down first, even more majestic in person than he had seemed over the comm channel. Heralded by the bos'n's whistle, he approached Kirk.

"Chancellor Gorkon," the captain said, with a slight bow from the shoulders.

Solemnly Gorkon returned the gesture.

Kirk gestured toward his officers. "Chancellor, may I present my first officer, Captain Spock, whom I believe you know. Dr. Leonard McCoy, chief medical officer. Commander Montgomery Scott, chief engineer."

He directed a faintly warning glance at Scott, but the engineer returned Gorkon's nod with somber civility.

Gorkon turned back toward Spock and said, with honest warmth, "Captain Spock, face to face at last. You have my thanks."

Spock bowed silently.

Gorkon turned to gaze at the Klingon female with unabashed pride. His consort, Kirk thought at first, one worthy of the head of an empire, elegant and striking even by human standards. "Gentlemen, this is my daughter, Azetbur."

Slender, her waist-length black hair smoothed back by a silver skull ornament, Azetbur moved toward them with measured grace. Like her father, she was robed in black save for the dark red capelets that marked her as a ruling member of the High Council. She stood beside Gorkon and nodded graciously at her hosts as the chancellor continued the introductions.

"My military adviser, Brigadier Kerla."

Kirk nodded at the tall, bearded, long-haired young Klingon who stepped from the platform. He recognized Kerla from a tape Rear Admiral Smillie had supplied after the briefing. Kerla returned the gesture with a faint air of belligerence.

*So,* Kirk thought. *Scotty and I aren't the only ones with a bone to pick.*

"And this," Gorkon was saying, as Kerla took his place, "is General Chang, my chief of staff."

Physically, Chang appeared unthreatening—almost a head shorter than Kerla and bald save for a gray mustache and wisp of hair at the base of his ridged skull. His right eye gleamed coldly as he stared at Kirk; his left was hidden by a black patch.

Yet he emanated a fierce, cruel cunning that made the captain's blood run cold. He had heard of Chang the Merciless, who had ordered the death of thousands, killed countless times with his own hands.

Innocents on Kudao, on Themis. Innocents like David and Carol. Kirk felt a thrill of hatred.

Beside him McCoy fidgeted.

Chang advanced, wearing a grim little smile. "I've always wanted to meet you, Captain . . ." He abruptly stopped mere inches away from Kirk's face, as if testing his host's capacity to flinch.

Kirk felt an impulse to reach for the bronze neck before him; instead, he forced a faint smile. "I'm not sure how to take that."

"Sincere admiration, Kirk," Kerla said behind him. If there was sarcasm in his tone, Jim could not detect it.

"As one warrior to another," Chang growled softly.

*You're a murderer, not a warrior,* Kirk wanted to protest, but caught himself.

Kirk had killed, but only in self-defense. He had even tried to save Kruge's life, and had nearly been killed for his efforts. Yet would the Klingons say the same of him? He pulled himself away from Chang and motioned at the transporter room door. "Right this way, please. I thought you might enjoy a brief tour."

In the corridor, Lieutenant Valeris watched unobserved as Captain Kirk led the Klingon delegation past two crewmen who snapped to attention.

They relaxed as soon as the Klingons were out of sight. Valeris recognized them as Burke and Samno, two ensigns with undistinguished records.

"They all look alike," Burke said with a wink at his companion.

Valeris frowned, confused. Except for the fact that the group all shared two characteristics—the high domed forehead with prominent bony ridges and the typically light bronze to dark brown skin coloration—Valeris did not think they looked at all similar. Indeed, she could think of several characteristics that distinguished each from the other, beginning with General Chang's eye patch.

"What about that smell?" Samno asked darkly,

the look in his eyes not altogether different from the one Valeris had seen earlier in the captain's. "You know only the top-of-the-line models can even talk."

Burke giggled. Valeris inferred that Samno was suggesting the Klingons emitted an offensive odor. She had heard the charge before, but had never had an opportunity to test the theory empirically. Perhaps she would be able to now, but it occurred to her that because she was not human, she might not be able to detect it.

She understood the comment about top-of-the-line models. She had often heard humans joke about the stupidity of Klingons, a fact Vulcans had good reason to find privately amusing—humans could hardly be considered the galaxy's scholars themselves—but were far too polite to mention in public.

She also understood the reasons for Burke and Samno's hatred. She neither condoned it nor thought it logical, but she understood it.

Her parents had both served in the Vulcan Diplomatic Corps and had been stationed on Zorakis, a planet in the Boswellia sector, bordering Klingon space. Several months prior to the Organian intervention, a war between the Federation and the Klingon Empire had seemed imminent. The Vulcans had vowed to find a way to prevent it.

Valeris's parents had volunteered to try to establish negotiations with the Klingons. Her mother, T'Paal, a devout pacifist but scarcely a traditionalist, had named her newborn daughter Valeris, after one of the honored female heroes of the Klingon race, a warrior. The name could also be construed as having Vulcan roots, a variant of the word for "serenity" or "inward peace," as well as being related to the English word "valor." The Vulcan child, then, was to be a courageous warrior for peace—or so she had been told by others who remembered her mother before she died, and her father before he changed.

Acting outside the Federation as representatives of Vulcan, T'Paal and her mate, Sessl, contacted the Klingons and attempted a dialogue. Their attempt was met with treachery, and T'Paal was killed. The attempt failed.

Sessl did not return to his native planet, but remained instead on the border world and re-thought his philosophy. He decided that, in this instance, the great Vulcan philosopher Surak was wrong, that peace and the Klingon race were incompatible. Sessl published a treatise arguing that the use of force was justified in certain situations—especially against Klingons.

His arguments horrified his peers. His family on Vulcan formally renounced him. As time passed and his daughter grew, his behavior became reclusive, brooding, slightly irrational. He exposed Valeris to only the rudiments of a Vulcan upbringing, leaving her mostly in the care of the human house servant. She was not given a proper Vulcan education, nor was she initiated into the mind rules. Sessl seemed unconcerned. At times he seemed unaware of her existence.

She was seven, the traditional age for bonding, when a group of Klingons attacked Zorakis again. Perhaps they were not even Klingons; she had not seen them with her own eyes, only remembered that the housekeeper, Imea, had run into the house, screaming the word in the local dialect: *Klinzhai! Klinzhai!*

The world erupted around them in a fireball. They found Sessl in his study and dragged him into the skimmer. Imea was severely burned, but recovered; Sessl was unharmed, but did not.

They fled to a safer world, far from the border. Sessl became entirely irrational and had to be confined. He died within days. An autopsy revealed long-term degenerative brain disease.

Valeris remained with Imea until she was of an age to return to her parents' native planet, Vulcan, to request a reinstatement of her citizenship and formal training: to reclaim her heritage. Her experiences there led her to Starfleet.

She was not proud of what her father had become. She had grown up deploring his philosophy, even though she had as much cause as he or anyone else to despise the Klingons. As a Vulcan, she was sworn to logic, not to the indulgence of emotion.

But she had good reason to agree with Captain Kirk: the Klingons could not be trusted. They had proved themselves to be a dangerously violent race.

Even so, listening to Burke and Samno's ignorant, bigoted remarks, she found it difficult to keep the distaste she felt from registering in her expression.

Burke and Samno began moving in Valeris's direction, both still looking over their shoulders in the direction the Klingons had gone, with the result that they very nearly ran into Valeris without seeing her.

Startled, Burke did a double take; Samno gasped aloud and drew back. "We were just kidding, Lieutenant," Samno said sheepishly, realizing that they had been overheard.

"You men have work?" Valeris interrupted, wondering whether the coldness she felt was audible in her tone. No matter. Her duty required her to work with these men. She would do so logically and efficiently, but that did not mean she had to like them.

"Yes, sir," Burke answered, standing to attention. Samno struggled to follow suit.

"Then snap to it," Valeris told them, and wondered as she watched them go whether adequate precautions had been taken to ensure the Klingons' safety aboard the *Enterprise*.

"Your research laboratory is most impressive," Gorkon told Kirk as they stepped from the *Enterprise* science lab into the corridor.

The captain nodded. "Starfleet's been charting and cataloging planetary atmospheres. All vessels are equipped with analytical sensors." It was scarcely classified information; Kirk did not doubt the Klingons were well aware of the sensor—and weapons—capabilities of all Federation vessels, with the exception, perhaps, of *Excelsior*.

Despite his best efforts, Kirk found himself honestly liking the Klingon leader. It was impossible to imagine Gorkon allowing, much less ordering, the killings on Kudao or Themis. The chancellor was the antithesis of every Klingon Kirk had met: sincere, gracious, well educated in the ways of humans, possessed of a charismatic warmth. Even Chekov, who had joined the group at Gorkon's insistence after a chance encounter in the corridor, was smiling, put at ease by the chancellor's attempts to tell Federation jokes. Gorkon seemed devoted to the notion of peace between his Empire and the Federation, spoke as if he had been waiting for an incident such as Praxis in order to avert war. . . .

Was it all a skillful act? After all, this was a man—a Klingon, Kirk corrected himself—who listened to General Chang's advice.

Gorkon stopped abruptly; Kirk turned to face him.

"This cannot be easy for you, Captain," he said softly, as if reading Kirk's thoughts.

Kirk stared at him, startled, embarrassed, and angry all at once. Did Gorkon refer to David's death or to Carol? Or was he implying that he had sensed the hatred directed at him and his party? If so, his remark seemed inappropriate here, in front of others.

"I would feel awkward," Gorkon explained, in the face of Kirk's silence, "if I had to give you a tour of *our* vessel."

Kirk relaxed, feeling almost guilty that he had

mentally accused the chancellor of such an implication. "Would you care to go topside?"

It was General Chang who answered swiftly, with the same grim smile: "Very much."

Alarmed, Chekov motioned Kirk aside. "Captain," he whispered, "you're not going to show them the bridge?"

"Full diplomatic courtesy," Kirk replied between clenched teeth, angry at Chekov—and himself—for questioning his judgment.

Kirk turned back to Gorkon and his entourage. "Chancellor," he said, gesturing the way toward the lift.

The group filed into the turbolift. Just as the doors were closing, Kirk heard a question, so faint that at first he thought it must have been his imagination.

"Yes, but would you want to drink from the same glass?"

In the redecorated officers' mess, dinner was proceeding smoothly. Spock felt encouraged. Despite the tension he had sensed aboard the ship earlier in the day, the Klingons and the *Enterprise* bridge crew seemed to be getting along quite well. No one had reacted in the least when the Klingons spurned the proffered utensils in favor of eating with their fingers. Indeed, even the captain appeared to have relaxed and was enjoying a lively debate with Azetbur and Gorkon about the merits of various types of liquor. The Romulan ale had served its purpose, though Spock had been mildly shocked when Valeris suggested it. At times, her behavior surprised him. He often had to remind himself that being born Vulcan and being raised Vulcan were two very different things.

He regretted that her duty shift made it impossible for her to be present at the dinner. She was an interesting conversationalist—Valeris's background rendered her more comfortable around humans and other aliens than most Vulcans—and she was capable of understanding most attempts at humor, a trait Spock would have envied, had his emotional mastery been less complete. It would have been interesting to introduce her to the Klingons and note their reactions to her name. And it would have furthered diplomatic relations.

Against the backdrop of stars, Gorkon raised his crystal goblet, filled to the rim with smoking blue ale. "I give you a toast: the undiscovered country . . ."

Spock glanced sharply at the chancellor. He was familiar with the reference, which he thought more appropriate to a wake than to a diplomatic dinner. Indeed, to whose death did Gorkon refer?

". . . the future," Gorkon finished merrily, aware of the stir he had caused.

Those at the table echoed him and raised their glasses. "The undiscovered country."

Spock lifted his own goblet and took a perfunctory sip. The chancellor had insisted that Spock be served Romulan ale in order to make a proper toast. Aware of Klingon custom, Spock acquiesed in this instance, for the sake of intragalactic relations. He had never drunk Romulan ale and was apprehensive. While he was capable of imbibing a small amount of ethanol without any noticeable effect, he doubted the same could be said for the smoking brew before him. And, as his physiology was similar to that of Romulans . . .

The taste was startling, electric on his tongue. Spock swallowed and noted that even that small amount had an immediate, faintly perceptible effect on his thought processes. He replaced the goblet and resolved to drink no more.

Nearby, McCoy and Uhura had set their glasses down and were attempting to politely stifle coughs.

*"Hamlet,"* Spock stated reflexively. "Act three, scene one."

Gorkon smiled, delighted. "'But that the dread of something after death, the undiscovered country from whose bourn no traveler returns, puzzles the will, and makes us rather bear those ills we have than fly to others that we know not of?' Ah, Captain Spock, you have never experienced Shakespeare until you have read him in the original Klingon."

"I do not understand," Spock said. "The quote clearly refers to the fear of death."

Gorkon leaned forward, enthusiastic about his subject. "But do you not see that it is also a metaphor concerning fear of the unknown? Our people have been in what amounts to a state of undeclared war with your Federation for nearly seven decades—and why? Because war, battle, is all we know. Because peace is something new, different, frightening to us. But we must be willing to embrace the fear and move forward into what awaits us. Into the future. We must find a way to reconcile our warrior concepts of honor and glory with the concept of peaceful coexistence with other cultures. Otherwise"—his expression darkened as he sat back—"we will destroy ourselves."

Spock nodded thoughtfully, then watched as General Chang turned to Kirk with a maliciously pleasant expression. The captain had made significant progress toward draining his glass of ale. Spock began to seriously doubt the merits of Valeris's suggestion.

"'To be or not to be,'" Chang quoted. "That is the question which preoccupies our people, Captain Kirk." He glanced quickly in Gorkon's direction as if acknowledging a source of contention with the chancellor. "We need *breathing* room."

Spock caught the reference, which he hoped was unintentional. The captain did as well, for he muttered, "Earth, Germany, 1938."

The brow over Chang's good eye rose. "I beg your pardon?"

Brigadier Kerla leaned forward hastily—so hastily that Spock wondered whether he had been charged with the task of keeping General Chang in line—and changed the subject. "Captain Kirk, I thought Romulan ale was illegal."

Kirk started at the sudden switch in topic, then regained his composure and smiled faintly. "One of the advantages of being a thousand light-years from Federation headquarters."

McCoy broke the awkward silence that followed.

"To you, Chancellor Gorkon." Face flushed, eyes shining, the doctor lifted his glass with a surge of enthusiasm. "One of the architects of our future."

Spock lifted his glass but did not drink, concerned by how quickly the ale seemed to be affecting the humans. He wondered if the Klingons had noticed—and saw that Gorkon had drunk very little. The chancellor had settled back into his chair to listen carefully to what the humans were saying.

Thus far the humans were conducting themselves appropriately. Even Commander Scott, who sighed as he signaled the attendant for more ale, "Perhaps we are looking at something of that future here." He eyed Kerla beside him. "You know, this isna my first time drinking with Klingons."

Sober and reserved, Azetbur turned her face toward the Vulcan. "Captain Spock, mindful of all your work behind the scenes, and despite the cordiality at this mess, I do not sense an acceptance of our people throughout your ship."

Kirk cast a significant glance at Spock. The Vulcan understood; the Klingons, then, had heard the offhand remark just before the lift doors closed. It had not been the only disparaging comment about Klingons Spock had heard that day—though fortunately the others, with their less than Vulcan hearing, had been spared them.

"The crew is naturally wary, ma'am," Spock replied. "We have been at war a long time. Perhaps not technically, in view of the Organian treaty—"

"A peace forced down our throats," Chang growled.

Spock acknowledged the general with a look. "Precisely. Had the Organians not intervened, war would have been inevitable. Perhaps we might still have been at war."

Glass of sapphire liquid in hand, Uhura joined the exchange. "Our media have been playing on our feelings against Klingons with the Kudao ... incident."

"Just as our media constantly vilify the Federation," Azetbur acknowledged, ignoring Chang's and Kerla's disapproving stares.

Uhura nodded excitedly. "Both sides must overcome ingrained prejudice—but how?"

Chekov held out his goblet for the attendant to refill. "Perhaps with few small steps at a time. Like this one."

"And perhaps with a large step or two," Dr. McCoy interjected, beaming at Azetbur. Spock suspected that the sudden surge of previously undiscovered warm feelings was in no small way related to the amount of ale consumed. "Like a peace treaty."

The suggestion evoked murmurs of approval from all at the table with the exception of Gorkon, who still played the role of disinterested observer, and Chang.

The general addressed Kirk abruptly. "Captain Kirk, are you willing to give up Starfleet?"

Kirk stared at the Klingon without answering.

Spock intervened. "I believe the captain feels that Starfleet's mission has always been one of peace."

Still glaring at Chang, Kirk said, "Far be it from me to dispute my first officer. Starfleet has always—"

"Come now, Captain." Chang's tone grew patronizing. "No need to mince words. This dinner is off the record. In space all warriors are cold warriors."

Spock glanced at Gorkon. The chancellor made no effort to correct his adviser, but waited intently to hear the response. Perhaps Gorkon, too, believed that Starfleet's primary function was a military one.

"We have *never* tried to—" Scott began angrily.

Spock attempted to inject a note of logic into the discussion. "General Chang, I joined Starfleet because I know it to be an exploratory and research organization, a rare opportunity for one interested in the sciences—"

"Science?" Chang countered. "A great deal of science went into the construction of your photon torpedo banks, I daresay."

Spock continued in a patient tone, ignoring the outraged gasps of his crewmates. "That is true, General. Starfleet vessels are equipped with weaponry—for defense purposes only."

"Aye," Scott slurred. "To protect Federation planets from the likes of—"

"That will be enough, Mr. Scott," Spock warned.

Kerla wheeled on him. "You hypocritically presume that your democratic system gives you a moral prerogative to force other cultures to conform to your politics."

"That's not true!" McCoy half shouted.

Chekov leaned angrily across the table. "We do *not* impose democracy on others. We believe that every planet has a sovereign claim to inalienable human rights."

Azetbur laughed, more a sound of contempt than amusement. "In*alien* . . . If you could hear yourselves. *Human* rights? Even the name is racist. The Federation is a *Homo sapiens*–only club."

Spock raised a brow.

"Present company excepted, to be sure," Chang said cheerfully, as if he found the entire situation quite entertaining.

"Well," Uhura admitted, "I suppose we're not perfect—"

Palms on the table, Scott pushed himself to his feet. "Don't let them put words in your mouth! I haven't served thirty years in the engine room of a starship to be accused of gunboat diplomacy!"

"In any case, we know where this is leading," Brigadier Kerla said to no one in particular, his eyes glittering from the effects of the ale. "The annihilation of our culture. The Klingons will replace those on the lowest rung of the Federation employment ladder, taking menial jobs and performing them for lower pay—"

"That's economics," Chekov protested, "not racism."

Uhura gestured angrily with her goblet. "But you have to admit it adds up to the same thing."

McCoy turned on her. "Don't be naive, Commander!"

She frosted instantly. "Kindly do not patronize me, Doctor."

Spock turned to the captain, seeking help, but Kirk stared sullenly down the table, clearly unwilling to interfere.

"We're explorers, not diplomats!" Chekov insisted to Chang.

McCoy gave his shoulder a push. "Come on, Chekov. Starfleet's killed an awful lot of natural phenomena in the name of exploration."

"We follow orders!" Scott objected, still on his feet.

Chekov shook his head in disgust. "Since when has *that* been an excuse? Diplomacy must resolve these—"

"Right," Scott half shouted. "Leave it to the politicians to muck it up and leave us defenseless!"

A cough interrupted the argument. Spock turned to see Gorkon, his expression somber; the other Klingons were not so successful at concealing their amusement.

"Well," Gorkon said after several seconds of silence, "I see we have a long way to go."

He rose. As Spock and the others followed suit, the Vulcan succeeded in mastering the keen embarrassment evoked by the *Enterprise* crew's behavior. The sense of futility proved far more difficult to shake. The past few days had revealed a startling degree of anger and bitterness that Spock had never expected to find among Federation members, least of all his friends. He understood the captain's difficulties, in light of Carol Marcus's condition and David's murder at the hands of Kruge, but he had not anticipated such hostility among the other crew members.

Had all this emotion been stirred up by the media coverage of the events on Kudao? Were humans so enormously susceptible to influence?

Valeris's judgment concerning the Romulan ale had been only partially correct. It had served to relax the diners initially, but it had also stripped away the thin veil of civilization to reveal the hatred lurking beneath. Spock wondered if he had totally misjudged the capacity of human beings for rational behavior, for peaceful coexistence.

If Gorkon felt the same way, their chances of attaining peace in the galaxy were remote indeed.

Jim Kirk stood in the transporter room and waited for the Klingons to take their leave. He felt a distant shame that he knew would grow as the effects of ale passed, but for now it was eclipsed by a pleasantly freeing vertigo and a tingling numbness in his nose and extremities. His feet no longer seemed connected to his legs, and he'd had to concentrate to keep from stumbling in the corridor. The others seemed in no better shape; McCoy kept yawning as he swayed on his feet, on the verge of nodding off, while Scott's broad face was flushed an alarming shade of pink. Uhura's cool demeanor indicated that she was still angry with the doctor and disgusted with the lot of them. As for Chekov, he wore an expression of contrived politeness that failed to entirely hide his sullen anger—an expression Kirk feared matched his own.

Thank God, at least Spock hadn't embarrassed them tonight—although the reverse certainly wasn't true. Kirk pitied the Vulcan, trying to establish a diplomatic dialogue with the Klingons while surrounded by a bunch of angry drunks.

Well, tomorrow he'd make it up to Spock. And to the Klingons, if they still wanted to have anything to do with the Federation after tonight. But for now the ale had freed Kirk's anger beyond the point of denial; his thoughts kept returning to Carol, to her deathly pale waxen profile, to the sight of her chest rising and falling gently, prompted only by the respirator. . . .

The best he could do was be civil.

Gorkon was speaking; Kirk frowned, tried to make sense of what the Klingon was saying.

"Thank you, Captain Kirk. The evening has been most . . . edifying."

Kirk felt a distant prickle of shame and anger and replied woodenly, "We must do this again soon."

Gorkon gazed at him with an intensity that made Kirk shift uncomfortably. "You don't trust me."

The captain looked away.

"I don't blame you," Gorkon continued softly. "You see me as a—what is the word?—a cliché. If there is to be a brave new world, we old people will have the hardest time living in it."

Kirk felt a flush of anger warm his cheeks. *We old people . . .*

"Captain Spock." Gorkon nodded at the Vulcan.

"Chancellor." Spock turned to Azetbur. "A pleasure to meet you, madam."

"Captain Spock." Azetbur bowed as she took her place beside her father.

"General Chang," Kirk said suddenly, surprising the others as well as himself. "A pleasure . . ."

Chang faced him, once again standing too close, as if daring the captain to step back. Chang's posture, voice, sly grin, all spoke of challenge. "Parting is such sweet sorrow, shall we say goodnight till it be morrow?"

Kirk clenched his fist, wanting nothing more than to drive it into Chang's midsection—but knowing Spock's and Gorkon's worried gazes were upon him, he struck it against his own chest and extended his arm in a Klingon salute.

Infuriatingly, Chang seemed highly amused as he stepped with his party onto the transporter platform. He pulled his communicator from his belt, spoke a few words into it, and nodded to Kirk.

"Energize," Kirk said, and did not try to hide the relief in his tone.

The whine of the transporter filled the room; the forms of the Klingons shimmered and were gone.

"Thank God," Scott sighed, leaning heavily against the controls.

"Did you see the way they ate?" Chekov complained, his Russian accent grown thicker than usual under the ale's influence. "Terrible table manners—"

"I do not believe," Spock interrupted, in as frosted a tone as Kirk had ever heard him use, "that our own conduct will distinguish us in the annals of diplomacy."

Kirk ran a hand across his forehead, trying to ease the headache that was already starting. He would attempt any necessary apologies and figure out what, if anything, could be done to improve the situation with the Klingons—tomorrow, when he could think. For now, recuperation seemed the only choice. "I'm going to sleep this off," he said in a low voice to Spock. "Let me know if there's some other way we can screw up tonight."

He stumbled to his quarters under the misguided impression that the evening's troubles had ended.

# Chapter Four

UNDER THE watchful eye of her bodyguard, Azetbur hesitated at the door to her father's quarters.

Although it was midday aboard *Kronos One,* the Romulan ale had left her dizzy, and she had gone immediately to her cabin to lie down until the effects passed. She had wakened from a light doze only moments later, heart pounding with the dread that had been disrupting her sleep ever since she set foot on the ship. Without thinking, she had come to Gorkon's cabin, followed silently by the sentinel who had been standing watch outside her own door.

Her fingers hovered above the buzzer. She did not know why she had come here, except to verify with her own eyes that her father still lived. The nights before they set sail for Earth had been plagued by troubling dreams of his death. Now, influenced by the ale, she was running to her father like a nightmare-frightened child.

Such behavior was very unbecoming in a member of the High Council. Azetbur felt shame.

At the same time, she pressed the buzzer, and felt an unspeakable relief when the door opened to reveal Gorkon, minus his impressive appointments, dressed in a simple dark tunic.

Before entering the cabin, Azetbur turned to her guard and signaled for him to remain outside. When the door closed behind them, she scolded him: "Father, where are your guards?"

It was a constant source of contention between them, his cavalier attitude toward his own safety—though he took extravagant, unnecessary pains to ensure his daughter's. Gorkon surveyed his surroundings with a mildly vacant expression, as if surprised to see the guards missing, and combed his graying beard with his fingers. The light by his chair burned. Azetbur saw text scrolled on the viewer. He had been reading, no doubt preparing for the next hour's meeting with his advisers. She was accustomed to his distractedness, a side effect of the intensity with which he approached his work.

"Gone," he said, focusing his dark amber eyes on her and seeing her at last. He smiled. "The ale rendered them useless; I suppose they're napping in their quarters or seeking some other appropriately warriorlike pursuit. I deemed it more prudent to trust the security devices. Come, sit." He motioned. "Have you come as a council member or as a daughter?"

"Both," Azetbur said, continuing to stand while Gorkon settled back into his chair and studied her. "Father—" She broke off, uncertain, realizing that she had come to him for comfort and had nothing rational to say. "I am . . . concerned."

Gorkon nodded, encouraging, focused now only on her, listening deeply to each word with disconcerting intentness.

"For your safety. I did not realize the depth of hatred that awaits us on Earth until we went aboard the *Enterprise.*"

He sighed. "It . . . startled me as well. Not that it existed—certainly, the fact that our peoples have cause to despise each other has been no secret for the past seventy years—but that it was so overt. I suspect Kudao has brought it to the surface."

"Kirk," Azetbur said, with sudden heat. "Kirk hates us. I do not trust him. Father, don't go aboard his ship again."

He tilted his broad, whiskered face quizzically. "Kirk is not dangerous, Zeta. His hatred is an honest one; his son was killed by Captain Kruge. But I suspect he has the intelligence—"

"If his son was killed," she countered, with a vehemence that surprised them both, "then why should he not seek revenge?"

"He is not a Klingon warrior. He is not sworn to blood revenge."

"I do not trust him," Azetbur insisted, letting the anguish she felt creep into her voice. "Father, I fear for your safety. I cannot sleep."

Gorkon looked away for a time—choosing his

words carefully, Azetbur knew, so that he would not unnecessarily alarm his daughter.

"Perhaps it is just as well that we have this discussion now," he said finally. "I do not believe Kirk means me harm. He is angry, resentful. He feels he has suffered much at our hands. I suspect he is right." He gave a faint, ironic smile. "And you are right, daughter. We both know my chances of surviving beyond this peace conference are remote."

Azetbur stared at him, stricken, tempted to lift a hand to her heart, yet restrained by pride.

"Sit," Gorkon said. It was not a request. Azetbur obeyed and took the chair opposite her father.

His gaze grew sympathetic, then hardened again. "If I die, you must succeed me."

"You will not die—"

"Listen to me!"

The uncharacteristic anger in his tone startled her into silence.

He began again, quietly, calmly. "I have been lucky, Zeta, that the warriors have permitted me to come this far. That I have managed to avoid assassination long enough to get the entire High Council to agree on the necessity of a peace treaty is nothing short of a miracle. Surely you have always realized that. Our security measures are nothing short of drastic. But now we must fear not only those within our own Empire. We must fear factions within the Federation and Romulan governments as well." He smiled faintly. "My child, indulge me. Does it not make sense to plan for the future? Or would you rather we leave the Empire in the hands of the military, to do with as they will?"

She drew in a breath and hardened herself against grief. "It seems reasonable to plan for such an emergency, Chancellor. What do you suggest?"

"You must succeed me," he repeated. "Zeta, there is no one else on the council I can trust. Korrd, perhaps, but he is too old and ill."

"Brigadier Kerla—" she began.

"Kerla is too hot-blooded, too easily swayed. He is a warrior at heart. Even now I do not know where his loyalties lie. And Chang is too shrewd to trust." He shook his head. "No, daughter. You are the only one."

She laughed softly, unhappily. "A female chancellor, Father?"

"I have the right to name my successor. Klingon law does not prohibit it."

"Klingon custom *assumes*—"

"Warrior custom, not Klingon. You must learn to make the distinction. The position of chancellor is not controlled by the military. The people will accept it, even if the military does not."

"And if you are assassinated, what makes you think I would not be?"

"I have made special arrangements with other members of the High Council. They have all sworn to protect you and confirm your appointment."

"All of them?" Azetbur asked, feeling, for reasons she could not yet fathom, a dull pang of suspicion. "You have spoken with all of them about this?"

"Yes."

She rose. "Father, you will not die."

"Of course not." Smiling, he leaned forward to touch her. "But will you promise me, Zeta?"

She felt the sudden, irrational anger of a rejected child. She had come to him for comfort, reassurance, and all he could do was speak to her of death.

"Promise me." He brushed her arm with his fingertips.

"You will not die," she said curtly, "so long as you can manage to keep your guards from getting drunk." She swept from the room, unable to look at him, knowing the sight of his face would break her heart.

Kirk made it to his quarters with only a small amount of difficulty. The euphoric numbing effects of the Romulan liquor had faded, replaced by an unpleasant thrumming in his head and a fatigue that made his limbs heavy, as if he were trying to move upstream against a strong current. He sat on his bunk and rubbed his eyes as the ship's bells chimed 0100.

He was half tempted to contact the hospital on Starbase Twenty-three again, though he had managed to get through earlier that afternoon. Kwanmei had been friendly but apologetic: still no change in Carol's condition. She promised to notify Jim aboard *Enterprise* the instant anything happened.

In the meantime there was nothing to do but

wait . . . and find something, anything, to keep his mind off Carol.

"Captain's log," Jim dictated. "Stardate 9523.8. The *Enterprise* hosted Chancellor Gorkon and company for dinner last night. Our manners were not exactly Emily Post. Note to the galley: Romulan ale no longer to be served at diplomatic functions."

He sighed and leaned back on the bunk, thinking. In one way, he felt embarrassed that he and his senior bridge crew had behaved as they did in front of the Klingons; in another, more philosophic way, he was glad it had happened. It would not make negotiations any easier, but a clearing of the air was necessary to the process. And if Gorkon was truly the shrewd, wise statesman Kirk perceived him to be, he would not allow the evening's unpleasantries to interfere with his goal.

Kirk yawned, then began dictating again, his voice low and drowsy. "But it wasn't the ale. That was just the excuse we needed to say all the things that were really on our minds. . . ."

His voice trailed off. For a time, he drifted on the verge of sleep, then started at the intercom's shrill signal.

The uncharacteristic urgency in Spock's voice made Jim sit up and shake himself awake.

"Captain Kirk, will you please join me on the bridge? Captain Kirk . . ."

A half hour before Kirk received the summons, Azetbur had scarcely returned to her quarters when the buzzer summoned her to the door. It opened to reveal Brigadier Kerla. His dark hair fell onto his shoulders as he bowed, stiffly formal, mindful of the guard.

"Councillor Azetbur," he said politely. "There is an urgent matter I wish to discuss to you."

She gave the guard a dismissive glance and nodded for Kerla to enter. He stepped past her and, once the doors had snapped shut, turned and reached for her.

She pulled back. In the dim light, his dark eyes glittered; his breath reeked of ale. "You're still drunk," Azetbur said, her tone heavy with contempt.

For an instant he hesitated, his eyes reflecting puzzlement and restrained fury. He *was* drunk, she knew—at least slightly, though the ale's effects were fading and he was probably in far better command of himself than he had been during the dinner aboard *Enterprise*.

"What have I done?" he demanded.

She had no answer for that. She knew only that the encounter with her father had left her full of unreasoning fury. She forced it from her tone and spoke calmly. "Nothing. But you should be on your way to a meeting, Councillor. Why—"

He caught her wrist, lifted her palm to his face, drew in her scent. "Azetbur. Zeta . . . I had to see you." The words came swiftly, urgently, from his lips. "I can wait no longer. Let us take the oath."

Her expression hardened. They had spoken of

this many times; always she had given him the same answer, more out of duty to her father than from a lack of love for Kerla. He was dynamic, strong, given more to passion than to thought, the opposite of everything Azetbur had been raised to respect, and she found him and his honesty of emotion undeniably attractive. When she was not preoccupied with worry, she realized she desired him equally.

But now his proposition seemed callous in light of her distressing conversation with Gorkon. How could she consider her own future when her father's was in such grave danger? She pulled her hand away.

"How many times must I repeat myself, Ker—"

Eyes burning, he leaned over her. "Do not reject me again. I cannot wait until after the conference."

"You must." She forced her tone to be cold, rejecting further argument. She pushed past him toward the door, turned, and stood beside it to indicate he should leave.

His breathing quickened by emotion, heavy brows knitted in disbelief, he watched her. Azetbur expected the usual quick display of rage, but instead, Kerla calmed himself and studied her face with an intensity uncannily like her father's. At last he released a single grudging sigh and moved for the door.

He paused beside her and spoke with a gentleness she had not heard in him before. "This anger is not meant for me. Something troubles you."

Taken aback, she raised a hand to her throat. They stared at each other a time before she said, "I . . . spoke with my father today."

He listened, waiting.

"We talked of the future." She lowered her voice to a whisper. "I fear for his life, Kerla."

"Your father is well protected. Were he not, he would not be alive now."

"You saw the hatred aboard *Enterprise.* There are many who do not want him to reach the conference, who wish him dead . . ."

Kerla straightened. "So long as I am able, I will protect him with my life, as I swear to protect you, Zeta."

He caught her wrist, gently this time, and drew her to him. She did not resist, but settled against him and let herself be comforted by the rapid beating of his heart.

Spock studied the deceptively peaceful display on the bridge viewscreen: the great battle cruiser *Kronos One* gliding silently alongside. The Vulcan was no longer concerned by the potentially awkward diplomatic situation that could result from the encounter between the *Enterprise* crew and the Klingons.

At the moment he had far greater things to worry about.

Spock leaned over the viewer at his station and confirmed the readout's accuracy for the sixth time, then straightened at the sound of the turbolift doors opening.

"Captain."

Kirk entered, squinted at the main viewscreen, then rubbed his eyes. "What is it, Spock?"

Valeris vacated the conn and took her place beside Chekov at the helm. Kirk remained on his feet, trying to focus his eyes on his first officer.

"I am . . . uncertain," Spock replied, at a loss to explain his certainty that some catastrophe was about to befall them. As a rule he scorned premonitions, and yet some peculiar instinct insisted he listen to this one.

The captain released a soft sound of exasperation. "Spock, I'm really tired . . ."

"We are reading an enormous amount of neutron radiation, Captain."

To Spock's relief, Kirk caught the implication and seemed to recover instantly from the effects of the Romulan ale. "Where?" He glanced quickly at *Kronos* on the screen.

"Curiously it appears to emanate from us," the Vulcan replied. The fact troubled him far more than it would have had the power surge come from the Klingon vessel. An unexpected surge of neutron radiation aboard the *Enterprise* signaled one of two possibilities: the first, that there had been a breach in the matter-antimatter reactor unit, with catastrophic results; the second, that the starship's photon torpedoes had been armed and brought to bear on a target.

"From us? From *Enterprise?*" Kirk's tone was one of disbelief.

Spock nodded. "I have checked with Engineering. All systems are normal. No loss of integrity in the reactor core."

Kirk strode over to the helm and placed a hand on the back of Valeris's chair. "Lieutenant, do you know anything about a neutron energy surge?"

"Sir?" Puzzled, she wheeled to face him.

"Mr. Chekov, anything unusual?"

"Just the size of my head," Chekov moaned.

"I know what you mean," Kirk said softly.

As he spoke, a photon torpedo streaked from the bottom of the viewscreen and struck *Kronos*'s hull with dazzling white-hot force.

"What the—" Kirk raised a hand to shield his eyes.

Spock blinked to clear the afterimage, then bent over his readout to verify the impossible. "We have fired on the chancellor's ship," he stated heavily.

Kirk wheeled, his expression stunned. "Uhura, monitor! Chekov, find out what's going on down in Weapons!"

"Torpedo room?" Chekov said into his monitor, over the calm drone of Valeris's voice, saying: "Direct hit."

Uhura swiveled to face Kirk. "Confirmed, Captain!"

A second torpedo flared in the bottom corner of the screen.

*"Who's doing that?"* Kirk cried as it hurtled at the battle cruiser. He forced himself not to turn from the blinding explosion.

"The Klingon ship's hull has been breached," Spock reported. "They have lost gravity and are slowly losing life support. Damage to the vessel is severe." He straightened and faced his captain. "Jim, they never even raised their shields."

Kirk closed his eyes.

Moments earlier, surrounded by advisers and security guards in his stateroom aboard *Kronos One,* Gorkon had found himself in the midst of a debate that made the humans' argument at dinner seem like a most civilized exchange of pleasantries. He did not allow himself to be overly disturbed by Azetbur's failure to promise to succeed him. He knew his daughter well: she would not fail him. At the moment she was filled with emotion and Romulan ale. If and when the time came, she would do what was best.

Besides, he had no choice but to trust her.

The chancellor remained silent, content to listen and learn what he could; it was a strategy he employed often, for it taught him much. The three who argued now—General Korrd and Brigadiers Kerla and Kamerg—were most useful to him, for they rarely agreed, which meant Gorkon heard three very different viewpoints on virtually every issue.

Chang, though cold-bloodedly efficient, was of little use as an adviser. Chang was closemouthed, too shrewd to let his opinion be known until he had tested the political waters. It was Chancellor Gorkon's custom to dismiss both Chang and Azetbur from such discussions. Azetbur was too outspokenly loyal to her father to allow free discussion of the issues to proceed, and Chang, like Gorkon, listened much and said little.

Gorkon had enough of a healthy mistrust of Chang not to want him to know too much.

Kerla, who had joined the discussion less than a minute before, was already on his feet and shouting. He made an impassioned gesture at Gorkon, who listened calmly. "How can we hold our heads up after the humans have so insulted us? Chancellor, did you not hear the things the captain allowed his underlings to say? Did you not hear what the soldier in the hall said when we entered the lift? They despise us! I have heard their jokes, but for the sake of decency will not repeat them here. They refer to us as simians, the speechless primates they evolved from! They think of us as unintelligent creatures, without feelings or thought!"

"Sit down!" General Korrd rumbled, in a voice that rattled the bulkhead. Obese, aged, but uncannily shrewd, and—amazing in one his age, who had seen so many battles, spilled so much blood—capable of extending his thoughts beyond the barriers of his own culture.

Perhaps, Gorkon thought, it was precisely because Korrd had seen so many brave warriors, including his own children, die beside him, that the old general now argued the case for peace.

Sullenly, Kerla sat, not out of fear of Korrd's bellowing, but out of respect for an elder's wishes.

"But he's right, General," Kamerg, far younger than Korrd, not so young or hot-blooded as Kerla, averred. "How can we deal peace with the Federation when the humans hate us so?"

"Not all humans hate us," Korrd said. "And there are others in the Federation besides humans."

Kamerg nodded thoughtfully. "Perhaps. But they are the driving force within it. If the humans do not deal fairly with us, we have no hope."

"You are discounting the Vulcans," Korrd said. "But more to the point: do we not have a thousand insulting names for humans? Do we not hate them as much as they hate us? Despise them for their weaknesses, even as they despise us for our strengths? Such feelings extend both ways.

"Try to understand: their culture abhors war; they see no glory in dying in battle, only waste. They fight only when it is necessary to defend themselves—and even then the Vulcans will not fight. Therefore, they see those who have died at our hands as victims, and us as murderers."

"They call us liars." Kerla's voice rose excitedly; he had scarcely been able to contain himself during the others' exchange. "Their own press accuses our government of murdering the Kudao settlers, then refuses to believe us when we explain they acted without the sanction of the High Council. Chancellor, I must speak my mind."

Korrd shot Gorkon an amused, long-suffering look, as if to ask, *And just what does he think he's been doing up to now?* Gorkon saw, but for Kerla's sake, did not react.

"I implore you," Kerla continued. "Forget the

notion of a treaty with the humans. We must strengthen our ties with the Romulans. Together we can force the Federation to its knees!"

Korrd gave a loud snort. "The Romulans don't possess the resources the Federation does. Stop thinking with your glands, Kerla. Even if we allied ourselves with the Romulans, we could never defeat the Federation. And the Romulans don't like us any better than the humans do."

"At least they understand what a warrior's honor means," Kerla countered hotly.

Old Korrd narrowed his eyes, then belched loudly to show what he thought of the implied insult.

On his feet once more, Kerla faced Gorkon. "Chancellor, I believe if we forge an alliance with the Romulans, we *can* defeat the Federation, then claim the resources for ourselves. There is still time."

"I see," Gorkon replied slowly. "Tell me, did Chang discuss this with you?"

Kerla's eyes blazed. "I act on no one's behalf but my own." He stiffened to attention. "With your permission, Chancellor . . ."

Gorkon nodded.

Furious, Kerla strode, long hair flowing, from the stateroom.

Gorkon sighed as the doors snapped shut behind the young Klingon's retreating form. He trusted Kerla, as he did all of his advisers—to an extent. The brigadier was loyal to the chancellor, but he could be persuaded to betray Gorkon if he became convinced that the good of the Empire was at stake.

Gorkon was well aware of the growing dissatisfaction among his military leaders over the new peace treaty. For that reason Gorkon had increased his and Azetbur's personal security, though he knew there was no way to be truly safe. Foolish was the leader who failed to realize that he was just as likely to be struck down by his own bodyguard as killed by a declared enemy.

He turned to see General Korrd studying him. The older Klingon rested his hands atop his impressive girth and made a low, soft rumble in his throat that said, *Ah, youth . . .*

Kamerg shook his head. "The brigadier is a fool."

"The brigadier is still young," old Korrd said by way of apology for Kerla's rudeness. "He perceives a warrior's honor as consisting of black-and-white choices. I once saw the universe through such a romantic filter."

"Kerla is not alone," Gorkon said carefully. "Others agree with him—others who wield a great deal of military power." He did not say more, nor did he mention the names of those he suspected of plotting against him. While he felt comfortable speaking of such things in front of Korrd and Kamerg, he was unsure of the loyalties of the security guards. More than likely at least one of them was a spy.

Korrd's ancient eyes gleamed; he nodded in understanding and opened his mouth to say something.

Gorkon never heard the words. With dizzying

impact, the room's axis swung ninety degrees; the port bulkhead became the floor. Gorkon was caught in an insane tumble of arms, legs, furniture —all outlined against the pulsing amber light of the alert.

The momentum dashed him against the bulkhead, forcing the air from his lungs. For an instant, no more, the ship hovered on its side, then righted itself with a groan. Gorkon was flung back against the cold metal floor and the softer, more forgiving surface of General Korrd.

He knew what had happened even before the general said it.

"We're hit!" Korrd roared beneath him, a half breath before another blast shook the ship.

Gorkon felt himself being catapulted once more —but this time a curious lightness filled him. Instead of colliding with the bulkhead, he lingered weightless in the air. Around him, chairs, advisers, soldiers, rose and began to float. With the detachment of one who realizes escape is impossible, death inevitable, Gorkon watched as his security guards flailed vainly in pursuit of weapons that floated just out of reach.

"Gravity generator!" someone called behind him.

*"Enterprise!"* Kamerg roared in helpless fury.

"Not *Enterprise*," Gorkon whispered. He knew Spock and trusted him utterly, more than he trusted his own people, and he had instinctively liked and trusted James Kirk. Kirk had good reason to hate, but, Kerla's words notwithstanding, he was a human who understood a warrior's honor, even if he did not understand killing. Kirk would perform his duty well, despite personal feelings.

Kirk was not behind this.

The sounds of weapons fire and screaming issued beyond the door of the stateroom.

*Azetbur,* Gorkon thought with a pang of alarm. *If they kill me, they will also try to kill Azetbur. I must warn her. . . .* He ignored the vertigo and clawed at the air in a wasted attempt to find purchase. The others in the room, clearly realizing what was coming, were trying desperately to move away from the chancellor.

Beyond the door, the sizzle of phaserfire searing flesh. Screams. The sounds drew closer.

Gorkon tried hopelessly to swim through the air, push his way past the floating debris to the intercom on the bulkhead. Even if he could not save Azetbur, if he could hear her voice again, speak to her one more time—

An agonized scream. A body sailed through the opening door, followed by a floating slick of blood, violet turned brown in the pulsing amber light. A severed arm followed after, spewing a bloody trail that pooled on the ceiling. The arm sailed forward end over end, bumping into its former owner's corpse, and finally ending up in the midst of the horrified onlookers.

Two Starfleet crewmen stood in the doorway, heavy gravity boots on their feet, blasters in their hands, raised and ready to fire.

On either side of Gorkon, security guards raised

their weapons and struggled awkwardly to take aim at the armed intruders.

Kamerg had managed to pull himself to the bulkhead intercom and was screaming to the bridge: *"Enterprise officers are assassinating the chancellor! Enterprise— Kirk—"*

No, Gorkon wanted to say. Not *Enterprise.* Not Kirk. Someone else is responsible.

The men in Starfleet uniforms fired on the guards. Not standard Fleet-issue phasers, Gorkon saw, but burning phasers, illegal in the Federation, capable of inflicting far more damage, far more pain. Capable of searing through flesh and bone.

Blood spattered him. Gorkon closed his eyes, felt a guard's body bump gently against him.

*Azetbur,* he thought desperately, hoping that sheer intensity of will would carry his message to her, *my child, continue my work.*

He opened his eyes again and calmly met his killers' gazes. He wanted to tell them their deception would not work; he knew they had not come from the *Enterprise.*

There was not time. One of the men fired. Gorkon shuddered at the fiery agony that consumed him from chest to abdomen but did not permit himself to cry out. Instead he sighed and thought of Azetbur before surrendering to darkness.

# Chapter Five

ABOARD *ENTERPRISE*, the captain and his horrified crew watched the main viewscreen as Chang, his contorted features bathed in amber glow, screamed at Kirk in his native language.

The visual went abruptly, ominously dark.

Finger to her earpiece, Uhura swung toward the conn. "He says we've fired on them in a blatant act of war."

"We *haven't* fired—" Kirk began.

From his station, Spock interrupted. "According to the data bank, we *have*, Captain. Twice."

Valeris glanced down at the helm console. "Captain, they're coming about!"

She punched a control. On the screen, *Kronos* slowly rotated, then closed on the *Enterprise.*

Spock bent over his viewer. "Confirmed. They're preparing to fire."

Chekov swiveled his head to gaze at Kirk. "Shields up, Captain?"

Kirk stared at the screen. Impossible, of course. *Enterprise* could not have fired on *Kronos*—unless sabotage was involved.

Kwan-mei Suarez's words echoed meaninglessly in his mind: *Out of nowhere. The ships fired out of nowhere. . . .*

At the moment Chang wasn't willing to listen. Something drastic had to be done to get the Klingons' attention, to convince them that Kirk had not given the order to fire.

"Captain." Valeris's voice rose to a notably un-Vulcan pitch. "Our shields . . . !"

Kirk studied her calmly. "Uhura," he said, holding Valeris's gaze, "signal our surrender."

Uhura turned to stare at him. "Captain—"

He faced her. *"We surrender."*

She returned to her board and complied as Chekov protested, "Captain, if they fire at us with our shields down—"

Kirk struck a toggle on the console arm. "Torpedo bay! *Did* we fire those torpedoes?"

"Negative, Captain," Scott's voice replied. "According to inventory, we're still fully loaded."

Kirk felt only infinitesimal relief. At least his ship wasn't responsible for the damage to the Klingon vessel—but it remained for him to convince Chang of that.

Spock frowned as he checked the information on his viewer. "Data banks reconfirm, Captain. Two photon torpedoes fired."

"Stand down your weapons," Kirk told Scott.

He heard a sharp intake of breath on the other side of the communication. "Captain, if—"

"Stand *down*, Mr. Scott. All stop. Do you hear me, mister?"

"Aye, sir," Scott said reluctantly.

Kirk closed the channel and held his breath.

*Come on, Chang, figure it out.*

Nothing happened.

Spock bent over his viewer. "They appear to be holding their fire, Captain."

Kirk almost started as, behind him, the lift doors snapped open and shut. McCoy appeared at the captain's side, medikit in hand.

"What the hell's going on?"

"I wish I knew," Kirk said. "Uhura?"

"It's pretty chaotic over there, sir. There's been weapons fire and a lot of shouting."

"I'm going aboard." He rose and glanced over his shoulder at his first officer. "Spock, you have the conn."

Spock stepped in front of the lift, blocking him.

"I am responsible for involving you in this, Captain. I will go."

Kirk shook his head. "I'm going. As captain, I have to convince them I didn't give the order to fire; your presence wouldn't be half as convincing."

Spock hovered, uncertain; Kirk continued. "Besides, you're going to be responsible for getting me out of this. Meantime"—he lowered his voice—"we're not going to be the instigators of a full-scale war on the eve of universal peace."

The Vulcan nodded; Kirk saw the hint of gratitude in his eyes. Surprisingly, Spock patted him firmly, once, on the shoulder blade. "Perhaps you're right, Captain."

Kirk looked at him, slightly startled, as McCoy stated, in a tone that allowed for no argument: "I'm going, too. They may need a doctor."

Kirk didn't protest. "Uhura, tell them we're coming. And tell them we're unarmed."

Aboard *Kronos One,* General Chang left the bridge and painstakingly made his way to the stateroom by grasping the bulkhead handholds. Above his head, victims of the slaughter floated beneath growing pools of violet blood.

He had been deeply tempted to fire on *Enterprise,* but he'd restrained himself. Even now the sight of the dead—some of them officers he had served with for years and respected—made him clench his teeth and promise himself revenge on Kirk.

Soon. Soon enough. But it would not have been honorable to fire on a surrendered vessel.

Chang paused at the stateroom door. Here the sea of airborne blood increased as he saw before him a scene as chilling as any from Kudao: disembodied heads, limbs, a torso severed at the waist, drifted in an ocean of death, the silence marred by the occasional groans of the wounded.

Chang did not shrink from the sight. As a warrior, he had long ago learned to accept the cost of battle. But for this, he promised himself grimly, Kirk would have to die.

In the midst of this obscene tide, Chancellor Gorkon floated face down like a drowned victim— alive, for bright violet blood still seeped across his chest and arm to pool just above his back. Chang cried out to him and swiped at the air in an effort to reach him, nearly losing his grip on the handhold. Others arrived to help. Chang shouted at them as well, but all attempts to grab Gorkon failed.

The lighting flickered. Chang lurched suddenly, jerked downward in the grip of an invisible giant as *Kronos*'s gravity returned. He fell to his knees and bowed his head beneath the thunderous downpour of bodies and blood.

Seconds before gravity was restored, Azetbur screamed with frustration as she clawed the air.

Her efforts did no good. She floated just out of reach of the smooth metal ceiling, unable to get her balance, even to control her direction.

Outside the door to her cabin, they were killing her father. She could hear muffled screams of slaughter. Soon they would come for her.

The thought did not frighten her, did not inspire her useless scrabbling, her helpless fury. She wanted to be free only so she could go to Gorkon and die with him. If he was not yet dead, she wanted to explain to him that she had always intended to obey his wishes, to succeed him.

She had known, even as she had allowed Kerla's

words to comfort her, that his promises were empty. How could he protect her father now, when all of them were reduced to such a vulnerable state? This was not the quiet assassination attempt of a councillor aboard *Kronos*—against such, Kerla might have proven effective.

This was an outright attack by a hostile vessel. A Romulan warbird, perhaps, laying waste to both *Kronos* and *Enterprise,* then stealing away to leave the Empire and the Federation to accuse each other.

Or was Captain Kirk so insane with hatred and grief that he would fire, unprovoked, on the Klingons? Impossible. Or so her father would say.

*Too trusting. Father, you are too trusting. . . .*

She did not trust Kirk, but she had expected greater cunning from him, not a blatant attack.

Gravity returned abruptly, hurling her to the floor like a stone. Azetbur pushed herself to her feet, ignoring the personal belongings that rained down about her, and staggered from the cabin.

The ever-present guard had deserted his post outside her door; Azetbur ran down the corridor and found him some distance away, dead, his torso crosshatched with phaser wounds, the walls and ceiling spattered with his blood.

She did not allow herself to react, to slow her pace. She stumbled over the bodies of those she had known, over detached limbs whose former owners she could no longer identify, and at last arrived at her father's stateroom.

The doors stood open; inside was a scene of

unbearable carnage, of mangled bodies and blood. Only two officers were standing. At the sight of Azetbur, they stepped back to reveal Chang and Kerla, crouched over Gorkon's still form.

She cried out, more in outrage than sorrow, and ran to her father's side. She did not see his wounds, only saw that he was covered with blood and unconscious, but still breathing.

Chang and Kerla both moved back to allow her to take Gorkon, limp but warm, in her arms. She glanced up at them both. Chang's face reflected hatred for what had happened here; Kerla's eyes were as stricken and angry as her own.

"Where is the physician?" she demanded of Chang.

"Dead," he said bitterly, "and sickbay is destroyed. We are searching for someone who can help, but can find no survivor with the medical skills—"

Gorkon stirred and released a small, sighing breath; Azetbur moaned and rocked him.

"Father," she whispered, "I will succeed you. I swear it. I will succeed you. Only live . . ."

The intercom crackled. Chang rose and responded, then crouched low to speak again to Azetbur.

"Kirk is coming. He says *Enterprise* did not attack, that they wish to offer help. He is bringing a doctor."

"*Enterprise* is undamaged? Then who attacked us?" Azetbur asked.

"Kirk lies," Chang said grimly. "We did not

monitor it—we were not expecting to be fired on by our escort! But there were no other vessels in this quadrant, and the trajectory of the photon torpedoes is clear. *Enterprise* fired them."

Kerla pulled himself to his feet swiftly, angrily. "Let Kirk come! *I* will deal with him!"

"No," Azetbur said, her voice shrill with desperation. "They have a doctor. Let my father be taken care of. Then we will deal with them."

For a moment Chang and Kerla hesitated; Chang nodded. Kerla spoke, his voice tight, grudging. "I will return shortly."

Gorkon moaned, but his eyes remained closed. Azetbur rocked him and felt his blood trickle down her arms.

"Why?" she whispered, her face bent low to her father's. "Why didn't they kill me? Why do they let me live?"

Chang turned away.

In the garish light of *Kronos*'s transporter room, Jim Kirk squinted at the phasers held so close to his head that he could see they were set to kill. Cautiously he held out his hands to indicate he was unarmed; neither he nor McCoy stirred as they were roughly searched.

Brigadier Kerla stormed into the room, able at last to openly show his contempt.

"Are you mad?" he demanded, thrusting his face into Kirk's. "Have you lost your mind? You attack us, then tell us you're beaming aboard—"

"I give you my word," Kirk said solemnly, "I don't understand what has happened. I gave no order to fire."

"We're here to help," McCoy added, nodding at his medikit, which was being skeptically inspected by one of the guards.

"How bad was it?" Kirk asked. "Were there any casualties?"

Quaking with fury, Kerla began to answer, then stopped and glared intently at them both. At last, his anger unabated, he said, "Follow me."

He led Kirk, McCoy, and two of the guards into the corridor. They did not go far before Jim saw it: bulkhead, ceiling, floors, stained with red-violet blood. He drew in a breath; Kerla turned his head sharply to study the humans' reactions as they passed corpses of slain soldiers, severed limbs, violet pools.

"But what— Who . . . ?" Jim asked, unable to believe, not wanting to understand, what he saw. "How did this happen?"

Kerla did not answer, did not slow his pace. Sickened, Jim followed him past the bodies, listening as the doctor scanned them with the tricorder, searching in vain for signs of life.

Kerla led them to what had once been the chancellor's stateroom; the scene inside was one of utter carnage. Bodies, pieces of bodies, arms and legs, tables and chairs, were strewn crazily across the floor, all of it splattered with blood.

In the center of the room Chang crouched beside

Azetbur as she sat cradling her father in her arms. Stricken, bloodied, she stared mutely up at Kerla, at the humans. Kerla hurried to her side.

"Chancellor Gorkon!" McCoy rushed to him immediately. "Jim, he's still alive!"

Chang rose.

"My God," Kirk breathed. "What happened here?"

Chang's eyes were insane with outrage. "You feign ignorance?"

*"What happened?"* Kirk demanded.

"You crippled our gravitational field with a direct torpedo hit, and two Starfleet crewmen beamed aboard in magnetic boots and did *this!"* Chang roared, with a sweep of his arm at the dead, at Azetbur and Gorkon. *"We have witnesses!"*

Kirk turned away, stunned.

"Jim!" McCoy struggled to free himself from the grasp of the security guards, to reach Gorkon.

"He's a *doctor!"* Kirk wheeled on Chang. "Let him help—"

"How can I trust—" the general began.

McCoy outshouted him. "Are you carrying a surgeon?"

"We *were!"* Chang bellowed.

"Then let me help!"

Chang glanced uncertainly at the pietà of Azetbur and Gorkon, then grudgingly signaled the guards.

McCoy hastened to Gorkon's side, motioned at a nearby conference table. "I need some light. Can we get him onto the table?"

The Klingons lifted the chancellor gently onto the table. Huddled between Azetbur and McCoy, Jim stood at Gorkon's head and forced himself not to flinch at the sight of the man's wounds. It seemed impossible that he was still alive; the phaser beam had ripped a bloody seam from his chest to his abdomen.

With General Chang hovering over his shoulder, McCoy scanned Gorkon once more, then produced a sonic stimulator and began trying to heal the injury. The chancellor stirred, groaned. "Hold him," McCoy said. His voice was steady, but his hands trembled.

Kirk leaned forward and gently pinned down the dying Klingon's arms; Jim's fingers grew slick with warm blood. As difficult as confronting the Klingons had been for him, he had no quarrel with Gorkon. In fact, he realized now that he liked and respected the chancellor and believed him sincere —more than he could say about any other Klingon in the room. Gorkon had the foresight to see beyond war, beyond Klingon tradition. And if they lost him now . . .

"Sweet Jesus," McCoy whispered. "He's lost a lot of whatever this stuff is."

Kirk stared down into Gorkon's face; the chancellor's bronze complexion had gone ashen. Panicked, Jim glanced up at McCoy. "Can you—"

"Jim," the doctor's voice was stricken, "I don't even know his anatomy." With growing desperation, he ran the stimulator over Gorkon's torso a second time, then looked at Kirk and shook his head.

"The wounds aren't closing."

Gorkon groaned and reached out. His hands closed on Kirk's wrists.

"You're killing him!" Kerla shouted beside McCoy.

Chang lunged at the doctor.

Jim held him back. "No!"

Gorkon moaned again, then grew silent. His grip loosened; his hands fell away.

"Chancellor Gorkon," McCoy cried, "can you hear me? Chancellor!"

Gorkon remained still.

"Father!" Azetbur cried.

Frantically McCoy tore open Gorkon's collar.

"Bones . . . ?" Jim asked, feeling as if he were watching humanity's last chance for peace die before his eyes.

"He's gone into some kind of arrest. Come on, dammit!" McCoy swore at Gorkon, then pounded the Klingon's chest.

The chancellor opened his eyes and looked up into Jim's face.

"Are you all right?" Gorkon asked feebly.

Jim heard his own voice telling Spock: *They're animals. Let them die . . .*

*No*, Jim tried to whisper. *Don't let it end this way.*

The chancellor's eyes dulled; his jaw slackened.

Alarmed, Kirk glanced quickly at McCoy. The

doctor was staring at the bright red indicator on his scanner in disbelief.

"I lost him," McCoy whispered, shaken.

Kirk moved to him, tried to pull him away. Azetbur gathered her father into her arms.

Chang faced the two humans, his expression one of grim triumph. "Under Article One-eight-four of Interstellar Law, I place you both under arrest. You are charged with assassinating the chancellor of the High Council." He motioned to the guards.

"He just tried to save him!" Kirk shouted, angry not for himself but for McCoy, who had never taken losing a patient well, no matter how hopeless the situation.

Chang barked an order at the guards.

Jim was too stunned even to struggle as the Klingons led them both away.

Azetbur rocked her dead father like a child.

During his life, he had been wise enough to reserve his trust for only a few: his late wife, his daughter, General Korrd. But he had made the mistake of trusting James Kirk, and Kirk had killed him.

Even now, stunned by grief, the fact made little sense to Azetbur, but she was beyond reason. She knew only that her father had died without the comfort of knowing his daughter would succeed him, would carry out his mission of peace.

Even in the repose of death, his expression showed exhaustion and strain. Azetbur gently smoothed the traces of weariness away—then started as Kerla's hands appeared on either side of Gorkon's face.

Chang knelt beside them, at Gorkon's head, and carefully raised the chancellor's eyelids with his thumbs.

A rumble started low in Kerla's throat.

*"No!"* Azetbur pushed their hands away. She knew what they intended: to send her father into the afterlife in a manner befitting a warrior, with a cry that warned the dead of his coming.

Kerla and Chang regarded her with confusion.

"No," she repeated, steadying her voice. "My father wanted peace; he was no warrior. I know his wishes. He came to break tradition, not keep it."

Kerla made a quick, furious movement as if to push past her and continue the ceremony without her permission, but Chang lifted an arm to hold him back.

"Do as she wishes," he said quietly. He stood and motioned for Kerla to do likewise.

The younger Klingon withdrew and stepped back, eyes ablaze with rage and sorrow. Chang's cold expression spoke of a hatred that ran very deep.

They left her alone, to hold her father and whisper to him of promises.

# Chapter Six

THE SENIOR OFFICERS had gathered on the bridge and listened solemnly as Uhura faced them.

"They've been arrested," Uhura said, her own expression stunned, "for the assassination of Chancellor Gorkon."

Outwardly Spock did not react, but he was filled with regret, not just for the predicament of his friends but also for the death of Gorkon, for his own sake and for that of the Klingon Empire and the Federation. With Gorkon heading the High Council, peace had seemed an attainable goal; now it receded once more into the realm of improbability.

Why is it a constant, the Vulcan wondered, that the universe resists favorable change, particularly in the realm of politics? Why is it that those who are most likely to instigate such change—no matter how rational, how reasonable, how humane and necessary—are also most likely to be murdered or deposed before they see their reforms enacted?

"Mr. Spock," Chekov cried, "we've got to do something!"

The others—Scott, Uhura, Valeris—turned to Spock expectantly.

He straightened. He was not altogether surprised at the turn of events. He had known there was a chance the Klingons would react by arresting the captain, but he had also known that Kirk had the best chance of convincing the Klingons that he had given no order to fire on *Kronos.* And no doubt the captain had realized that, if he had remained aboard *Enterprise,* the Klingons would have opened fire.

No, the captain was the logical one to go. Yet Spock could not entirely shake the very human twinge of guilt he now felt.

He had been responsible for involving Kirk and the *Enterprise* in this mission. And, as he had promised, he would find a way to extract Kirk from the current situation.

"I assume command of this ship as of oh-two-thirty hours," Spock said. "Uhura, notify Starfleet Headquarters. Explain precisely what has taken place and request instructions."

"Yes, sir." She moved to comply.

He turned to find Valeris staring at him, one brow lifted in disbelief. "But, Captain Spock," she protested, "we cannot allow them to be taken back to the Klingon homeworld as prisoners."

He looked at her calmly, wondering if she detected the emotional implication of her statement.

Apparently she did, for she quickly added, "It is logical to assume that the doctor and the captain are innocent of any crime, is it not? Based on what you know of their character . . ."

"I feel it is a rational assumption, yes. But the Klingons have not had the years of experience that I have had in dealing with the doctor and the captain. They therefore lack the basis to make such an assumption."

"But since *we* do, should we not intervene?"

"What do you suggest, Lieutenant? Opening fire on the Klingon vessel will not retrieve the captain; and an armed engagement was precisely what he wished to avoid. Nor can we simply transport them to the *Enterprise,* as *Kronos* has raised her shields."

"At least we must keep track of where they are taken, sir," Scott put in. "I—"

"I have already addressed that question, Mr. Scott. We will be able to follow the captain's movements."

The crew regarded him with astonishment.

"How did you achieve—" Valeris began.

"Time is precious, Lieutenant," Spock interrupted. "We must endeavor to ascertain what happened here tonight. According to our data banks, this ship fired those torpedoes."

*"No way!"* Scott protested.

"Mr. Scott, you forget yourself. Please accompany me to the torpedo bay." Spock started toward the lift.

"And if we can't piece together what happened?" Chekov asked. "What then, sir?"

Spock sighed. He would have preferred to avoid the question altogether. "Then, Mr. Chekov, it resides in the purview of the diplomats."

He was relieved when Chekov did not ask what the outcome of *that* would be.

Sarek, ambassador from Vulcan, sat in the office of the Federation president beside the Romulan ambassador and listened politely as Kamarag, their Klingon counterpart, stated his government's case against Leonard McCoy and James Kirk.

Unfortunately it was the most logical, well reasoned argument Sarek had ever heard Kamarag put forth. Sarek knew James Kirk—had touched his mind, had sensed his loyalty to and admiration for Sarek's son, Spock. Sarek had once trusted Kirk with a dangerous task: that of rescuing Spock's body that it might be reunited with his spirit. Kirk had not failed.

Sarek knew Leonard McCoy as well, though he had never joined his mind with the doctor's. But Spock had trusted McCoy enough to make him the living receptacle of Spock's spirit, his *katra,* moments before Spock's death. The fact revealed much about the doctor's character.

True, he had touched the captain's mind before Kirk learned of the death of his son, David, at Klingon hands, and before his lover, Carol Marcus, had suffered injuries in a Klingon attack. But even if there was room in Kirk's heart to harbor hatred on his loved ones' account, Sarek knew it could never harbor an intent to murder.

If Sarek had been asked to choose the three humans he most trusted, he would have named his wife, Amanda, Captain James T. Kirk, and Dr. Leonard H. McCoy.

He therefore doubted Kamarag's assessment of the matter: that Kirk had ordered the *Enterprise* to fire on the Klingon vessel with the specific intent of damaging the gravitational system, then ordering Starfleet crew members to board *Kronos* and assassinate the chancellor.

In the first place, Kirk was far too shrewd to carry out an assassination attempt in such a blatant manner. In the second, the act was inconsistent with Kirk's usual behavior.

"The chancellor of the High Council is dead," Kamarag said, "the result of an unprovoked attack while he traveled to see *you* under a flag of truce on a mission of peace." He pointedly directed the words at the Federation president, who sighed and rubbed his forehead as if trying to postpone the onset of a headache. Ra-ghoratrei was Deltan, pale-skinned, white-haired, and at the moment possessed of numerous concerns, not the least of which was preventing a war.

"Captain Kirk was legally arrested for the crime," Kamarag continued in an uncharacteristically reasonable tone. "May I remind you that he and Dr. McCoy boarded *Kronos One* of their own free will. None of these facts are in dispute, Mr. President."

"I will demand a full investigation," Raghoratrei promised. "You can be assured we will cooperate with all our power to get to the bottom of the matter. In the meantime—"

"In the meantime," Kamarag finished for him, "we expect the Federation to abide by the articles of Interstellar Law you claim to cherish. Captain Kirk and Dr. McCoy will stand trial for the assassination of Chancellor Gorkon."

The president's lips thinned. "Out of the question." He turned to Sarek. "Ambassador, there must be some way to extradite these men—"

"They are guilty!" Kamarag shouted. "They have killed the chancellor! Under Interstellar Law—"

"I do not believe that Captain Kirk and Dr. McCoy are guilty of the crimes with which they are charged," Sarek began quietly, ignoring the Klingon's tirade. "Evidence against them seems circumstantial at best."

"Circumstantial!" Kamarag sputtered. "The *Enterprise* fired on *Kronos One!* Starfleet officers then beamed aboard and cold-bloodedly slaughtered dozens of innocents, including the chancellor! This is clearly nothing more than revenge on us for Kudao and Themis—and for David and Carol Marcus! And Kirk masterminded it all. I should have known peace was impossible while Kirk still lived!"

*"Enterprise* appeared to fire on *Kronos,"* Sarek stated calmly. "And two individuals wearing Starfleet uniforms committed the murders. Tell

me, Ambassador, has anyone testified that they heard Kirk issue these alleged orders to kill?"

Kamarag's face darkened. "Mr. President! Our esteemed colleague is clearly prejudiced in this situation, despite his claim that he is influenced only by logic. His son is Kirk's first officer—"

"And special Federation envoy, who opened negotiations with your High Council, in the interests of peace. Mr. President," Sarek said, "I share a measure of personal responsibility in this matter, but I am obliged to agree with my esteemed colleague's legal interpretation: Kirk and Dr. McCoy were properly arrested, and the Klingons are within their rights to try them."

The president stared at him unhappily. Sarek knew it was not what he had wanted to hear. It was not what Sarek had wanted to say, but it was the truth. Legally the Federation was bound by Interstellar Law to let the trial proceed, as enough circumstantial evidence existed to charge Kirk and McCoy with the crime.

He did not mention that there were other, not entirely legal, methods of extraditing the two men. Such methods were beyond the purview of those present—though not necessarily beyond that of certain Starfleet officers, one of whom was a very close relative of the Vulcan ambassador.

The president turned with fading hopes to the Romulan. "And what is the position of the Romulan government, Ambassador Nanclus?"

Nanclus's face was as stony and unreadable as a

Vulcan's. "In the absence of specific instructions from my government, I must concur with my colleagues."

"But surely," Ra-ghoratrei said, exasperated, "you cannot believe James Kirk assassinated the chancellor of the High Council."

Nanclus feigned reluctance. "Mr. President, I don't know what to believe."

"I am waiting for your answer, Mr. President," Kamarag insisted.

Ra-ghoratrei closed his eyes for a long moment, opened them, and sighed. "This president is not above the law."

Mollified, Kamarag rose, bowed, and exited.

The desk intercom sounded. "Mr. President, Starfleet Command is here from San Francisco."

Ra-ghoratrei sighed, overwhelmed. "Send them in."

Three officers entered. Sarek recognized two of them: Rear Admiral William Smillie, Starfleet commander in chief, and Admiral Cartwright. The third was a young lieutenant Sarek had never seen before. The officers bowed to the two seated diplomats before turning their attention to Ra-ghoratrei.

"Mr. President," Cartwright said.

The president nodded. "Admiral Cartwright . . . Bill . . . Lieutenant . . ."

Cartwright spoke urgently. "Mr. President, we cannot allow Federation citizens to be abducted."

Ra-ghoratrei absently rubbed his forehead. "I'm afraid we've just been through all that with the

Klingon ambassador. Pending a full report, I am constrained to observe Interstellar Law."

Smillie and Cartwright stiffened and exchanged glances. Then Cartwright nodded at the lieutenant.

"Mr. President," he said, "we've prepared Operation Retrieve based on the rising danger of terrorism between the Klingon Empire and the Federation. Sir, we can go in and rescue the hostages and be out within twenty-four hours with an acceptable rate of loss in manpower and equipment. We have the technology to—"

"Suppose," Ra-ghoratrei interrupted irritably, "you precipitate a full-scale war?"

The lieutenant straightened proudly. "Then quite frankly, Mr. President, we can clean their chronometers."

The president stared, aghast at the young human's enthusiasm.

"Mr. President," Nanclus added, "they *are* vulnerable. There will never be a better time."

Ra-ghoratrei sought Sarek's gaze, as if to say, *And you? You think it's reasonable to risk war, too?*

Sarek lowered his gaze. He was a Vulcan, obliged to control his emotions, but at the moment the temptation was great to show his disgust. He knew the hostages well, and expected they would prefer to go to their deaths rather than precipitate a war.

"The longer we wait, the less accessible those hostages will be, sir," Cartwright prodded.

The president paused. "I'll bear that in mind, Admiral. I think that's all."

Cartwright turned to go, but Rear Admiral Smillie lingered. "Sir."

The president looked at him.

"Those men have literally saved this planet, and you know it."

Sarek knew he referred to the mysterious probe that had once disrupted Earth's climate and would have made the planet a frozen wasteland had Kirk and his crew not intervened.

"I do know it," Ra-ghoratrei replied glumly. "And now I'm afraid they're going to have to save it again. By standing trial."

He motioned for them to go. Smillie lingered a half second, then turned and followed Cartwright out. Ra-ghoratrei put his head in his hands and rubbed his temples for a moment before looking up at Sarek.

"I want the crew of *Enterprise* in my office tomorrow morning."

Sarek blinked. He doubted the crew of the *Enterprise* had any intention of heading back for Earth at the moment, but it would have been most unwise to mention his suspicion to the president. Instead, he said, "They are still in space, Mr. President—adjacent to the Klingon Neutral Zone."

Ra-ghoratrei narrowed his pale eyes. "Then tell your son to get the hell back here before the end of the week. I don't want *Enterprise* any more involved in this than she already is."

"Of course, Mr. President," Sarek answered smoothly, knowing that, as either father or Vulcan ambassador, he had no jurisdiction over Spock in his capacity as a Starfleet officer. Despite his headache, the president would realize that soon enough, and the order for *Enterprise* to return would be issued by Starfleet Command.

Even then, Sarek was quite certain Spock would refuse to obey it.

Hours after her father's death Azetbur responded to the buzzer by instructing the door to her dimly lit cabin to open. Gorkon's body had already been incinerated without ado or ceremony; in the Empire, life was too short, resources too precious, to waste on the dead.

General Chang stepped inside, his manner somber and, as always, exceedingly formal. She did not rise, but sat in the gloom and studied him.

He bowed. "My lady Azetbur," he said, using the archaic mode of address to indicate respect rather than title, to show that he approached her not as the new head of the High Council but rather as a friend of her father's.

She had always assumed her dislike for Chang was returned in kind, but in the midst of her grief, his old-fashioned courtesy seemed oddly touching.

*Clever Chang. A warrior you may be, but you are just as canny a diplomat.*

He glanced around the room and frowned. "Have you no guards?"

"Mine was killed," Azetbur replied wearily. "My father's are dead or injured. I see little point in resisting the inevitable, General. If Kirk was going to kill me, he would already have done so." Her tone grew faintly challenging. "Why have you come? Are there problems with the prisoners?"

Chang stepped toward her, his posture one of contained urgency. "No, my lady. They have been . . . secured. I came to inform you it is time to speak with the Federation." He paused; for the first time since she had known him, a look of uncertainty crossed his features. "And to warn you to take precautions. It is unwise to be without security measures. Perhaps at present you are unconcerned for your own safety, but I urge you to think not of your loss but of the Empire's need. If you are killed, who will continue your father's work?"

"Why not you, General?" She could not keep the irony out of her voice; if he heard it, for courtesy's sake, he gave no sign.

"I am a soldier. I was your father's adviser . . . and friend, but we were never in agreement." He smiled thinly. "I think we are both aware that I would not be a fit successor. I know more of killing than of life . . . and at the moment our people must learn how to survive. You no longer have anything to fear from Kirk, but there are others, some of them aboard this vessel—"

"Who?" Azetbur demanded.

He met her gaze directly. "Kerla."

She drew back in mute protest, unable, unwilling, to believe what she had heard; he began talking rapidly to convince her otherwise. "I must speak openly, and quickly, because I fear the danger to you is great."

"I do not believe this," Azetbur whispered,

though her thoughts began to race. She had not spoken with Kerla, had not seen him, since Gorkon's assassination. She had assumed that he left her alone now to mourn her father's death in private. . . .

She had always wondered at the change of heart that had made Kerla, an avowed warrior, swear fealty to Gorkon and court his daughter. Had he loved her only as a means to power? Had he somehow aided the assassins—perhaps even been the motivating force behind the attack—intending from the beginning to become the chancellor's consort?

Had he somehow been in league with Kirk? Or had Kirk merely acted before Kerla had the chance?

The thought added fresh pain to her sorrow. She narrowed her eyes at Chang. "What proof do you have?"

"No proof," Chang admitted. "Merely suspicion. Instinct born of experience with treachery. I do not ask you to believe me or to take any action against Kerla—merely to take the necessary precautions. And to trust no one. In the meantime let me assure you that, for your father's sake, I have done what is necessary to see to your protection. I promise you, my lady, that you will arrive at the peace conference safely." His expression grew grim. "I swear it, on my life." He bowed once more. "Permit me to serve as your guard until you are prepared to go to the stateroom."

Before she could answer, he stepped outside.

Azetbur waited for the doors to close behind him before lowering her face into her hands.

At her post at *Enterprise*'s helm after the departure of Spock and Scott, Valeris had not yet resolved the ambiguity she felt concerning the situation with the Klingons. Technically the Klingons were within their rights under Interstellar Law to hold Captain Kirk and Dr. McCoy, but Valeris knew a means to circumvent such restrictions must exist.

She felt abashed by her emotional outburst on the bridge, when she had told Spock they could not abandon Kirk and McCoy. She had not meant to suggest engaging the ship in battle; she had not meant to suggest any specific action at the moment. She only knew that one had to be taken.

Spock had been logically correct, as always. There was no action at that moment, short of precipitating a war, that could have been taken in order to rescue the captain and the doctor. And a Vulcan, of course, would take no action to directly precipitate a war.

He had misinterpreted her meaning, but he had not misinterpreted the emotion in her voice, and for that she was ashamed. Despite his earlier praise, she felt once again that she had proved a disappointment to him, the one person she wanted to make proud.

She swiveled to watch as Commander Chekov left his post beside her to cross over to Communications, where Commander Uhura listened tensely to what Valeris suspected were orders from Starfleet. Indeed, even from where she sat, she could detect the faint shouting that issued from Uhura's earpiece. The human's eyes were narrowed in pain at the volume; her posture telegraphed anger, disappointment, and stubborn resolve all at once.

Clearly the orders were not what she wanted to hear.

Valeris did not know the captain, though she had known of him for some time. But she knew and admired Spock and knew that this human Kirk must be a worthy individual indeed if Spock deemed him friend. And he had inspired an uncommon loyalty in these exceptionally gifted officers, who had turned down career-advancing assignments in order to serve at Kirk's side.

She watched as Uhura turned to Chekov and said, in a calm voice Valeris found humorously incongruous with the screaming in her ear, "We're to report back at once."

Chekov's forehead creased with concern. He echoed Valeris's statement of the night before: "We cannot abandon Captain Kirk and Dr. McCoy." He looked at the rest of the crew, as if seeking help.

Tentatively Valeris rose from her chair and approached them.

"Of course not—" Uhura began, then broke off as she caught Valeris's gaze. Chekov turned toward her expectantly.

Valeris caught her breath. Once again she felt her resolve divided between two courses of action. As a

Vulcan, she wanted to follow the most logical path, which presupposed strict adherence to regulations, but she also wanted to rescue the captain and doctor at any cost.

She suspected Spock felt the same way, but as acting captain of the *Enterprise,* he would feel compelled to follow orders—unless the crew cooperated in providing a way to circumvent those orders without necessarily disobeying them.

"Four hundred years ago, on the planet Earth," Valeris told Chekov and Uhura, "workers whose lives were threatened by automation flung their wooden shoes, called sabots, into the machines to stop them. Hence the term 'sabotage.'"

She did not need to explain further. Uhura's gaze warmed with understanding, then went blank, as she said, with computerlike intonation: "We are experiencing a technical malfunction. All backup systems inoperative."

"Excellent," Chekov said with a grin, then shook his head slightly to remove the smile. He forced a grim expression. "I mean, too bad. Who will tell Captain Spock?"

"A fellow Vulcan?" Uhura asked, deadpan.

They gazed up at Valeris.

She felt an impulse to smile. She liked these humans—their loyalty, their ability to improvise in the face of crisis. Having been raised by a human, she felt far more comfortable among them than among her own people. It was one of many reasons she had requested an assignment aboard *Enterprise* instead of an all-Vulcan ship. Humans' standards were far less rigid; compared to their emotional, irrational behavior, Valeris's was judged to be perfect, logical. Humans were far less likely to notice any lapses of control.

It had occurred to her that perhaps Spock had chosen to serve aboard *Enterprise* for the same reason.

Valeris did not smile at her co-conspirators. Instead, she kept her expression carefully impassive and signaled her complicity by heading for the lift—and Spock, in the torpedo bay.

In the instant as she turned and faced the closing lift doors, she caught a glimpse of their amazed expressions.

At Ra-ghoratrei's request, Sarek remained and listened patiently as the president consulted his civilian advisers.

"As the ambassador noted"—Dr. Thlema, a xenopsychologist from Andor specializing in Klingon culture, politely tipped her blue-skinned antennae in Sarek's direction—"the Klingons are quite capable of using logic when it suits their purposes. I agree with Kamarag; their case against Kirk and McCoy is airtight. And if we interfere, if we attempt a rescue mission, it will probably cause a war."

Ra-ghoratrei nodded, hands clasped tightly atop his desk, milky eyes narrowed beneath long white brows. "Then you agree: no intervention."

Thlema drew back in surprise. "Quite the contrary. I'm simply outlining the most likely scenario.

I said it would *probably,* but not definitely, cause a war. But if we *don't* react, the Klingons will perceive that as weakness, which will put us in a bad bargaining position in terms of a peace treaty. Frankly, I think the risks of a quick military strike to retrieve Kirk and McCoy are acceptable. War with the Klingons is not to be feared—not at the present time. They're at a disadvantage, and they know it."

Ra-ghoratrei's lips tightened into a thin line. He raised his long, pale fingers to his forehead and rubbed as if to erase troubling thoughts.

Sarek closed his eyes and heard the Romulan Nanclus's words: *They are vulnerable. There will never be a better time. . . .*

There had been growing hostility between the Romulan and Klingon empires; mutual trade had slacked off. The Romulans had nothing to gain and everything to fear from an alliance between the Klingons and the Federation. Sarek did not doubt that the Romulan government was doing everything in its power to influence the Federation to sever relations with the Klingon Empire. Indeed, war would be to the Romulans' advantage.

Sarek had expected to hear such words of war from Nanclus. He had not been surprised to hear them from Admirals Smillie and Cartwright.

But now, hearing them issue from the mouths of Federation civilian advisers, Sarek began to realize how alarmingly the galaxy teetered on the precipice of war.

Henry Mulwray, a middle-aged human, spoke.

Sarek had not met Mulwray before this meeting, though he had heard of him often. Mulwray was the largest contractor of Starfleet's defensive weaponry —though rumor had it that at least part of his wealth had been accumulated by illegal sales of arms to non-Federation customers. Sarek saw only one reason for Mulwray's presence at the meeting: to provide the information he offered Ra-ghoratrei now.

"You have our total support, Mister President," Mulwray said somberly. "My factories can gear up to full weapons production in less than a week."

Ra-ghoratrei's tone was wooden; he did not quite meet the human's gaze. "Thank you, Henry. Right now, we're pursuing diplomatic channels."

"Of course," Mulwray reassured him. "No one wants a war."

Ra-ghoratrei wavered; Sarek realized it was time to speak, and quickly.

"If I may, Mr. President . . ."

Ra-ghoratrei faced him.

"The important thing," Sarek reminded him, "is to keep the peace process alive. If the new chancellor is so disposed, perhaps we can attach a rider, assurance that these men won't be executed. Then—"

An urgent voice filtered through Ra-ghoratrei's intercom, cutting him off: "Mr. President, you have the new chancellor of the Klingon High Council calling."

The president swung around to look at the visual on the far wall; the others followed suit.

Azetbur, regal and splendid in her new appointments, appeared. Most intriguing, Sarek thought; beside him, Dr. Thlema released a small noise of surprise. Klingon leadership generally excluded females as being intrinsically unfit, which meant that Azetbur must have been an exceptionally qualified contender—or she had exceptionally powerful supporters.

The choice made Sarek hopeful. He had met Azetbur and knew her to be a most fervent proponent of her father's policies. The specter of war receded slightly in Sarek's consciousness. Perhaps there was still chance for a peace treaty.

"Mr. President," Azetbur said, ignoring the surprised reactions her appearance had evoked, "I have been named chancellor of the High Council in my father's place."

Ra-ghoratrei had already recovered and wore an expression of sympathy. "Madam Chancellor, you have my sincerest condolences on your recent loss. I want to assure you that this shameful deed . . ."

She brushed aside personal matters with a sweep of her hand and spoke with such force and intensity that her listeners sat motionless, stunned by the transformation. She had indeed assumed her father's role; Sarek fancied he had even heard a trace of Gorkon's intonation in her speech. "Mr. President, let us come to the point: you want the conference to go forward, and so did my father. I will attend in one week—after I've had the opportunity to master the details of his position—on one condition: we will not extradite the prisoners, and you will not attempt to rescue them in a military operation." Azetbur paused to give her next words weight. "We would consider any such attempt an act of war."

Ra-ghoratrei had relaxed with relief at her first words, then paled to an even more bloodless shade at her last. Yet his tone and expression were cordial. "We look forward to meeting with you next week, Madam Chancellor. I hope you will be our guest here on—"

"After recent events," Azetbur said brusquely, "you will understand I prefer a neutral site. And in the interests of security, let us keep the location secret."

Ra-ghoratrei smiled weakly. "As you wish, Madam Chancellor."

The screen darkened abruptly in reply. The president turned toward his advisers.

"I will do what I must to avoid a war"—he swiveled to face Sarek—"even if it costs the lives of your son's friends."

# Chapter Seven

AZETBUR TURNED SLOWLY from the screen to face her council.

Of her father's advisers, only two, Chang and Kerla, remained, and at the moment she did not trust either of them.

She yearned for old Korrd's advice, but his condition was still grave; because of his advanced age, the wounds inflicted on him by Gorkon's assassins were slow to heal.

She studied Kerla for signs of betrayal. His manner toward her in front of the others was as exceedingly formal as ever. Was his behavior when they were alone together the act?

With a flourish, Kerla unfurled battle plans and laid them before her. Chang stood back without comment and watched them all carefully—like a predator, Azetbur thought, always silent, always watching. She would take his words to heart: *Trust no one.* Not even Chang.

"Attack them now, Madam Chancellor, while we still can!" Kerla cried.

She leaned forward to study the plans dispassionately.

"Attack," General Khmarr, young—too young, younger even than Kerla—and eager for battle, insisted, "or be slaves in their worlds!"

"We can take whole by force what they propose to divide!" Grokh said, gesturing at the star map. General Grokh was not quite so young, but even he could scarcely be called middle-aged.

It disturbed Azetbur that the most experienced minds of the Empire had been lost in the attack; of her remaining advisers, Chang was the most cunning, the most experienced. Logically, she should depend on him now most of all, but she shared her father's fear of him. Dared she trust him?

And if she could not trust Kerla, not trust Chang, then there was no one on the council she could trust—save herself and her dead father.

Why had the assassins allowed her to remain alive thus far?

She sighed wearily and looked up at Grokh. "You don't seem to grasp our situation, General. War is . . . obsolete. As we are in danger of becoming."

Kerla's tone held a rebuke. "Better to die on our feet than live on our knees."

"That wasn't what my father wanted—"

145

Chang interrupted softly, bitterly. "He was killed for what he wanted."

Azetbur's face hardened as she remembered the instant when her father's body went limp in her arms.

She had heard it said that Kirk had the heart of a Klingon; upon reflection, she now believed it true. A Klingon who sought revenge for the death of a family member—a son, a mate—would not have entrusted the task to others.

Kirk had come aboard *Kronos* to make certain Gorkon was dead; no matter that he would have to pay with his own life, and that of his friend, for the satisfaction.

To complete the cycle, Azetbur would now make certain of Kirk's fate. But she would do so in a way that did not jeopardize all that her father had worked toward.

She faced Chang. "Kirk must have a fair trial."

"Klingon law will take its course," Chang said grimly.

"No. Kirk must be tried according to Interstellar Law."

The three younger generals began to protest; she ignored them. "You will represent the state, General Chang."

Chang's good eye narrowed. "The Federation will pay dearly," he promised.

"Not the Federation; the peace process must go forward." Azetbur's voice dropped to a whisper. "Kirk. Kirk must pay for my father's death."

Chang bowed. "With pleasure, Madam Chancellor."

Spock stood in the torpedo bay and stared down at the impossible.

Beside him, Scott studied the same console readout and shook his head. "It's as I said, Mr. Spock: inventory still registers every torpedo."

"Yet the data banks insist we fired," the Vulcan mused. Impossible, that *Enterprise* had fired on the Klingon vessel—and yet Spock had witnessed the attack with his own eyes.

Or had he?

He turned to Scott. "One computer is lying."

Scott frowned. "A computer canna lie, sir."

Inwardly, Spock was amused by the engineer's remark. The Vulcan had become so accustomed to hearing the figurative expressions of human speech that he occasionally indulged in them himself. Given the engineer's distressed state, Spock decided in favor of being literal.

He nodded. "Correct, Mr. Scott. Therefore we must check the torpedoes visually."

"That could take hours!"

"Nevertheless . . ." Spock said. It would take some hours for the Klingons to transport the captain and doctor to the trial site and to conduct the trial itself. And Spock knew of no other way to proceed.

"And if they're all in one place?" Scott asked.

Spock drew in a breath, released it. "Then someone aboard this ship forged a data bank entry." It was the most likely possibility, one he found distasteful to contemplate.

It did not occur to him to consider Kirk a suspect.

Both men glanced up as Valeris descended into the bay.

"Captain Spock," she said. "They have named Gorkon's daughter chancellor. I heard the report."

Scott made a low sound in his throat, shook his head. "I'll bet that Klingon bitch killed her father."

Spock glanced sharply at him, astonished at the depth of hatred in Scott's tone—and reminded more than slightly of his encounter with Jim Kirk after Admiral Smillie's briefing. "Her own father?"

"It is an old story, sir," Valeris said calmly. At Spock's look, she added, "Patricide as a means to power has been practiced for centuries within the Klingon Empire."

"As it once was on Earth," Spock reminded her, "and in Romulan culture. The fact that it *has* been practiced in no way proves that Azetbur—"

"They don't place the same value on life that we do, Spock," Scott interrupted bitterly. "You know that. Take my word: she didn't shed one bloody tear."

Spock experienced a sense of frustration that threatened to verge on futility. How were they to rescue the captain without provoking a war and then attempt to establish peaceful relations with the Klingons if such an attitude persisted among

Starfleet's top officers? "That is hardly conclusive, Mr. Scott, as Klingons have no tear ducts." He turned to Valeris before the engineer could react. "Any reply from Starfleet to our dispatch, Lieutenant?"

"Yes, sir."

Spock noted her hesitation and studied her keenly. "And . . . ?"

Under his scrutiny, she straightened; her expression became utterly impassive. "Commander Uhura has been experiencing technical difficulties, sir."

"Curious," Spock said softly. He had been fully prepared to commandeer *Enterprise* on his own and release the crew from any obligation to follow his orders, but he also realized that the crew would insist on aiding him in the rescue and would thus be deemed as guilty as he.

Uhura, it seemed, had provided a way that might spare them all courts-martial.

"Very well," he told Valeris. "For twenty-four hours we will agree that this conversation did not take place."

"A lie?" She did not shrink from the word, nor did her tone imply disapproval.

"An omission," Spock corrected her. "After that—"

Scott had listened to the exchange with growing anxiety; now he could contain himself no longer. "Twenty-four hours from now we won't have a clue where the captain is!"

"I know precisely where he'll be," Spock said. Scott gaped at the Vulcan. "Where?"

As *Kronos One* warped toward home and Kirk's trial, Azetbur sifted through her father's notes, preparing for the conference.

She had moved into Gorkon's quarters, partly at Chang's insistence: the chancellor's cabin was better equipped with security devices, more easily defensible by guards. She had feared it might renew her pain, but being surrounded by her father's effects had brought a curious comfort. Now she sat in Gorkon's reading chair, where she had last seen her father whole, and massaged the deepening crease between her brows as she frowned at the glowing viewer.

Gorkon's notes were incomplete; apparently he had kept much of his intended negotiating strategy in his head. Azetbur remembered all that he had discussed with her, privately and in the presence of the other councillors, but she knew he had kept much to himself.

He had not trusted his own High Council. *And I,* Azetbur thought grimly, *shall follow his lead.* She had trusted Kerla completely, and still loved him —but Chang's words had fostered doubt. She could trust no one, not even Chang, who had taken charge of arranging her security. These days her mood swung between two extremes: sometimes she wanted urgently to live, to carry Gorkon's work forward; at other times she lost all desire to go on, for it seemed useless to try. She suspected she would not live long enough to sign a peace treaty with the Federation, but perhaps she would survive to see Kirk tried. That would have to be satisfaction enough.

But, unlike her father, she had no successor she could trust.

Azetbur closed her burning eyes, then opened them as the viewer signaled. She pressed a control; the picture toggled to that of the guard, Katris, outside her quarters.

"Madam Chancellor," he said, his speech as thick and ponderous as his oversized features. "Brigadier Kerla wishes to speak with you alone in your quarters."

She straightened and sighed inaudibly. "Let him in."

Katris nodded. The screen blinked, then flashed the same report the two guards outside saw: that Kerla bore no concealed weapons other than the phaser he had turned over to them.

Even if he had been armed, Azetbur would have felt no fear. She had been ready to die since the assassination. Besides, their conversation would be monitored from three separate locations aboard ship.

She did not rise as Kerla entered. She knew precisely why he had come after allowing her a brief period of mourning, knew that it would be easier for both of them if she was direct and cruel.

The instant the doors closed behind him, his formal comportment vanished. He strode over to her, knelt by her side, and took her wrist.

She did not resist, but yielded without responding as he raised her open palm to his face. Her arm was limp; she forced herself to gaze at him without emotion, without warmth. It was difficult: he was strong, full of fire. She yearned to stroke his long, beautiful hair, to bury her face in it and take comfort from its scent as she had only days before.

He seemed not to notice her coolness. "Zeta, let us take the oath tonight. There is nothing now to stop us."

*Nothing,* Azetbur thought, *now that my father is dead.*

He tried to pull her closer, but she resisted, drawing back in the chair. He looked up at her, bewildered.

"What, Zeta? Have I not allowed you sufficient time? If so, I beg forgiveness."

She forced her expression to remain cold. "Things have changed between us, Brigadier Kerla."

Slowly he released her wrist and withdrew his hand. She saw rage flare in him, saw him struggle to contain it. "I do not understand."

"Were you loyal to my father?" she asked abruptly. The question surprised them both. She had intended merely to end the relationship without explanation. *Fool,* she told herself. *If Chang's suspicions are correct, you have just hastened your own execution.*

This time Kerla did not hide his fury at the insult to his honor. Azetbur watched him without reaction; if Kerla was merely playing a role, he was an accomplished actor indeed.

"What are you suggesting, Chancellor? That I betrayed Gorkon? That I was responsible for his death?" He sprang to his feet. "I did not always agree with him. I never made a secret of that. But I took an oath of allegiance to him! I do not need to repeat it for it to be valid!"

"You have taken no oath of allegiance to me."

The statement diluted his anger. He crouched to face her at eye level. "I will gladly take such an oath, Chancellor. You have my loyalty; I thought you knew."

*"Do* I?" she asked softly.

She expected the question to infuriate him again; instead, he gazed intently at her and lowered himself, one hand on the arm of Gorkon's chair.

"You are angered by the death of your father," Kerla said at last, with disarming gentleness. "I do not hear your words of accusation; you do not mean them. You have much on your mind. After the peace conference, we will speak again, when you have come to yourself." He reached out to touch her hand.

She pulled it away. "No. We will not speak of this later, even if I should survive. We will not speak of this again. You are not to come to my cabin again, save on official business."

"Azetbur . . ."

She signaled for the guard. Kerla rose swiftly, angrily.

"You do not trust me," he said, his voice low, bitter. "The time will come when you will regret that you have sent me away."

She returned to her reading and did not permit herself to watch as he left.

McCoy stood beside Kirk in the center of the courtroom and was frightened.

Not that the Klingons had treated them badly. On the contrary, they'd taken care of their prisoners far better than the doctor had anticipated. He and Jim had been put in a comfortable cell with padded bunks and given fairly decent food, if you allowed for the fact it was Klingon. Not that he'd been able to eat more than a bite.

Azetbur was continuing her father's humane policies, McCoy figured, wincing as he realized the semantic evolution of the word "humane." The only degrading part was being denied a shave and a shower.

And McCoy was doing a lot of sweating.

The Klingons were being *too* kind. Which meant they were saving up for something.

Probably for this. The courtroom was a curious blend of cathedral and circus: a cavernous stadium arranged in rising circular tiers hewn from jagged rock.

And at its center, at the very base, was the prisoners' dock, a circular enclosure that came to McCoy's waist. The dock was spotlighted, the rest of the cavern dim, shadowed; McCoy squinted and could just make out the cameras suspended from the high stone walls.

At first the realization made him even more nervous—so everyone in the galaxy would be watching the debacle; and then he realized with hope that Spock and the *Enterprise* crew would be watching, too.

He scanned the high tiers jutting above them just as Chancellor Azetbur, majestic and unapproachably beautiful, entered with her entourage. He had not seen or spoken to her since the night her father died, when she had been speechless with grief. The sight of her gave him hope. Azetbur, like her father, was reasonable, compassionate, intelligent. Surely she couldn't believe the captain had conspired to kill Gorkon. . . .

The audience began to chant, softly at first, increasing to a thunderous roar until McCoy felt it in the soles of his feet: "Kirk! Kirk! *Kirk! KIRK!*"

The doctor gripped the edge of the dock lest his wobbly knees betray him. Jim didn't react. He had remained morosely silent throughout the ordeal. McCoy knew that the chancellor's death had hit him hard. Jim grieved for Gorkon, as a living being and as the last hope for peace in the galaxy, and was grieved by the hatred that had possessed him since David's death and Carol's injury—the same hatred that had spurred the assassins.

McCoy hadn't felt much like talking himself. He had admired and respected Gorkon as much as anyone he'd met—but the chancellor had died

J. M. Dillard

because McCoy, a Starfleet medical officer, hadn't been required to study Klingon anatomy. Sure, he could have learned it on his own, but he'd been too busy—and besides, the theory had always been that Federation ships stayed in Federation space and never encountered Klingons.

Theoretically.

*Or was the underlying assumption so ugly we couldn't admit it to ourselves?* McCoy wondered. *That a Klingon life wasn't worth saving . . .*

The crowd's chanting grew so loud he could no longer think. The defense attorney—dark-skinned, broad-shouldered, powerfully built—entered the arena. McCoy had been too distraught at their first and only brief meeting to remember his name. He remembered only his surprise at the fact that the likable young Klingon seemed sincerely interested in trying to help his clients, though he offered little hope of a favorable verdict.

The attorney proffered two unfamiliar-looking devices to McCoy and Kirk. McCoy took one, frowning at it uncertainly until the attorney showed them how to hold it. Jim caught on and leaned over to shout in McCoy's ear.

"Translators!"

McCoy nodded and held his translator to his ear as General Chang emerged from the shadows. The audience stilled expectantly.

*Prisoners, prosecution, defense,* McCoy thought. *But where are the judge and jury?*

General Chang began to speak, his expression

one of utter smugness and satisfaction. McCoy glared, convinced that Chang had been waiting a long time for this moment. He adjusted the translator against his ear and listened.

"The state will show," Chang said, "that *Enterprise* fired on *Kronos One* without provocation, the chancellor and his advisers having been lulled into a false sense of security with an invitation to a state dinner aboard Captain Kirk's vessel at nineteen-thirty hours that same evening." He turned to Kirk with a slight, insulting smile. "Do you deny all this?"

"Kirk! Kirk!" the spectators hooted.

McCoy heard metal strike stone and gazed up into the darkness directly behind them in time to catch a fleeting glimpse of the ghostly pale features of the judge.

The crowd stilled.

"The prisoner will respond," the judge commanded. He wore a studded glove to which was attached a dull metal sphere that McCoy realized served as gavel.

A muscle in Jim's jaw danced. "I don't deny we invited them to dinner."

"Were you drunk at that dinner?" Chang asked silkily.

"What?" Jim drew back, confused and angered.

"Isn't it a fact," Chang continued, "that you served Romulan ale, a beverage illegal in the Federation because of its overwhelming potency?"

"The drink was served," Jim admitted.

McCoy looked down and shook his head.

*Why doesn't our attorney object? This is a damned show trial.*

"This is a damned show trial," Rear Admiral Smillie said hotly to President Ra-ghoratrei. He did not want war, but he knew both Jim Kirk and Leonard McCoy—two of Starfleet's best. They had served the Federation well and were due to retire. They deserved a better fate than this.

If he could just persuade Ra-ghoratrei to try *some*thing in terms of a rescue mission . . . Once Kirk and McCoy were safe, the diplomats could go in and clean up the pieces. Smillie felt certain that the Klingons' situation was too desperate for them to attempt war. He glanced sharply at Sarek, who he felt was responsible for Ra-ghoratrei's reluctance.

Sarek did not react; the president ignored Smillie as well, his attention riveted on the trial proceedings.

Smillie sighed and returned his attention to the screen.

McCoy watched as Chang strutted back and forth in front of the prisoners' dock.

"And you still maintain that your ship did not fire on *Kronos One?* Would you have known if she had? Come now, Captain. The record clearly shows there were no other ships in the sector."

"There were no other ships in the sector," Kirk confirmed.

*Dammit, Jim,* McCoy wanted to shout at him, *are you* trying *to get us the death penalty?*

"Did you have occasion to refer to your ship's data banks during that night?"

"I checked the data banks, yes," Jim answered stonily.

"And what did they tell you?"

Jim hesitated. "That we fired two photon torpedoes. But—"

The rest of his answer was drowned out by the mob's howls.

Chang gave a faint hateful smile. "The witness is excused—for the time being."

He strode off as the judge gaveled for order.

McCoy's fear turned to honest anger as he recognized the next witness: one of Chancellor Gorkon's guards, minus his right arm. The arm could have been located—and, if too damaged, recloned—and reattached, or at the very least, replaced by a prosthesis. But the prosecution had chosen to use this unfortunate victim to play on the crowd's sympathies.

Or perhaps the guard had chosen, as had Chang, to shun medical intervention and sport the disfigurement as a badge of courage.

The defense attorney approached the witness. "Tell us what you saw the night Chancellor Gorkon was assassinated."

The guard nodded. "We were fired on by the *Enterprise*—"

"Let that remark be stricken from the record." The attorney turned and raised a hand toward the judge. "The witness assumes *Kronos One* was fired on by the *Enterprise,* but has no direct knowledge of such."

"Denied," the judge intoned.

The attorney sighed and directed his attention back to his witness. "Continue."

"After the first hit," the guard said, "we lost our gravitational field. I found myself weightless and unable to function. Then two Starfleet crewmen came walking toward us."

"Perhaps they merely wore Starfleet uniforms—" the attorney began.

Chang called from the shadows. "I move that remark be stricken as purely speculative."

"So ordered," the judge said. "Colonel Worf, we are interested in facts, not theories."

Colonel Worf—odd name for a Klingon; no wondered he hadn't remembered it, McCoy thought—contained his frustration and continued his questioning. "Did you see their faces? Could you identify them if you saw them again?"

The guard hesitated. "No. But they were human, I'm sure of that."

Worf tilted his head skeptically. "If you didn't see their faces, how do you know they were human?"

*Bless you,* McCoy directed the grateful thought at Worf. *You're trying; you're actually trying.*

"I couldn't— I didn't . . . I didn't get a *good* look at them; that's what I mean. But I could tell they were human."

"Hmm." Worf turned away thoughtfully, then

swiveled suddenly and fired a question at the startled witness. "If the gravitational field was not functioning, how could these men have been walking?"

"They appeared to be wearing gravity boots," the guard said.

A murmur traveled through the crowd. Colonel Worf seemed sorry he had asked. "No further questions."

Chang stepped forward to take over. "They fired on you?" he asked the guard.

The Klingon nodded. "With Starfleet-issue phasers. They dashed into the chancellor's stateroom. We could hear more phaserfire. Then they went back the way they'd come."

"Toward the transporter room?"

"Yes, sir."

"Thank you," Chang said solicitously. "That will be all."

The guard exited. Chang turned a glittering eye on McCoy.

"Dr. McCoy, what is your current medical status?"

McCoy felt a thrill of fear at the sound of his own name, but he faced Chang squarely and purposely misunderstood the question. Damned if he'd do anything to make Chang's work any easier for him.

"Aside from a touch of arthritis," he answered jauntily, "I'd say pretty good."

Next to him, Jim almost smiled.

Chang was not amused; he stared silently at the doctor. McCoy yielded first.

"For twenty-seven years I have been ship's surgeon and later chief medical officer aboard the USS *Enterprise*. In three months I'm due to stand down."

Chang frowned at the idiom. "Stand . . . ?"

"Retire."

"Ah," Chang said softly. "I believe you also consumed Romulan ale at the officers' mess on the night in question, Doctor?"

"Objection!" Worf shouted with such force that McCoy started.

"Sustained," the judge replied, to everyone's surprise.

"We all did." McCoy's voice quavered with anger. "But that doesn't mean—"

The judge interrupted. "General Chang, come to the point or abandon this line of inquiry."

Chang acknowledged the request with a gracious nod, then studied McCoy with that damnably smug expression. "Was Chancellor Gorkon alive when you first examined him?"

"Barely." McCoy lowered his voice as he remembered.

"Have you saved patients as 'barely' alive as he was?"

For a moment anger, guilt, and pain rendered McCoy speechless. "I didn't . . ." He faltered, shamed by the recollection. "I didn't have the knowledge of Klingon anatomy I needed."

The great hall went silent; McCoy's words echoed.

"You say you are due for retirement," Chang persisted gently. "May I ask: do your hands shake?"

"Objection!" Worf cried.

McCoy jerked his chin up and stared at Chang with unmasked hatred, scarcely aware that Jim had laid a reassuring hand on his shoulder. A half dozen obscene racial epithets concerning Klingons filled his head, all of which he longed to hurl at Chang and none of which applied, in his own mind, to Azetbur or her late father.

"Overruled," the judge thundered.

"I was nervous," McCoy said heatedly.

"You were incompetent!" Chang leaned over the dock and shouted in McCoy's face; Jim moved toward him threateningly. "Whether deliberately or as a result of age combined with drink, this court will determine."

"I tried to save him!" McCoy's voice broke. "I was desperate to save him! He was the last best hope in the universe for real peace!" He gazed up into the shadows, in Azetbur's direction, hoping that she understood.

"The chancellor herself will testify that the defendant's hands shook."

McCoy bowed his head in shame.

Chang stepped back and gestured grandly at Kirk. "And now we come to the architect of this tragic affair, Captain James Tiberius Kirk. I put it to you, Captain, that you were seeking revenge for the death of your son."

Jim paled in the harsh light. "That isn't true!"

Relentlessly Chang continued. "That, either as an instrument of Federation policy or acting on your own drunken initiative, you and your fellow conspirators crippled *Kronos One* and cold-bloodedly assassinated the chancellor of the High Council. Then you and Dr. McCoy went aboard to make certain the job was complete."

"Objection!" Colonel Worf protested. "Captain Kirk has not been identified as the assassin."

The judge sounded faintly bored, anxious to be finished with the proceedings. "Sustained."

"I offer into the record the following excerpt from Captain Kirk's personal log." Chang signaled someone at the far end of the room.

Kirk's recorded voice filled the room: "I've never trusted Klingons and never will. . . . I have never been able to forgive them for the death of my son. . . ."

An explosive babble filled the room; the judge pounded his metal glove for silence. McCoy turned to Jim, who stood stiff and expressionless except for the utter disbelief in his eyes. It wasn't true, wasn't true, McCoy told himself. The tape had to have been faked. He looked to Kirk for reassurance, but Jim refused to meet his eyes.

"Are those your words?" Chang demanded.

"Yes," Jim whispered.

McCoy stared at him, mute with horror.

"Spoken by you?"

"Yes."

"Louder, please," Chang insisted. "We cannot hear you."

Jim straightened and said firmly, "Those words *were* spoken by me."

McCoy closed his eyes and surrendered all hope.

From the bridge of the USS *Excelsior,* Captain Sulu watched.

Before the trial began, Sulu had known nothing whatsoever of the circumstances surrounding Gorkon's assassination—except that Kirk was innocent. Of that there could be no question—at least, not in Sulu's mind—even after hearing Kirk's recorded statement. And he felt certain that the Federation, Starfleet, and even the Klingons were aware of the fact as well.

As the trial proceeded, Sulu's anger grew. He hadn't seen the *Enterprise* crew in several years, and to see the captain and Dr. McCoy in such circumstances was acutely painful, though he had been forced to smile at McCoy's tongue-in-cheek response to the question about his medical status. It soon became clear the Klingons had no intention of conducting a fair trial; it was also clear that Starfleet and the Federation intended to do nothing about it. They were going to let Kirk and McCoy serve as scapegoats, ostensibly to prevent a war, while the real assassins went unpunished.

Sulu did not want war. But he knew that Gorkon's murderers did. If sacrificing Kirk and McCoy brought peace, the killers would do whatever was necessary to destroy that peace. The sacrifice would be wasted.

Sulu made a decision, one that might cost him a career in Starfleet. It was not the first time he had been willing to take such a risk for a particular captain and a particular crew.

"Communications," he said, swiveling in his chair.

Rand turned, expectant. "Sir?"

He lowered his voice confidentially. "Send to commander, *Enterprise:* 'We stand ready to assist you. Captain Sulu. USS *Excelsior.*' Attach our coordinates. Use a secured channel."

Rand hesitated as she raised her pale gold brows in surprise. "Is that wise, sir? I mean, given their situation—"

Sulu's look silenced her in mid-sentence. He did not need to explain himself. Years before, Rand had served aboard the *Enterprise* under Kirk's command.

"Aye, sir," she said.

Unhappily, Sulu returned his gaze to the screen.

Aboard *Enterprise,* Uhura forced her attention away from the trial and onto the incoming communication. The message from *Excelsior*'s captain brought an inward smile; she turned to Spock. "Sulu's giving us his position and telling us he's standing by."

The Vulcan's gaze never left the screen. "He's placing himself in a most awkward position," Spock murmured.

No worse, Uhura thought, as she turned back to

watch the trial, than the position Spock would soon be placing himself in—if she knew her Vulcans.

Kirk leaned wearily against the dock as Colonel Worf spread his arms in appeal to a judge presiding above them.

"Objection, your honors! My clients' political views are not on trial here."

Jim listened to it all with sudden detachment, exhausted by the emotions Chang's questioning had evoked in him.

Gorkon's death tormented him. At the moment, the trial and whatever sentence might follow seemed meaningless. Only two things mattered: that Gorkon's killers be brought to justice and that the peace process continue. Jim was helpless to do either at the moment, but he suspected that Spock would find a way to accomplish both.

Hearing his earlier words about David repeated before the court had stunned him. The Klingons could not have obtained his personal log without the help of a conspirator aboard *Enterprise*—a conspirator who might very well still be aboard her. He could only hope that Spock had already come to the same conclusion.

Nearby, McCoy wearily lowered his face into his hand, defeated.

Jim felt pity for him, mixed with a sudden curious detachment. Had the doctor ever really thought they had a chance in hell of being found innocent? McCoy had seemed frustrated, scandalized by the captain's honest, and thoroughly incriminating, answers.

It wouldn't have mattered if he'd lied. Nothing anyone did here mattered; the judges would still find them both guilty. He had understood that the instant he heard the excerpt from his personal log.

Chang moved closer to the prisoners' dock—circling like a hawk, Kirk thought, moving in for the kill. "On the contrary," the general began, his volume slowly increasing, "Captain Kirk's views and motives are at the heart of this matter. This officer's record shows the accused to be an insubordinate, unprincipled career opportunist with a history of violating the chain of command when it suited him.

"Indeed, the record will show that 'Captain' Kirk was once 'Admiral' Kirk and that Admiral Kirk was broken for taking matters into his own hands in defiance of regulations and the law." He wheeled and swooped down on Kirk, grabbing the edge of the dock. "Do you deny you were demoted on these charges, Captain?"

Kirk hesitated and adjusted the translator against his ear, pretending not to understand.

Chang thrust his face into Kirk's and screamed, veins standing out on his neck, *Do not wait for the translation! Answer me now!*

"Don't answer!" Worf shouted, leaning against the other side of the dock. He swung around to thrust a beseeching hand up at the judges. "Objection!"

Jim knew what the answer would be before it came.

"Objection overruled. The prisoner will answer the question."

"I cannot deny it," Kirk said.

Chang's lips curved upward in triumph. "You were demoted."

"Yes."

McCoy groaned softly.

"For insubordination," Chang continued.

Jim shrugged cavalierly. "I have on occasion disobeyed orders."

"And were you obeying or disobeying orders the night you arranged the assassination of Chancellor Gorkon?"

"I ob—" the defense attorney began.

"I was unaware of the assassination until I boarded his ship!" Jim shouted.

Chang's eye widened with theatrically exaggerated amazement. "You deny *Enterprise* fired on *Kronos One?*"

"Well, I—"

"You deny," Chang said, louder, "that *your* men beamed aboard *Kronos One* and shot the chancellor?"

Jim stiffened as he understood where the general's logic was headed. Chang was nothing if not brilliant, and there was no point in trying to resist, to argue. The outcome would be the same.

"I cannot confirm or deny actions which I did not witness," Jim replied.

"Captain Kirk, are you aware that, under Federation law, the captain of a starship is considered responsible for the actions of his crew?"

He heard McCoy's sharp intake of breath as the doctor, too, realized, and Jim did not look at McCoy as he answered: "I am."

Chang nodded grimly. "So if it should prove members of your crew did in fact carry out such an assassination . . ."

McCoy desperately clutched his arm. "Jim! They're setting us up!" He turned toward the judge's box. "Your honor, I protest!"

"The defendant will be silent!" the judge thundered. "Captain Kirk, you will answer the question."

"As captain," Jim said heavily, "I am responsible for the conduct of the crew under my command."

Chang's posture and expression radiated victory. He faced the judge. "Your honor, the state rests."

McCoy turned to Colonel Worf with a hopefulness Jim thought pathetic. "Is it our turn, now?"

The Klingon's dark, broad face wore a grim expression. "According to Klingon law, both sides present their cases at the same time. We've *had* our turn."

McCoy paled and opened his mouth to speak, then started as the judge's gauntlet crashed against stone with a flurry of sparks.

"It is the judgment of this court that the defendants are guilty as charged."

The spectators roared, then began to chant a

single, booming word; Kirk had no doubt as to its meaning.

*Death* . . .

He stared with honest hatred at Chang, whose own expression was unreadable.

The judge pounded his mailed glove against stone once more; the crowd fell silent. "Captain James T. Kirk, Dr. Leonard McCoy . . ."

Kirk and McCoy turned. Jim squinted through the harsh light at the judge's ghostly white countenance, partially obscured by the shadow of his upturned cowl.

"Have either of you anything to say before this court passes sentence?"

Jim and Bones shared a look.

"We were framed," McCoy said.

Their attorney stepped in front of them and addressed the judge, his tone impassioned. Jim watched with amazement. The Klingon was actually angry and disappointed for his clients' sake.

"I wish to note for the record that the evidence against my clients is entirely circumstantial. I beg the court to consider this when pronouncing its sentence."

"So noted." The judge paused. Jim steeled himself. He had no doubt that the sentence would be death. For him it didn't matter, but for McCoy . . .

He turned and gave the doctor a glance that reassured and apologized at the same time. McCoy shrugged, cleared his throat, and looked at the judge.

"In the interests of amity for the upcoming peace

talks," the judge said, "the sentence of death is commuted."

McCoy sagged against the dock. Jim forced himself to keep his balance. The crowd roared angrily, then quieted to hear the rest of the sentence.

"It is the judgment of this court that, without possibility of reprieve or parole, you be taken from this place to the dilithium mines on the penal asteroid archipelago of Rura Penthe, there to spend the rest of your natural lives."

# Chapter Eight

FROM THE SAFETY of the *Enterprise* bridge, Spock watched with the others as the prisoners were led away.

"Rura Penthe!" Uhura recoiled, horrified, from the sight.

"Known throughout the galaxy as the aliens' graveyard," Chekov whispered, his face slack with shock. Beside him at her post, Valeris kept her expression taut, controlled, belying the agitation in her eyes.

"Better to kill them now and get it over with," Scott muttered bitterly behind them.

Spock stared mutely at the screen. Impossible to deny that the trial had evoked deep emotion within him. After many years spent among humans, he had learned to accept his heritage and the fact that he possessed emotions. He had even come to see

173

how he had overcompensated for the fact—which Dr. McCoy had taken great pains to point out, on one occasion accusing Spock of "trying to out-Vulcan the Vulcans."

Yet he remained devoted to logic. He was most comfortable in his role as a Vulcan and saw no advantage in abandoning it now. While certain positive emotions, experienced judiciously, might enhance life, none could be permitted to control it.

And so Spock contained those he experienced now: frustration, anger, despair, and, strongest of all, an entirely irrational guilt.

Guilt, because he had volunteered the *Enterprise* and James T. Kirk for the Kronos mission. To some degree, he had been guilty of manipulation. Yet his reasons for doing so were logical beyond reproach. The *Enterprise* under James T. Kirk was the safest choice for transporting the Klingon chancellor; it was merely incidental that Kirk would have the opportunity to meet Chancellor Gorkon, to know that Klingons other than Kruge existed in the universe. Both Kirk and Gorkon stood to benefit from the encounter.

But circumstance had conspired against them. And more, Spock realized now, than circumstance. The real conspirators were free, while Kirk and McCoy stood trial, which meant that Azetbur's life and the chance for peace were still endangered.

Spock also felt guilt for not boarding *Kronos* in Kirk's place. He argued most logically with himself: had Kirk not gone, the Klingons would simply have destroyed *Enterprise*. The captain's gamble had saved the ship—and now would save the peace conference.

Nevertheless, Spock could not quite free himself of the nagging conviction that it would have been better for him to stand in Kirk's place in the prisoners' dock.

Initially he had experienced relief on learning that his two friends had escaped the sentence of death. He had prepared himself to face that outcome with some measure of acceptance.

Yet a small internal voice—one he had almost silenced during the emotion-denying discipline of Kolinahr, one that had led him back to the *Enterprise* and V'Ger, one he had learned in recent years to carefully attend—refused to accept the possibility and insisted, even in that grim instant before sentence was passed, on hope.

His relief was immediately outweighed by alarm. Rura Penthe had attained legendary status as the cruelest penal colony in the Klingon archipelago. Spock agreed with Commander Scott; a swift execution would have been more merciful. No one survived a stay of any length on Rura Penthe. Death was inevitable.

Spock had no intention of allowing the inevitable to occur, nor would he hesitate to disobey a direct order and violate Starfleet regulations. He was simply repaying a favor. And, as he had once told Jim Kirk, some things transcended the discipline of the service.

He turned to Valeris. "Let's see the torpedo hit again, Lieutenant."

She glanced back at him; only a Vulcan could have seen the dark emotion that burned in her eyes. She saw that he noticed, and lowered her gaze. Spock felt a stirring of compassion as her fingers flew over the controls. He would have liked to reassure her, but his words would have been meaningless. The odds were great that the captain and Dr. McCoy would be dead before rescue arrived.

As the image of *Kronos One* reappeared on the monitor, Spock raised his fingers to his brow, then consciously forced himself to lower them before anyone caught the gesture.

The bridge crew watched in silence as a photon torpedo streaked across the screen and pounded the unwary Klingon vessel.

"It is *Enterprise,*" Chekov said, hopeless. "We fired."

Spock was not so certain. He watched as, on the visual, *Kronos* reeled from the impact of a second hit.

"It's na possible!" Scott directed his protest at the Vulcan. "All weapons *visually* accounted for. Sir."

Valeris swiveled to face Spock. "Captain . . .?" Her tone was unusually diffident, soft. "Is it not logical to consider *all* possibilities? This is most difficult to say, but has it occurred to"—Scott turned sharply to frown at her, and she recoiled slightly—"to any of us that Captain Kirk is . . . that is, we know his feelings about Klingons, what they did to his . . ."

Uhura and Chekov were both glaring in open

disapproval at her; Spock's own gaze was impenetrable. She broke off, then lifted her chin in pale defiance. "Well, it *is* a possibility."

Spock held her gaze a few seconds, then said tonelessly: "Again."

The scene returned to *Kronos*, hovering placidly in starry space. A flash appeared in the bottom right sector of the screen.

"Hold," Spock ordered. He studied the frozen image. They had all been making the same assumption based on sheerly visual evidence. The torpedoes' trajectory made it *appear* that they had been fired from the *Enterprise*. However . . .

An image rose unbidden in his consciousness: Jim Kirk, his features twisted with anger, saying, *They never even saw the ship that attacked them; the phaserfire seemed to come out of nowhere . . .*

He gazed back at the expectant crew. "An ancestor of mine maintained that if you eliminate the impossible, whatever remains—however improbable—must be the truth."

"What exactly does that mean?" Uhura asked, desperation and impatience in her voice.

"It means," Spock replied slowly, "that if we cannot have fired those torpedoes, someone else did."

Valeris's left eyebrow rose sharply.

Scott shook his head in confusion. "They dinna fire on themselves. And there were no other ships present."

"No. But there *was* an enormous neutron energy surge."

"Not from us!" the engineer protested.

"Precisely," Spock said. Using Occam's razor and—though it was difficult to admit to himself—intuition, he had already come to the simplest, most logical conclusion possible, one so unbelievable the crew would reject it unless they were led to the same deduction.

Chekov frowned thoughtfully and tilted his head. "I don't understand, Mr. Spock. A neutron surge that big could only be produced by another ship . . ."

*"Kronos One?"* Uhura suggested.

Spock shook his head. "Too far off. This ship had to have been very near us. Perhaps underneath us . . ."

"If another ship had been beneath us, the Klingons would have seen her," Scott said.

Spock turned to him. "Would they?"

The others gazed at him in confusion, but Valeris understood.

"A Bird of Prey?" she asked softly.

"A Bird of Prey," Spock confirmed.

"Cloaked?" Chekov's intonation rose in disbelief.

"A Bird of Prey canna fire when she's cloaked!" Scott protested.

"All things being equal, Mr. Scott, I would agree. Normally, the power drain caused by a cloaking device is too great to allow simultaneous use of weaponry. However, all things are not equal: this one can."

Scott's ruddy complexion paled. "Then you're

talking about a dreadful new engine of destruction, Mr. Spock."

"I believe I am."

"We must inform Starfleet Comm—" Valeris began, but Scott interrupted angrily.

"Inform them of what? A new weapon that isn't visible? Raving lunatics—that's what they'll call us! They'll say we're so desperate to exonerate the captain we'll say anything."

Spock released a small sigh. "And they would be correct. We have no evidence, only a theory that happens to fit the facts."

"Even assuming you're correct, Mr. Spock," Uhura asked, "why would they fire on their own chancellor?"

Spock evaded the question, not for lack of an answer, but rather because he hoped his unstated suspicion was incorrect.

He made a decision and faced Valeris. "I want this ship searched from bow to stern. Lieutenant Valeris, you are in charge. Start with the transporter room and proceed outward."

The young Vulcan rose. "Aye, sir."

Chekov's expression remained puzzled. "I do not understand. If there was a ship underneath us, surely the assassins beamed aboard from that vessel, not *Enterprise.*"

"You have forgotten something," Spock told him. "The data banks claim *we* fired. If we did, the killers are here; if we did not, whoever altered the data banks is here. In any event, what we are searching for is here."

Chekov's frown deepened. "What *are* we searching for, Mr. Spock?"

He turned toward Valeris, certain that she understood—in her studies, she had excelled in logical deduction. "Tell him, Lieutenant."

She straightened self-consciously in response to his scrutiny. "Two pairs of gravity boots."

McCoy raised stinging eyes against the bitter wind. Overhead, Rura Penthe's three suns floated, ghostly and pale, providing no warmth. The doctor blinked. The wind and cold made his eyes tear, but the drops froze before reaching his cheeks.

He hadn't thought the human body capable of withstanding such temperatures—at least, not *his* human body. At first he'd been glad for it, in a way. Freezing to death seemed preferable to death at the hands of the guards. He'd go numb all over, fall asleep, and that would be it. A quick, fairly painless end.

That was before he'd spent any time in the cold. Now his hands and feet ached viciously, and the agony threatened to spread. The heavy leg irons didn't help.

Painless, hell. Freezing to death was definitely *not* the way to go.

McCoy struggled to keep his balance on the snow-covered ice, leg irons clanking as he maintained pace with fourteen other prisoners. Beside them trudged five Klingon guards attended by vicious-looking jackal-mastiffs.

The scene struck McCoy as surrealistic; this was barbarianism from a bygone era. *We knew they read Shakespeare; something tells me they read Dumas, too.*

He squinted, snow-blind, into the distance, but saw no possible destination—only white, extending into infinite horizon. McCoy clutched his ragged furs more tightly as he shivered. Any hope he'd cherished of Spock coming to rescue them had long vanished. The doctor alternated between sullen apathy born of despair and irrational anger at Jim, who trudged ahead of him and hadn't said a word since they'd arrived.

Come to think of it, neither had McCoy. Too damned cold even to talk. . . .

He almost stumbled into Jim before he realized that the head guard had signaled the prisoners to stop. The Klingon—hard to tell, with everyone wrapped in the same raggedy furs—pressed an instrument on his belt that produced a high-pitched whine.

Rumbling. Snow slid aside to reveal a huge trapdoor. It yawned open; another Klingon guard emerged and placed a box in the swirling snow.

A third Klingon emerged, attended, like the others, by a snarling, snaggle-toothed mastiff. The commandant, McCoy guessed, judging from the way he stepped onto the box and surveyed the shivering group with an air of cruel indifference. The Klingon seemed more hardened than his prisoners, and certainly no happier to be there.

"This is the gulag Rura Penthe," he growled. "Observe." He gestured with a fur-covered arm at a barren sweep of snow. "There is no stockade, no guard tower, no electrified frontier. They are not needed. Only a magnetic shield prevents beaming. Your new home is underground."

He lifted a whistle to his lips. McCoy started at the shrill blast.

Two guards emerged from the trapdoor, dragging a struggling convict, a human, stripped of his protective wrappings. The prisoner screamed, "No! Nooo!"

The commandant watched impassively, then addressed his listeners. "Punishment means exile from prison to the surface. On the surface nothing can survive."

The guards hurled the screaming convict onto the ice. His cries abruptly faded; he lay immobilized by the cold. McCoy looked away.

The commandant's expression was one of unutterable boredom, as if he had seen this scene performed countless times. "Below, no one can escape. Work well and you will be treated well. Work badly and you will die."

He stepped off the box, which was immediately retrieved by one of the guards, and descended through the trapdoor. The prisoners were herded after him.

McCoy was grateful to head someplace warmer, but as he was prodded into the entryway, he turned his head to take one last look at the wasteland outside—and at the frozen corpse of the convict, already half covered by the swirling snow.

Below was a huge underground labyrinth with a large open yard, ringed by crude huts. McCoy found it a bleak improvement: sheltered from the bitter wind, but still freezing. Much to his disappointment, the leg irons were not removed. At least they were allowed to wander freely in the courtyard —though, after catching sight of the other inmates, McCoy wasn't so sure that was a good thing. Every one of them seemed twice his size and ready to prove it.

And the minute word got out that James Kirk had arrived . . .

McCoy glanced surreptitiously at the guards above them on the scaffolding, then hissed at Kirk, "Jim, let's find someplace where we can stay out of trouble."

Kirk glanced at the less than friendly crowd milling around the yard and nodded, then jerked his head toward the outer wall. Legs aching, McCoy followed.

"Maybe I shouldn't even tell you to not try and get yourself killed," the doctor said glumly, when they were out of earshot of the others. "Actually, that might be the easiest way to go."

Kirk's expression brightened; he raised his brows at McCoy in mock surprise. "We'll manage until Spock gets here," Jim said easily.

McCoy felt a surge of irritation, fueled by exhaustion, cold, and hunger. "Why do you always have to be such a damn Pollyanna in these situations? Spock doesn't know where Rura Penthe is. No one in the Federation does, and even if they did, they'd never be able to get here. We're somewhere in the Klingon Empire."

"Spock will find us," Jim said firmly.

"Find our *corpses,* you mean—" McCoy began bitterly, but stopped as a shadow fell across them. He glanced up.

The creature blocking the light was gigantic and unlike anything the doctor had ever seen: silver-scaled, with horny growths extending from temple to chin. The left side of his face bore brilliant red welts that might have been a scar from a previous battle or a perfectly normal marking for his species.

As the doctor had feared, the word was out: the alien loomed menacingly over Kirk and growled something that sounded to McCoy like *"Quog wok na pushnat!"*

Jim spread his hands in a "you-have-me-at-a-disadvantage" gesture. "I'm afraid our universal translator was confiscated."

The alien leaned closer and rumbled something totally incomprehensible.

Kirk smiled. "Sorry . . ."

His reaction infuriated the alien, who roared, *"Ragnit ascru, unto pram moreoscue shondik!"*

"He's definitely on about something," McCoy offered timidly, trying not to be too obvious about sidling out of the way.

*"Quog wok na pushnat!"* the creature threatened,

and to show he meant business, lifted Kirk into the air with one arm.

"If this is your spot," Jim began, "we'll move on."

He choked as the alien lifted him in the air. McCoy considered coming to Jim's rescue for precisely one second, then looked about desperately for help.

"He wants your obedience to the Brotherhood of Aliens," a low, feminine voice said. McCoy turned, startled. The speaker was humanoid, female, dark-skinned, and golden-eyed, strikingly beautiful.

"He's got it," Kirk gasped, red-faced. Distracted by the woman, the alien eased his grip. Kirk gulped in air.

"And your coat," the woman said.

"'Fraid not." Kirk eyed his adversary. "It wouldn't fit him, anyway."

The woman did not quite smile as she spoke to the alien in his guttural tongue. Somewhat reluctantly, the creature lowered Kirk to the ground. Jim adjusted his wrappings against the cold.

*"Fendo pomsky,"* she told the alien, who made an affirmative gesture and wandered off.

Kirk faced his savior and studied her appreciatively. "Thanks."

"What's the Brotherhood of Aliens?" McCoy asked.

"Prisoners from outside the Klingon system. They tend to band together." The woman raised a dark and faintly noxious-smelling object to her lips—a hand-rolled tobacco cigarette, illegal as hell, McCoy thought at first—and inhaled smoke. "I'm Martia."

She offered them the burning cigarette. McCoy drew back at first, but she persisted. "This'll help keep you warm. You're Kirk and McCoy."

Kirk took the cigarette and inhaled; his surprised reaction convinced McCoy, who took a healthy drag. A rush of warmth spread from his throat downward. He coughed and handed the cigarette back to its owner.

"How did you know?" Kirk asked.

Martia shrugged. "We don't get many chancellors' assassins."

Jim's expression hardened. "We didn't kill Gorkon."

Martia's eyes widened with mock innocence. "Of course not." She glanced casually over one shoulder to be sure no one else was within earshot. "There's a reward for your death."

Nervously, McCoy followed her gaze. "Figures."

Jim showed no surprise. "We've been set up all along."

Martia nodded, leaned forward conspiratorially. "Somebody up there wants you out of the way."

"I don't believe we can get more out of the way than this," McCoy sighed.

"They'll make it look like an accident," she whispered. "It's easy enough to do here."

McCoy shivered, though not from cold. Martia saw, took another drag off the cigarette, and passed it back to him.

The doctor took it gratefully and tried not to

cough this time as the astringent smoke hit the back of his throat. "What are you in for, if you don't mind my asking?"

She showed a flash of perfect white teeth; McCoy found himself mesmerized by her eyes—golden, flecked with black—and noticed Jim was not immune to their effect, either.

"I don't mind. Smuggling—guilty. I come from Arc. Smuggling is an ancient and respected trade there."

"How much time's left of your sentence?" Kirk asked.

Her smile twisted grimly. "Don't you know? Everyone on Rura Penthe is here for life."

At Dr. Marcus's bedside, Kwan-mei Suarez smiled as Carol opened her eyes.

Kwan-mei did not particularly feel like smiling. She was glad to see Carol awake at last, but at the same time, she dreaded this moment.

Two days before, she had been helping Jackson through the hospital corridors. He took small, tentative steps, one brown hand clutching the railing, the other holding Kwan-mei's arm. She had been happy again; Jackson was recuperating, cheerful, and they had heard earlier that morning from the doctors that Carol's treatment had been successful.

And then they had passed a wall monitor carrying the news about Chancellor Gorkon's assassination. The fact was almost a day old, due to the starbase's remote location. Both had frozen, com-

J. M. Dillard

pelled to watch; she had not been able to meet
Jackson's eyes. She knew he had reacted just as she
had, with initial horror and pity, followed by a cold
reassessment: so Gorkon was dead. She could not
help seeing a degree of justice in the fact. The
chancellor's fate had been no worse than that of the
victims on Kudao or of those on Themis. Certainly
no worse than Sohlar's.

As the news commentator droned on, Gorkon's
official portrait had flashed onto the screen, followed by bloody scenes from Kudao and the ruins
of the stations on Themis. Kwan-mei had found
herself hoping Gorkon had bled to death slowly,
aware to the end. She had turned away, ashamed.

The stunning news about Jim Kirk's arrest drew
her back. She had been close enough to Carol to
know about her son, David, and how he died; she
also knew Kirk was his father. She felt that, through
knowing Carol, she also knew Jim, and she thought
the charges were insane.

That night they had watched excerpts from the
trial in Jackson's room.

Carol groaned and gently fingered her forehead,
touching the gold and white hair that Kwan-mei
had brushed an hour before.

Kwan-mei leaned forward, grateful to know that
doctors were monitoring Carol in the next room;
her skin still had an unhealthy ivory cast. She tried
to decide if Carol had always been so pale. Certainly she had always seemed tired, overworked. "Carol? How do you feel?"

Carol tried to sit up; Kwan-mei pressed a control

that silently raised the head of the bed. "Rotten," Carol croaked, still rubbing her forehead. "What the hell happened?"

Kwan-mei drew a breath to reply. Before she could, Carol closed her eyes. "The building . . . the whole damn building . . ." She opened them again and stared at the walls, then accusingly at Kwan-mei. "This isn't Themis, is it?"

Kwan-mei's smile had faded entirely. "No. It isn't. You had a head injury; you've been out for a few days. How much do you remember?"

"The walls." Carol let her head loll against the pillow. "I remember the walls coming down. The damn building was collapsing on us. You ran to the window . . ."

Kwan-mei nodded. "The station was attacked."

"Klingons," Carol whispered. Kwan-mei heard the hatred in her tone.

"Yes. Their government denies it, of course, but there were witnesses who saw the warbirds—"

"The others," Carol interrupted. "Gods, are they all right? Jackson, Sohlar—"

Kwan-mei's throat constricted painfully. "Jackson's all right. Broke his spine in a couple of places, but he's been up and walking for a few days now. Just about mended. And I walked away without a scratch. Can you believe it?"

Carol looked steadily at her, eyes widening with dread at the omission.

Kwan-mei bowed her head. "Carol, I'm so sorry. We lost Sohlar."

Slowly, stiffly, Carol turned her head away and

gazed through the window at the garden. When she turned back toward Kwan-mei, there were tears in her eyes.

"How did it happen?"

"Quickly," she lied. "He never knew . . ."

She held Carol's hand and let her cry for a while. She felt no guilt over the lie about Sohlar; she had been the only one with him when he died, the only one who knew what had happened. She hadn't even told Jackson about it, so Carol would never have to know the truth. But she fully intended to tell her about Kirk, as difficult as that might be. It would be impossible to protect her from the news.

Carol turned toward her, still wiping tears from her cheeks, and asked, "Has anyone contacted Jim?"

Kwan-mei's heart skipped a beat. If she didn't tell Carol now, there was a real danger someone else might refer to the trial or turn on a monitor carrying the news.

Yet, looking at Carol's anguished expression, she simply couldn't find the words. "He was here. He was very upset and wanted to stay, but he was called back to Starfleet Headquarters. Some kind of emergency . . ."

"Typical Starfleet timing," Carol said, not quite able to smile. "Poor Jim . . ." Her expression darkened. "Maybe because of Themis. Do you think there's going to be a war?"

"I don't know," Kwan-mei answered honestly. "I really don't know."

# Chapter Nine

ESCORTED BY Commander Chekov, Spock entered the galley to find the servitors dismantled. Crew members were sifting through the dishes and cutlery that covered every surface.

Spock carefully picked his way through the debris to where Valeris stood. "Any progress?"

He could easily have asked the question via intercom from the bridge, but at the moment the bridge was the place of least activity aboard the ship. Spock trusted Valeris to oversee the search efficiently; but perhaps his presence there would facilitate matters.

And perhaps his desire to check on the search in person was motivated by anxiety. In reality he had nothing to do at the moment except wait while *Enterprise*'s long-range scanners sought the captain and McCoy—and think. He had already done all he could do thus far for his friends by ordering the search and by earlier taking advantage of the supply of viridium patches on the bridge. The rest was up to Kirk—and Lieutenant Valeris.

Valeris caught sight of Spock and Chekov and stiffened to attention. "None, sir. We have a crew of three hundred examining their own quarters, but the killers may be among them."

Spock nodded, though the notion was a discomfiting one.

Valeris continued. "Surely they have disposed of the boots by now. Wouldn't it have been more logical to leave them on Gorkon's ship?"

"Such logic must give way to physics," Spock replied. "Gravitational systems aboard *Kronos* had not been restored by the time the killers escaped. Without their boots, they would not have remained on the Klingon transporter pads."

Chekov extended thumb and forefinger in imitation of a phaser. "Why not simply vaporize them?"

"Like this?" Valeris asked. She removed a phaser from a wall mount, set it to kill, and incinerated a nearby dish.

Chekov winced and covered his ears as the alarm sounded. Spock endeavored not to be amused by her none-too-Vulcan brashness. At times she reminded him strongly of James Kirk, though he suspected she would be insulted at the thought.

Valeris calmly returned the weapon to its mount and switched off the alarm. "As you know, Commander Chekov, no one can fire an unauthorized phaser set on kill aboard a starship." She turned to

Spock. "Captain . . . suppose that when the killers returned, they disposed of the boots in the refuse?"

Spock nodded; he had already considered that possibility. "I am having the refuse searched."

"But the incinerator—" Chekov began.

"All Starfleet-issue clothing is fireproof, Commander," Spock reminded him. "If my surmise is correct, those boots will cling to the killers' necks like Tiberian bats. They could not make their escape without them, nor could they simply eject them out the airlock for all to see; no . . . they are here. Somewhere."

He swiveled his head as Commander Uhura entered the galley, carefully stepping over the scattered utensils. She was frowning. "Did someone fire a phaser?" Distracted, she did not wait for an answer. "Mr. Spock . . ."

The Vulcan met her gaze.

"I've pulled out my . . . um, wooden shoe, and Starfleet is screaming for us to return to port."

As she spoke, Scott entered.

"Mr. Scott," Spock said. "Any progress on repairing our warp drive?"

Scott had been in an exceptionally surly mood ever since Admiral Smillie's briefing; he puckered his forehead. "There's nothing wrong with the bloody—"

"Mr. Scott," Spock reminded him smoothly, "if we return to spacedock, the assassins will manage to dispose of their incriminating footwear, and we will never see the captain or Dr. McCoy alive again."

"—could take weeks, sir," Scott finished without missing a beat, his demeanor suddenly earnest.

Spock nodded approvingly. "Thank you, Mr. Scott. Commander Uhura, notify Starfleet that our warp drive is inoperative."

Valeris, who had followed the exchange intently, raised a disapproving brow. "A lie?"

Spock faced her unwaveringly. "An error." He experienced no internal dissonance at the thought of prevaricating, so long as the benefit achieved in so doing outweighed any harm. In this case, the benefit was Kirk and McCoy's lives.

"I'll tell them someone threw a gravity boot into it," Uhura said unhappily.

Spock noted Valeris's hesitation. If she ascribed to the galactic myth, as many did, that Vulcans did not lie, she might very well be tempted to notify Starfleet Command on her own initiative. Spock watched her and waited.

"Right," Valeris said at last. A strange look had come into her eyes, one that Spock interpreted as repressed amusement and mild exasperation. "A gravity boot in the warp drive . . ." She paused. "With your permission, Captain Spock, I wish to see how the search is proceeding in sickbay."

Spock dismissed her with a nod.

Uhura watched her leave, then said, in a hushed, worried voice, "You understand that we have lost all contact with the captain and Dr. McCoy?"

"At present they are surrounded by a magnetic shield," Spock replied. He had expected as much.

While the captain and doctor were being transported to Rura Penthe, they could be traced; the inability of *Enterprise*'s scanners to detect them meant that they had arrived on the penal colony . . . and that there was not much time left.

Spock did not like the thought of his two friends spending any amount of time on Rura Penthe, but such was unavoidable. Until the captain's precise location was known, it would be foolhardy to order the *Enterprise* blindly into Klingon space. To do so would be to risk three hundred lives instead of two.

"If my calculations are correct," he told Uhura, "the captain should be deep into his escape planning by this time."

He did not say, *If he has survived* . . .

At that moment Jim Kirk was standing in the prison yard thinking only of survival. He was unclear about how, exactly, the fight had started. All he knew was that the alien—who, to Jim's mind, resembled nothing so much as a brightly painted horned toad—had approached once more and made a few threatening sounds. This time, Martia didn't even have a chance to interpret. She and Bones had watched, horrified, as the alien had slammed a rough, scaly paw into Jim's face.

Within a light-second Kirk and the alien were squared off, encircled by jeering prisoners, and Jim was wiping blood from his nose. He could hear McCoy calling for the guards. No point in that; they had already joined the raucous crowd.

Before Jim could gather himself, his opponent struck again with a horny fist. This time Jim staggered back and fell, but fought the dizziness and scrambled to his feet to begin circling. He would not make the same mistake again: his foe might be huge and lumbering in appearance, but it could move with deadly speed.

The next time the creature swung, Jim ducked and managed to come back with an uppercut. He caught the alien square on the chin. The blow seemed to cause the creature no discomfort, but Jim grimaced at the pain—the hornlike growths on the creature's chin had gored his fist.

The alien lunged at Kirk and pulled him down; the two wrestled on the frozen ground until Jim managed to slip free. A kick to the chest, a slam to the neck, and the giant at last was down. Jim staggered toward his friends.

Until a hand around his ankle pulled him back. The alien lay, grinning, reeling Kirk in with an inexorable grip. In an instant the creature was on its feet and crushing Kirk, chest to back, in a bear hug. The pressure increased until Jim was lifted off his feet, unable to breathe.

In desperation, Kirk drew his legs up and swung down hard, smashing the creature in the knee.

To his grateful surprise, the alien dropped with an earsplitting scream. Gasping, Jim stumbled away.

Bones hurried to his elbow. "You okay?"

Jim nodded, unable to speak.

Martia smiled, triumphant and calm, as if she had never doubted Kirk would emerge the victor. Jim hadn't been so sure. "They'll respect you now," she said.

"That's a comfort," Jim managed, catching his breath. "I was lucky that . . . thing had knees." He looked back; the giant toad was still on the ground, clutching his injured leg.

Martia followed his gaze. "That's not his knee." She showed a crescent of white teeth at his confused reaction. "Not everybody keeps their genitals in the same place, Captain."

"Anything else you want to tell me?" Kirk shot back, then addressed McCoy before she could respond. "Bones, why don't you see what you can do? Let him know we're not holding a grudge."

McCoy studied the injured behemoth dubiously. "Suppose *he's* holding a grudge." Tentatively the doctor approached the alien and knelt down to examine the knee.

Jim turned to Martia; she read the question in his eyes and answered it before he could ask.

She shook her head. "When whoever it is makes his move, you won't be here to ask if he's the one." She hesitated; for the first time, Kirk saw a trace of fear in her expression. "You want to get out of here?"

"There's got to be a way," Kirk said.

She glanced around anxiously, then opened her mouth to speak—and closed it again, no longer trying to hide the fear. She shook her head and moved off.

Kirk watched her go, then glanced back as the alien cried out in pain.

McCoy was gingerly attempting to manipulate the leg. He looked up at Jim, then back down at the knee, in amazement.

"Hot damn, Jim, she's right!"

The buzzer summoned Sulu from an unpleasant dream in which he was aboard *Enterprise* and Spock was dead.

He sat up instantly, pulse racing, and ordered a lamp on. "Come in."

Janice Rand entered hesitantly and lingered by the door, lowering her gaze at the sight of her commanding officer in such a disheveled state. Her face was shadowed and drawn; she had volunteered for an extended duty shift. Sulu had allowed it because he trusted Rand—and because the fewer among the crew who knew what he intended in advance, the easier it would be for them later, when Starfleet started asking questions.

He had asked Rand to relay any communications from *Enterprise* or Starfleet Command directly to him in person. Conversations via intercom aboard ship would directly become part of ship's record, and Sulu preferred for now to keep certain things off the record.

"Sorry to wake you, sir," Rand said, looking as though she envied him. "But Starfleet urgently requests any data we may have on the whereabouts of *Enterprise*."

"What?" Sulu rubbed his eyes. He had heard the statement, but registered it a half second later than normal, by which time the question was already out of his mouth.

"Apparently they're refusing to acknowledge the signal to return to spacedock, sir."

Sulu did not allow himself to smile; Rand would not have understood that he was thinking of Spock and wondering fondly what manipulation of logic the Vulcan intended to use to explain *that* one to headquarters. He paused, then said very seriously: "Signal Starfleet Command that we have no idea of *Enterprise*'s location."

Rand's pale eyes widened in astonishment. "Captain, are you sure—"

Sulu hardened his expression. "That will be all, Mister. Unless you have a problem . . ."

"No, sir." Rand straightened to attention, then left.

As the doors snapped shut behind her, Sulu sighed and sat back, now fully awake. Janice was a good officer; but if Sulu yielded to the temptation to explain what he was doing, she would be as liable as he. He had no desire to implicate any of his crew.

In fact, he had no real desire to implicate himself —it could very well mean losing *Excelsior,* the command he had awaited for so many years. But if it came to that, Sulu would accept it. Kirk's and McCoy's lives far outweighed such a small sacrifice.

Assuming they were still alive . . .

* * *

Kirk stretched out on the filthy tattered mattress beside McCoy and stared at the bunk overhead, which groaned uneasily as its occupant shifted his weight. The prisoners' quarters, a shabbily constructed hut, did little to block out the cold. Kirk tucked his coat more tightly around himself.

He needed to rest, to steel himself for another day here, but the cold, the throbbing in his nose and jaw, and his restless thoughts made sleep impossible.

At times like these, he envied Spock his Vulcan training; he would have liked now to be able to shut out the pain, the cold, the anxious thoughts about Carol. . . .

By now she had either died or regained consciousness, only to learn that he had been sentenced to a life term on Rura Penthe for murder.

Not that he was so horribly worried for his own sake. He knew that Spock would come for them as soon as Jim found a way around Rura Penthe's magnetic shield. In the meantime, if he could just keep from getting killed by one of the other prisoners, he could survive the brutal prison conditions. But he doubted McCoy could take more than a day.

Kirk turned his head. The doctor was staring wide-eyed into the darkness.

"Can't sleep?" Jim asked softly.

"Three months till retirement." McCoy's tone was beaten, hopeless. "What a way to finish."

"We're not finished," Jim said.

McCoy turned on him, bitter. "Speak for yourself. One day . . . one night . . ." He made a slashing gesture across his throat with a forefinger. "Kobayashi Maru . . . How are we supposed to protect ourselves? We don't even know who our enemies are!"

Kirk tried to sound reassuring. "We'll find a way out of here, Bones."

"If it's so damned simple," McCoy hissed, "how come no one's escaped?"

"That's what they tell the prisoners. I don't believe them. And I think Martia knows something she's not telling."

"You mean, like how to get out of here?"

Jim nodded.

"Fine," McCoy said caustically. "Then I suppose we'll all just take a little hike to the surface. And *then* what'll we do? Try to flag down a passing freighter? We couldn't last an hour."

"Spock will be waiting for us. Trust me."

McCoy squinted at him suspiciously, clearly wanting to believe, but remaining unconvinced. "Now I think *you* know something you're not telling."

"Bones?" Jim asked thoughtfully, changing the subject. The less McCoy knew about details, the safer it would be for him if things went wrong. "Are you afraid of the future?"

McCoy snorted as he shifted uncomfortably on the unforgiving mattress. "That *was* the general idea I intended to convey."

"I didn't mean *this* future."

"Are we playing multiple choice?"

An alien claw suddenly flopped over the side of the bunk above them. Jim noticed; McCoy didn't. Jim pretended not to and kept on talking. Maybe the alien was a very heavy sleeper.

Or maybe he was dead.

"Some people are afraid of the future," Jim continued, keeping an eye and an ear open. "Of what might happen." He paused. "I was frightened, really frightened."

A second claw dropped suddenly and dangled over the edge of the bunk.

McCoy's tone grew quietly sympathetic. "I've looked death in the eye a thousand times and tried to be professional about it. Of course, it wasn't usually *my* death I was looking at." He turned his head to look at Jim. "What frightened you specifically?"

A third, different, hand dropped. McCoy saw, and met Jim's gaze knowingly.

Someone was methodically knocking out—or killing—all the prisoners within earshot. Jim forced himself not to tense, to speak casually.

"I was frightened of . . . myself. What I had become after David's death, after . . . what happened to Carol. I was frightened of no more Neutral Zone. I was *used* to hating Klingons. That's why I failed in our assignment."

"You didn't fail," McCoy protested. "It wasn't your fault Gorkon died."

"If he hadn't, I would have failed. I couldn't play

diplomat with them, Bones. You saw that. It never even occurred to me to take Gorkon at his word. Spock was right. I was behaving like a bigot, blaming all Klingons for the act of one."

McCoy's eyes widened as a fourth alien hand fell and dangled above their heads. He swallowed. "Well, don't be too hard on yourself. We all felt exactly the same."

Jim shook his head. "No. Somebody felt much worse. And I'm starting to understand why."

"Well, if you've got any bright ideas, now's the time to—"

"Time's the problem," Kirk said. "You and I don't count. We're just a couple of pawns in someone else's chess game. But you heard the judge: the peace conference is on again. Whoever killed Gorkon will sandbag the thing all over . . . unless we find a way out of here."

McCoy started at a muffled sound and put a finger to his lips. Nearby, a stone came loose and rolled past them. McCoy closed his eyes and pretended to sleep; Jim did the same, listening intently as something crawled toward them in the dark.

Kirk tensed, ready . . .

"Kirk. It's me, Martia."

He opened his eyes to see her face, hovering above his in the darkness. She crouched low beside the bunk. Jim glanced back at McCoy, who still pretended to sleep.

"Listen," Martia whispered. "No one has ever escaped from Rura Penthe."

J. M. Dillard

"Except us," Jim said.

Martia did not quite smile. "It *is* possible. I know how to get outside the shield."

"Where do we come in?" Kirk asked warily.

"Getting outside the shield is easy. After that, it's up to you to get us off the surface before we freeze." She paused to search his face intently, drawing her long body closer to his. "Can you?"

"Possibly."

"Do you mean that? I won't risk it if—"

"I can get us off the surface," Jim answered firmly.

Desperate with hope, she leaned over him and grasped his arm; her large eyes glittered above him in the darkness. "I can't make it alone. You're the likeliest candidate to come to this hellhole in months."

"Candidate for what?" Jim asked.

She drew back her fur hood and kissed him. Jim didn't resist. The memory of Carol brought guilt, but he could not afford to discourage his only chance for escape.

She pulled away, eyes shining. "Go to Lift Seven in the morning for mining duty. I'll see you there."

Kirk watched as she vanished into the shadows.

Beside him, McCoy made a low noise of disgust and propped himself up on one elbow.

Jim raised his eyebrows in mock innocence. "I think I've been alienated."

McCoy rolled his eyes. "What is it with you, anyway?"

204

Jim shrugged. "Still think we're finished?"

The doctor sighed. "More than ever."

Chekov continued his painstaking examination of the transporter room and tried not to feel discouraged.

The situation was hopeless, of course. By now the assassins had carefully removed all traces of their activities. Chekov had volunteered to join the search, not with the hope of finding anything, but because it was better than sitting by idly, worrying about the captain and Dr. McCoy.

Now he was *busy*, worrying about the captain and Dr. McCoy.

And Lieutenant Valeris had needed extra hands. Chekov liked the lieutenant. Unlike the other Vulcans he had met, Valeris had a sense of humor and didn't take every expression she heard literally. He suspected that she was half human, like Spock —certainly she'd spent a lot of time in human company—but Chekov did not want to be impolite by asking her a personal question.

At the same time, Chekov felt she was overeager and inexperienced, as demonstrated by the zealousness with which she conducted the search. She was very obviously trying to impress Mr. Spock. Had she not been Vulcan, Chekov would have suspected that she had a crush on her mentor.

Despite his doubts about the usefulness of searching the transporter room, Chekov did his best not to leave a centimeter unscanned. If Mr.

Spock was right—and he could not remember a time when the Vulcan had been wrong—the killers had passed through here.

Chekov moved to the transporter platform, lifted his scanner . . . and froze.

On one of the pads, large enough to be seen by the unaided eye, were several small dark violet spatters.

With haste born of hope, he dropped to his knees and scraped a sample into an evidence tube.

In the science lab, Spock stared through the microscope at a cluster of delicate wine-colored cells. The distinctly bright violet hue had darkened with time, but Spock did not doubt what he saw before him. With forced intellectual detachment, he wondered whether these particular cells had once flowed in Chancellor Gorkon's veins.

The Vulcan straightened and turned to Chekov, who hovered nearby with intent expectancy.

"Klingon blood," Spock said. He pressed a control; a display lit up to reveal the flat disc-shaped cells.

Chekov stared at the visual, his expression a mixture of horror and triumph. "They must have walked through it when it was floating and tracked it back here."

Spock gave a single nod. "This is the first evidence that corroborates our theory."

"Now we go to Starfleet?" Chekov asked hopefully. Spock understood his concern; at this point the crew had committed no serious breach of regulations, if Command chose to accept their claim that the warp drive had malfunctioned. But once they ventured into Klingon space without Starfleet's sanction, they would become criminals.

This single piece of evidence proved only that the killers had returned to the vessel; it did nothing to clear the captain and Dr. McCoy.

"Now we expand our search to include uniforms," the Vulcan said.

Chekov's shoulders sagged slightly. *"All* uniforms?"

Spock simply looked at him.

"Aye, sir, *all* uniforms," Chekov replied, all hope gone from his tone. A daunting, time-consuming task, Spock knew, when time was the commodity they could most ill afford to waste, but the search had to be carried out. Chekov hesitated. "But, Mr. Spock, certainly by now the killers have cleaned them—"

"How, Commander? They could not use ship's laundry. They would have to input their personal code to do so, so the uniforms could be traced to them." In the event of undetected contamination on a planet surface or aboard ship, the affected individual would be notified and quarantined or, if necessary, treated. Inputting another's code, Spock knew, was impossible; to avoid errors, the computer was programmed to refuse a code that did not match a particular uniform. "I suggest you check laundry records first, especially those immediately after the assassination. Any unusual contaminants, such as Klingon blood, can still be found in the cleaning fluid. However, I do not expect you will find anything; the killers are well aware that they can avoid detection longer by simply hiding the uniforms aboard the ship."

"Yes, sir." Chekov sighed and moved wearily for the door.

"Mr. Chekov."

Chekov turned.

"The longer we take," Spock told him, "the greater danger in which we leave the captain and Dr. McCoy." Even if they failed to find the evidence Spock sought, he would go to his friends' aid, but to do so would be to risk even greater danger than Kirk and McCoy were in now. "If we attempt a rescue without clear proof of their innocence, all of Starfleet is bound by Interstellar Law to recapture them and extradite them to Klingon space.

"And the penalty in the Klingon Empire for prison escape is torture followed by execution." He did not mention the penalty that he and the crew would face for engineering the escape; the human's darkly determined expression indicated he was well aware of the consequences.

Chekov's tone was low, bitter. "In other words, if we bring them aboard the *Enterprise* and return to Federation space—"

"We would be attacked by Starfleet vessels," Spock finished. It seemed an insoluble dilemma; if Kirk and McCoy could not be cleared before the rescue attempt, then the *Enterprise* and her crew would have to fight their way out of Klingon space—and they would then be left with the option of fleeing to Romulan or Federation territory, where other attackers would await them. "They would be ordered to either capture or destroy this ship." The Vulcan paused. "And I for one do not intend to allow the *Enterprise* to be captured."

Chekov's gaze was grim but unflinching. "We will find the evidence, sir."

Spock nodded. Once Chekov had departed, the Vulcan released a silent sigh and wished he shared the human's certainty.

In a corridor on the level of the crew's quarters, Valeris stood before a light-plan of the *Enterprise* and checked off the locations that had been thoroughly searched: wardrobe, synthesizers, recycling area, sickbay, bridge, observation deck, Jeffries tubes, Engineering. . . . Few areas remained; it was simply a matter of time before more evidence was found.

As no one else was present, she allowed herself to lean against the console and close her eyes. Since the onset of the search, she had not rested; Spock had made it clear that time was of the essence. He had not even hinted that she should remain on duty until the search was over, but she knew her doing so would please him.

She had been without sleep fewer than forty-eight hours; a properly trained Vulcan was theoretically capable of eschewing rest for weeks. Valeris silently castigated herself for not having perfected that skill earlier, but there had been many other deficiencies in her training to remedy, and very little time.

She pressed a hand against her tired eyes. She did not believe that discovering the missing boots or uniforms would clear Captain Kirk and Dr. McCoy. Spock's efforts would prove futile, but Valeris did not feel it her place to tell him so.

A shouted exclamation at the corridor's far end, where others were conducting a search of crew quarters, caused her to open her eyes.

For dignity's sake, Valeris moved as quickly as possible without breaking into a dead run.

She stopped in front of the open cabin door in time to see a crewman remove a heavy boot from a locker and hold it aloft for all to see. As Valeris watched from the doorway, he pointed the toe of the boot ceilingward and pressed the sole against the side of the locker, then withdrew his hand.

The boot remained in place, defying gravity.

# Chapter Ten

SPOCK KNEW, even as he waited impassively beside Commanders Chekov and Uhura and Lieutenant Valeris inside Ensign Dax's quarters, that they had not come to the end of the search. It would have been foolhardy and illogical for the assassin to hide damning evidence against him in his own locker.

Ensign Dax was no doubt as blameless as Jim and McCoy. Yet Valeris seemed entirely unaware of the fact; her manner, when she notified Spock of the discovery, had been, and still was, faintly triumphant.

Perhaps she merely felt, as Spock did, that the discovery and resultant interrogation of Dax would lead them to further evidence. But the mystery of Gorkon's murder remained far from solved.

An ensign entered, one Spock knew instantly was incapable of having committed the crime. If the others noticed, they said nothing, but studied the suspect in silence. The Zeosian native's face reflected curiosity mixed with apprehension. He straightened and gazed anxiously at Spock, his commanding officer, with wide, innocent eyes.

"You are Technician Dax?" Spock asked.

The Zeosian nodded—from the shoulders, because his cervical spine was not designed for such movement. "Yes, sir." He glanced at the unreadable expressions of his superiors. "What's happened?"

"Perhaps you know the Russian epic of Cinderella," Chekov said coldly. "If the shoe fits, wear it."

Had Spock been entirely human, he would have been very hard pressed not to smile at that moment.

Dax frowned quizzically, then looked down at his own feet.

The others followed his gaze. Dax's feet, like those of all Zeosians, were large and webbed, quite incapable of fitting into the incriminating boots. Chekov emitted a barely audible groan.

Spock did not look at Valeris at that instant, but he suspected she was struggling to conceal her chagrin.

While the others fought to recover, Spock questioned Dax. "A pair of gravity boots was discovered in your locker. Do you have any idea how they arrived there?"

Dax's eyes widened. "No, sir. Were they the same gravity boots—"

"We shall know as soon as tests are performed,"

Spock replied. "If you obtain further information concerning the boots' appearance, please notify me at once. That is all. You may return to duty."

"Aye, sir. Thank you, sir." Blatantly relieved, Dax hurried out the door.

Spock turned to his fellow officers; Chekov's and Uhura's expressions were glum, Valeris's carefully impassive, but the sense of failure was palpable.

"There is still time," Spock told them. "Perhaps the boots will reveal some clue that will help us unravel the mystery. And soon we will find the uniforms." He turned toward Valeris. "Continue the search, Lieutenant."

"Aye, sir." As she headed for the corridor, Spock sensed that she as well as the others had given up hope for Kirk and McCoy.

As he was on the verge of doing . . .

Kirk stepped out of the hut into the unrelentingly bitter morning after a hellish night. He had been too cold, too painfully exhausted, to sleep much, and he had not been able to stop thinking about Carol and whether they would ever see each other alive again.

There had been time, too, to think about Martia's promise to help them to the surface. Kirk didn't trust her. She could very well be leading them both to their death, and yet, if he didn't take her up on her offer, he and Bones were doomed just as surely if they both remained inside the prisoners' compound.

And if they *did* make it to the surface in one

piece, what if Spock didn't make it in time? Or the *Enterprise* was destroyed en route by Klingons?

Jim flapped his arms against the cold and forced his thoughts onto the moment at hand. Beside him, Bones walked stiffly, dragging his leg irons with some difficulty. Jim glanced over at him. The doctor's face was almost entirely hidden by scraps of ragged fur, but what Jim could see of it looked haggard, pale; his blue eyes were deeply shadowed. The sight strengthened Jim's resolve to get out today. He quickened his pace.

"Hey, wait up," McCoy grumbled, hoarse from the cold. "Maybe you can run with these things on, but I can't."

Kirk strained to see over the heads of the other prisoners as they stood in several different queues. "C Lift." He gestured at the open wire cage, then lowered his voice so only the doctor could hear. "She said C Lift."

McCoy settled into line behind Jim and waited blearily as the aged lift door screeched open. Their group slowly pushed its way inside; the door clanged shut.

McCoy glanced around the caged lift—looking, Jim knew, for Martia, who was nowhere to be seen. Instead, the two humans were surrounded by brutes twice their size, one of which—a hideous seven-foot-tall simian with a shock of orange hair —appeared to be eyeing the pair with dangerous interest.

"I think we've been had," the doctor muttered

out of the side of his mouth. Jim agreed silently, expecting an attack at any second.

The gruesome creature leaned closer; Jim steeled himself for a fight . . . and started at the sound of Martia's voice.

"No, you haven't, Doctor."

Jim stared. The brute glanced furtively around them to be sure no one noticed, then said softly, in a voice that was unmistakably Martia's, "Get off at the first level and join the gang going into the mine." A whimsical expression crossed its simian features. "They don't take females."

Jim stood stunned into silence until the cage lurched to a stop; the metal doors squealed open. The creature inclined its head to indicate that he and McCoy should follow. Jim did so, tensing as the doctor grabbed his arm with a fur-wrapped hand.

"What kind of creature is this?" McCoy hissed, glancing with trepidation at the simian's huge back. "Last night you two were spooning—"

"Don't remind me," Jim snapped.

They shuffled behind the others into the dim mine; the cold increased to brutal intensity, seeming to emanate from frozen rock walls that glittered dully with embedded crystal. Jim waited, shivering, as he was issued a drill and a light helmet by one of the Klingon guards, who then shoved him toward the wall. Jim watched the miner next to him for a few seconds, then imitated him: drill the rock, pull the crystal free, set it on the flatbed shuttle. Nearby,

Martia—or the alien who claimed to be Martia—was already hard at work.

"I'll be," McCoy whispered at his elbow, gaping wide-eyed at the gleaming rock. "Do you have any idea what all this dilithium must be *worth?*"

The sudden proximity of a guard encouraged him to get busy.

The work was far less brutal than the cold, and it helped warm him. Jim burned his way into the rock with the drill, then tugged at the dilithium until it came free. The trick was to keep the jagged crystal from cutting his numbed hands by letting the drill remove most of the rock beforehand.

Beside him, McCoy cursed as he struggled to extract a crystal by hand. Jim reached out to help him and was promptly struck on the back by one of the guards. Jim swallowed his anger and turned back to his own work until the Klingon wandered away. Then he motioned for McCoy to use the drill.

The doctor nodded and this time managed to remove the crystal without difficulty. Jim continued drilling, one eye on the creature with Martia's voice. It didn't look like a setup, but at the moment the omnipresent guards made any attempt at escape impossible.

Out of the corner of his eye Jim saw the prisoner beside him slip a modest fortune in crystals under his coat.

In the next instant a blast of light left him phaser-blind; when his vision cleared, the prisoner was gone, and McCoy was staring at the empty space in mute horror.

With exaggerated deliberateness and one eye on the guards, the doctor set his crystal on the fast-growing pile in the flatbed shuttle.

Jim continued working grimly. Hours later the two of them were grimy and exhausted; despite the cold, Jim had managed to break a sweat. He had fallen into a meditative state brought on by repetitious action. His thoughts turned to the assassination. Had the torpedoes actually been fired from the *Enterprise?*

To think that they had was chilling; to think that they had not was even more so. Worst of all, no matter where the attack originated, there had to have been conspirators aboard *Enterprise.*

And there still were. The question was, did Spock know?

He started as his peripheral vision caught the simian motioning behind him. Kirk turned and saw that the guards sat eating lunch with their backs to the prisoners.

He glanced back at the creature—and his jaw dropped as the simian metamorphosed before his eyes into a young human girl. As he and McCoy watched, stunned, the girl stepped easily out of her leg irons and smiled at them.

"Follow me," she whispered.

Silently she set her drill down and walked into the depths of the mine. Kirk and McCoy glanced over their shoulders to make sure the guards weren't watching, then followed suit.

The slender girl crawled nimbly into a small hole in the frozen rock wall. Jim balked, unsure whether an adult, much less one wearing leg irons, could make it through.

The Martia-child motioned impatiently. Kirk cast a skeptical glance at McCoy, then got flat on his stomach and crawled in backwards. It was a claustrophobic fit, slow going with the chains. Kirk maneuvered himself end-first and pulled McCoy in after him.

The hole opened into a larger tunnel. Kirk got on his feet, panting as he struggled to keep up in the heavy leg irons, knowing that McCoy was having an even harder time.

He turned toward the girl again, only to find that she had changed back into the simian creature. The fact struck Jim as ominous; he would have felt far safer if she had remained the young girl or shifted back into Martia, though the huge creature was probably better able to withstand the surface cold.

And better able to win a hand-to-hand struggle against Jim and McCoy. . . .

In the distance, guards shouted.

The clanking of heavy metal grew louder as Kirk and McCoy increased their pace.

The tunnel opened at last onto a huge abandoned mine entrance abutting a high ice ledge. The creature scrambled down the ledge and jumped down onto a flat snowfield. Painfully, Kirk and Bones followed.

The killing cold on the surface stole Jim's breath; the air burned his face, eyes, lungs. He staggered to his feet, afraid to think how it affected McCoy, but the doctor had managed to keep up.

Jim kept moving: to stand still in the frigid air was to die. The Martia-creature led them across the snowy expanse to a broad frozen river. The alien stepped gingerly onto the thick ice, arms waving to keep its balance. Jim did the same, slipping on the slick surface, finally putting his hands against the ice and half crawling.

Beneath his feet the ice groaned and began to splinter under the weight of the leg chains.

Alarmed, Jim turned toward McCoy, ready to grab the doctor if the ice gave way.

McCoy's face had gone bloodless; he seemed to be scarcely moving. Jim reached out and pulled him along. They stumbled and slid over the ice, and at last made it across the river and up onto the high bank.

Jim dragged Bones the whole way, focusing on the doctor to keep himself going. Jim's hands and feet had gone numb; his face and ears ached fiercely from frostbite. If it got much worse . . .

At the top of the riverbank, the Martia-creature paused to stare at the horizon. Jim stopped gratefully, his limbs weighed down by an exhaustion more bitter than any he'd ever known. Yet he dared not rest too long, or it would be impossible for him to move farther.

Beside him, McCoy sighed and slipped his arm from Jim's grasp. "I can't . . ."

With numbed hands, Jim rubbed McCoy's arms and torso in an effort to keep the doctor's circulation going. At the same time he fought a sense of weary defeat. They would never make it. Bones was on the verge of collapse, and Jim wouldn't last much longer himself.

"We're at the edge of the shield," the Martia-creature announced triumphantly.

Jim followed her gaze. Beyond lay an endless ice desert, a sight that evoked both despair and hope.

If Spock could manage to find them in time . . . If they could only survive long enough on the surface . . .

Jim turned and glanced in the direction they had come.

He would not go back. Even if he had wanted to, he knew McCoy could never survive the return trip. At least there was a chance that he could survive on the surface until Spock arrived.

If Spock arrived . . .

"Come on." He gave McCoy a push. *"Keep moving!"*

They staggered on.

*Enterprise* hovered on the edge of Klingon space.

Having completed his evening meditation, Spock reclined on his berth. Now he gazed thoughtfully at the flickering votive candle as he awaited word from the bridge.

Once that word came, there would be little time to effect rescue; if the rumors Spock had heard were true, the climate on Rura Penthe's unshielded surface was lethally cold. Captain Kirk and Dr. McCoy would not survive exposure long—assuming they survived an escape attempt.

It was quite likely that they were already dead and that word from the bridge would never come. Spock had carefully considered the proper course of action in that instance; his responsibility lay in protecting the tenuous peace that currently existed between the Federation and the Klingon Empire.

In either event, the conspirators would do whatever was necessary to sabotage the peace conference. Chancellor Azetbur's life and the lives of all those attending the conference—including Spock's father, Sarek—were in grave danger. The fact that no attempt had yet been made on Azetbur's life suggested the conspiracy extended well beyond the Klingon Empire.

They had more pieces of the puzzle—the boots, the traces of Klingon blood on the transporter pad—but not enough to exonerate the captain. Disturbing, to think that some of the conspirators might still be here, aboard the *Enterprise.*

Were there those within Starfleet—indeed, aboard this vessel—who remained loyal to the Klingon warrior class?

Spock sighed soundlessly and relegated the subject to his subconscious. So far, conscious contemplation of the subject had yielded no further progress, and his life among humans had taught him the value of intuition and inspiration. From Jim Kirk he had learned the concept of trusting one's instincts. While instincts could never replace logical deduction, the two were most useful in balance.

J. M. Dillard

He regretted the fact that his life aboard *Enterprise* was about to end. It was time again to find his niche in the universe.

Many years before, when *Enterprise*'s first five-year mission ended, Spock had been afraid. He had despaired of finding a home as perfectly suited to his talents and unique background as the *Enterprise*. Now he looked forward to the chance to grow, to expand. He no longer feared the judgment of others: of his father, his family, other Vulcans. He was confident that he would find his own path once again.

Valeris reminded him very much of himself, of the young Spock—despairing at the reality of her emotions, struggling to master them. Spock found himself in the opposite situation now: he no longer feared his emotions, but valued them, desired to use them—in a controlled manner—to enhance his life.

He wished there were a means more effective than words through which to communicate this insight to Valeris. He would have liked to share more of his experience with her. He regretted that he now had to leave the *Enterprise* while she remained.

His gaze fell upon the Chagall and lingered there. He had taken to collecting human art because the contemplation of it instructed him in human symbols, human values. He allowed himself to become mindlessly absorbed by the picture, to appreciate its at once meaningful and meaningless beauty.

A strange conviction seized him—intuition, Jim

Kirk would have called it—that he knew the solution to the mystery, but was refusing to see the evidence that lay before his eyes.

The intercom whistled. Before Spock could sit up and touch the controls to respond, Uhura's excited voice filtered through on override.

"Mr. Spock, I've got them!"

On the bridge, Spock paused briefly to glance over Uhura's shoulder at the blinking display on her visual before heading to the science station to scan the indicated star system.

What he saw was most gratifying: although Rura Penthe was well within Klingon space, its distance was one the *Enterprise* could reach fairly swiftly. He straightened.

"They're outside the beaming shield. Mr. Scott, start your engines."

For the first time since Admiral Smillie's briefing, the engineer beamed. "Aye-aye, sir." He headed for the lift.

"Sir," Uhura said suddenly. Spock turned at the note of panic in her tone. "The universal translator—I was just programming it for Klingonese, but it's not responding. It's coming out all garbled."

Spock moved swiftly to the communications console and swiftly ran a diagnostics; both he and Uhura read the results and gave each other a knowing look.

Even if *Enterprise* ran cloaked into Klingon space, she still risked detection by specially equipped listening posts inside the Klingon border. And without the translator to aid them, the risk of attack escalated enormously.

The conspirators were at work again.

At the moment there was nothing to be done. Resolutely Spock returned to the command console. "Mr. Chekov, set a course for Rura Penthe."

At the helm Chekov swiveled to face the Vulcan. "Mr. Spock, Rura Penthe is deep within Klingon territory. If we're discovered—"

"Quite right, Mr. Chekov," Spock allowed smoothly before the helmsman could finish. "If, as I suspect, all of our computer data banks have been stripped of all information on the Klingon language, then we will have to rely on the archive library. What is now required is a feat of linguistic legerdemain—and a degree of intrepidity—before the captain and Dr. McCoy freeze to death."

Mortagh Outpost Three was understaffed, underfunded, decaying—in short, one of the least sought-after assignments in the Empire, which suited former gunner Kesla perfectly. His one taste of battle—years ago, in a pointless skirmish between his ship, *Beria,* and a Romulan vessel whose name he had never learned—had resulted in the death of his captain, most of his crewmates, and his closest friend. Kesla had escaped with severe injuries and a determination to leave the life of a warrior behind, Klingon honor be damned.

He knew his job was looked down upon by respectable Klingons; he knew that he fit the stereotype of the spineless, drunken, dozing outpost sentinel. He did not care. He welcomed the isolation and the lack of responsibility—in all his years at Mortagh, he had never heard so much as a rumor of a Federation ship attempting to steal across the border, though those who worked the outposts near the Romulan border told a far different story.

There the outposts were properly equipped with the latest detection devices. Mortagh Three creaked with age—a metaphor for the decaying Klingon government. Kesla and his peers were forced to perform their jobs with scanners that had been outdated a century ago, without proper visual displays for viewing passing ships. They were even without weapons; their only threat lay in informing the Empire of the offending vessel, then hoping the border patrol managed to destroy the right ship. Smugglers favored the route; the sentinels had long ago given up trying to stem the tide.

Kesla did not welcome the boredom, but there were ways of diluting it—for example, with the fiery Catullan liquor he'd consumed that evening. Access to black market wares was one of the occupational benefits of working the border. The Catullan liquor, qrokhang, had taken the edge off Kesla's restlessness, if not his boredom, and eased him into a pleasant numbness.

Now he sagged against his scanner console, skirting the edge of sleep, images from the long-ago battle clouding his euphoria.

The scanner beeped a warning.

Kesla straightened and tried to shake himself

awake. A feeble light on the aging screen blinked at him, indicating a cloaked vessel.

Klingon ships were forbidden by law to remain cloaked while passing the outpost. The smugglers were well aware of that fact and knew it was safer for an unregistered vessel to pass by openly—at least that way, the alarm wouldn't wake those working the outpost. They did not know that the halfhearted adjustments made to the ancient scanners to detect the more recent innovation worked only half the time.

Kesla frowned, displeased that his nap had been disturbed. This smuggler was apparently new to the business. He punched a toggle on his console.

"This is Sentinel Kesla of Mortagh Outpost Three. What ship is that? Identify yourselves."

A pause followed—one so long that the nearby operator, Genrah, yielded to curiosity and wandered over to listen next to Kesla. Kesla shifted to allow him room. Mortagh Three's unspoken rule insisted that the sentinels share any opportunities to alleviate boredom.

Both of them frowned at the console.

The reply came in a feminine voice laced with static. "We am thy freighter . . . *Ursva*, six weeks out of Kronos. Over."

Kesla shared a surprised look with Genrah. Female Klingon smugglers were rare indeed, but if this one was Klingon, Kesla was grandsire to an Earther.

"Whither are you bound?" Kesla asked gruffly,

responding in the odd archaic dialect the female had used. It was no small feat to keep the amusement from his voice. This smuggler was probably Rigellian or Catullan, in which case Kesla owed her a debt of gratitude. But if she knew so little of smugglers' protocol in the Klingon Empire, she would probably never reach her destination.

Genrah and Kesla waited, drowsy but mesmerized, through another delay.

"We is condemning food . . . things and . . . supplies to Rura Penthe. Over."

At this point, Kesla and Genrah both laughed aloud at the ridiculousness of the lie. The smuggler was so inept that Kesla pitied her. He waved at Genrah to let her pass. If she was hauling Catullan liquor, Kesla wished her good fortune in her task. She would need it.

To let her know he knew full well who she was and what she was doing, Kesla uttered a phrase which, in smugglers' code, wished her luck in avoiding border officials.

Uhura clutched the edges of her console and stared at the communications board. The last comment by the Klingon had left the crew entirely mystified, and if she failed to respond properly . . .

Nearby, Chekov and Spock glanced up from the antique paper dictionaries that littered the consoles. The past few minutes had been harrowing; had it not been for Spock's ability to rapidly scan the archaic alphabetized glossaries and to perfectly recall the few sentences in Klingon he had ever heard, *Enterprise* would probably have been nothing more than space flotsam by now.

But, according to Spock, the Klingon had just told her not to catch any bugs—then dissolved into raucous laughter.

Uhura glanced for guidance at the Vulcan, whose expression, though impassive, nonetheless conveyed his total bewilderment at the idiom.

The raucous laughter faded; Spock gave Uhura a nod.

She turned back to the board and did her best imitation of Klingon laughter; the effort made her throat sore.

The Klingon closed the channel. Uhura waited tensely for a few seconds until the realization settled in: the communication was over. They had, for reasons she could not fathom, been granted clearance.

She deflated against the board with a shaky sigh and only then realized she had been holding her breath.

Behind her, Spock said gently, "Was that so bad?"

She turned her head just enough to narrow her eyes at him.

McCoy watched Rura Penthe's setting suns throw warmthless coral light across the ice desert and knew that he was about to die. Impossibly, he dragged himself behind Jim and Martia across the ice; the act of movement provided a momentum that he found oddly difficult to overcome, even at the height of his weariness.

Frostbite had already claimed his feet, hands, ears, face. He did not care. He wanted only to stop moving, to surrender to the cold, to rest, even if it meant eternally. Spock and the others would feel bad, but at the moment, the doctor was too deeply tired to care.

But speaking seemed to require as much energy as motion—and so McCoy stumbled after the captain, until he could bear no more.

"Jim." He could manage no more than a whisper, and even that effort brought tears to his eyes. "Leave me. I'm . . . finished."

"No way," Jim said, trying to sound stubborn, but his voice was flat with exhaustion.

"Spock isn't coming. . . . This is insane, hoping he'll find us. I don't care anymore. Just let me die here."

"You see this?" Jim turned to display a red stain on the back of his ragged coat.

McCoy stared stupidly at it, his thoughts too slowed by the cold for him to make sense of what he saw.

"It's the viridium patch Spock slapped on my back right before we went aboard Gorkon's ship."

"That cunning little Vulcan," McCoy said faintly, too tired to smile, but not too tired to feel gratitude for Spock's quick thinking. An emergency supply of viridium patches was kept on the bridge for those occasions when haste prohibited stopping by sickbay for subcutaneous transponders. The patches were messier and less elegant—McCoy had always preferred the invisible transponders—but had far greater range.

"Once we're beyond the shield," Jim said, "they should be able to pick it up two sectors away."

"If they're even looking for us . . ."

Jim's tone hardened slightly. "Spock's looking for us."

In front of them, the apelike creature with Martia's voice interrupted, pointing to an icy ridge. "We're almost there. Once we're outside, we'll make camp."

The trickle of hope pushed McCoy past fatigue, past all pain.

By the time the three reached the ridge, dusk had given way to blackness littered with stars. The temperature dipped, but the doctor was heartened: using the viridium patch, Spock would be able to find them in time. The very real danger of freezing to death had receded, for the ridge sheltered them from the wind, and the creature—impossible to think of it as Martia—produced a flare from its coat and broke it in half. The flare blazed brightly for an instant, then formed a small fire.

McCoy ignored the prickles of pain as his numbed extremities began to warm. He huddled as close as possible to the flames without setting himself afire. Jim crouched beside him.

The creature sat nearby; shadows thrown by the flickering light made it look doubly ghoulish.

McCoy held his hands to the warmth; the sensation was pleasurable to the point of pain. He glanced at the creature. "Would you mind explaining that little trick you do?"

It shrugged. "I'm a chameloid. That's why we're such good smugglers."

Jim's tone was dulled by weariness. "I've heard of chameloids—shapeshifters. I thought you were mythical."

The creature graced him with a snaggle-toothed smile. "Give a girl a chance, Captain." As they watched, it began to metamorphose. McCoy stared, fascinated, as its features shifted, darkened, melted down into the smaller, finer ones of the beautiful Martia. "It takes a lot of effort."

"I don't wonder," McCoy replied. He hesitated. "Stop me if I'm wrong, but do we really have any way of knowing if this is the real you?"

She directed her now-enticing smile at Jim, who looked slightly sickened. "I thought I would assume a pleasing shape." Her tone became abruptly businesslike. "We're outside the shield. Now it's your turn, Kirk."

Jim smiled faintly. "If you say so." He rose slowly, stretched, then stepped forward and with a lightning-swift motion that startled McCoy, slugged the woman full force on the jaw. She fell back without a sound.

"Are you crazy?" McCoy jumped up and waved his arms in alarm, only peripherally aware of the agony caused by the expenditure of energy. Granted, he didn't *trust* her exactly, but she'd risked her life to get them this far. . . .

Martia gazed up at them with a wounded expression, a hand to her injured jaw. McCoy could see she was bleeding—green—from the mouth.

Jim's expression was pitiless as he looked down at her. "She didn't need our help getting anywhere. Where did she get these convenient clothes? And don't tell me that flare is standard prison issue."

McCoy had no answer. As Jim spoke, Martia began to metamorphose back into the brute. The blood trickling down her jaw changed from emerald to sapphire.

"It's to let them know where we are," Jim continued, stepping back in preparation for the fight. "Ask her what she's getting in return."

The brute rose to its full height. "A full pardon," it said, its tone as stone-hard as Jim's. "Which doesn't cover this. . . ."

McCoy made a small noise of despair and stepped back as Kirk and Martia began to circle each other. It was hardly a fair fight; the brute was two full heads taller and without the heavy leg chains that slowed Jim down.

"An accident wasn't good enough?" Jim said.

"Good enough for one," Martia replied in a silken voice incongruous with her true appearance. "Two would have looked suspicious. But 'killed while attempting escape'—now, *that's* convincing enough for both."

They lunged at each other. Kirk grabbed the brute and held on—and lost his grip as Martia's huge, shaggy form was transformed into little more than a pair of wide, sharp-fanged jaws.

The glistening, slavering jaws spat an obscene

viscous liquid at Jim before dragging him behind a snowbank. McCoy ran over to watch helplessly, then shrank back in disgust.

The creature had become a mass of slime-coated black tentacles that threatened to strangle the life out of Kirk. Somehow Jim struggled to his feet, only to be pulled back down.

By the time he rose again, the tentacled creature in his grasp had become a miniature female, who slipped easily from his hands and scrambled past McCoy. The doctor leapt with all his energy and managed to catch hold of a tiny ankle; even as he fell, rolling in the snow, he felt the ankle in his grip swell in size.

He looked up to see an exact replica of Jim Kirk.

"Surprise!" Martia-Kirk called, and struck McCoy full across the face. The doctor fell back in the snow and watched, dazed, as the real Jim faced his double.

"Your friends are late," Jim gasped.

"They'll be here," Martia replied.

They sprang at each other again. McCoy closed his eyes and fought dizziness. He could hear Jim speaking, faintly, as if calling out from a very great distance: "I can't believe I kissed you."

Even more faintly came Martia's voice, against an ever-growing buzzing in his ears: "Must have been your lifelong ambition . . ."

The buzzing increased to a painful level until McCoy slipped gratefully into darkness.

# Chapter Eleven

ALONE AND EXHAUSTED, Scott sat in the officers' mess and allowed himself a second cup of coffee. Like many of the others, he had volunteered for double duty until enough evidence had been found to satisfy Spock.

He glanced down at the *Enterprise* map on his datapad and blinked once, twice, to clear his blurred vision.

He was not so young as he had once been. None of them were. But if Spock expected the captain and Dr. McCoy to survive the horrors of Rura Penthe, then he, Scott, was more than happy to put up with losing a bit of sleep.

He drew a hand across his tired eyes and sighed. Of course, Spock was more like James Kirk than the Vulcan liked to admit—both stubborn, both refusing to give up hope even in the face of impossible odds. Scott glanced back at the map and this time was able to focus well enough to check off the areas of the ship that had been searched.

Few areas were left; the odds of finding the missing uniforms were getting worse by the second —almost as bad as the odds that *Enterprise* could safely make it into and out of Klingon space without a dent in her hull, or that the captain and the doctor could survive the freezing cold long enough to be rescued.

Scott ran a finger under his collar and realized that he was uncomfortably warm. Had he gotten so old that a wee bit of searching made him break a sweat? Instinctively he reached out toward the nearby air circulation vent to cool himself.

No air. The vent was blocked.

Scott frowned. This was a matter for maintenance, but the engineer in him asserted itself: it would take him longer to report it than to fix it himself. He quickly removed the cover and peered inside.

Something—wadded fabric—had been stuffed inside the vent, completely cutting off the airflow. Scott experienced wonderment for only a millisecond before he registered the colors: burgundy, mottled with violet—and a darker emotion set in.

He pulled the uniforms out and hurried to find Spock.

Out of the corner of his eye, Kirk saw McCoy weakly raise his head and shake it as he came to. Jim wanted to react, wanted to go to the doctor's aid, but at the moment he dared not look away from his foe for an instant. He and Martia-Kirk circled each other, arms locked in a restraining embrace.

"Isn't it about time you became something else?" Jim gasped. Martia's all-too-perfect performance as Kirk had disconcerted him only for a second; now he realized that it was to his advantage for Martia to retain this guise, especially if the guards arrived before the *Enterprise* did. . . . She seemed reluctant to change, as if the efforts of shifting so often had drained her.

The reverse psychology worked. "I like it here," Martia's voice said, though the lips that articulated the words were an exact replica of Jim's.

She pulled down with her entire weight, forcing Jim off his feet. They grappled, rolling through the snow. Against a dizzying spin of white, Jim saw his own face, contorted. . . .

The surprise sensation of moist heat on the back of his scalp made him turn his head—and stare, eyeball to eyeball, into the dripping jaws of a sharp-fanged Klingon mastiff.

He sprang to his feet immediately and faced the group of armed Klingon guards, led by the commandant, who stepped forward. The situation seemed utterly hopeless—unless Jim could react before Martia had a chance. "What took you so long?" he snapped.

He glanced over at her and was relieved to see that she had not yet changed from her Kirk disguise. Perhaps she really had exhausted her shapeshifting capacities. "Kill him! He's the one!"

Her voice—her *real* voice, Jim suspected—was harsher, more guttural, than Jim had ever heard it before. The guards hesitated, confused. The commandant raised his weapon and narrowed his eyes at them.

"Not me, idiot—*him!*" Jim shouted.

The commandant fired at the Martia-Kirk, who dissolved into oblivion before she could utter a sound. Jim did his best to separate himself from the horror he felt at the sight. Martia had meant to kill them both, but desperation had forced her to use anyone she could. He and Bones had simply been the most suitable victims.

He tensed, prepared to spring at the commandant and deflect the fire that would be intended next for McCoy, who had staggered forward to watch the drama. Jim stepped protectively in front of him.

The commandant turned to favor Kirk and McCoy with an ironic gap-toothed grin. "No witnesses . . ."

As Jim had suspected, the commandant had never meant to keep his bargain with Martia. He lifted his weapon and aimed it at Jim and Bones.

"Damned clever if you ask me," McCoy said conversationally, but Jim heard the utter weariness in his voice that said he'd had enough and didn't particularly care which way it ended now—as long as it ended swiftly.

Jim nodded, keeping his own tone casual. "Killed trying to escape—it's a classic."

"That's what he wanted," the Klingon agreed in a low growl; from his intonation, it was clear he wasn't speaking of Martia.

"Who?" Jim took a step closer, his eyes on the weapon in the commandant's hand. It was hopeless; even if he managed to wrest the phaser away, one of the dozen guards who surrounded him would shoot immediately—first him, then Bones.

But if, before he died, he could at least know who had arranged the assassination . . .

"Who wants us killed?" Jim insisted, watching the commandant intently.

The commandant's toothy grin became a sly half-moon smile. "I have heard you humans once had the custom of granting the condemned one wish before execution; we Klingons still have a similar custom. I will grant you this courtesy before death. Why not tell you? His name . . ."

The Klingon's words were drowned out by the growing hum of the transporter effect.

"Son of a bitch!" Kirk shouted, half in pure anger, half in surprise, as he felt the familiar brief spell of dizziness that accompanied dematerialization. The scene faded as the guards raised their weapons to fire . . .

. . . and became that of the *Enterprise* transporter room. Kirk shuddered at the ecstatic, overwhelming sensation of warmth, at the sight of his friends: Spock, Uhura, Chekov. Spock and Chekov stepped forward with heavy blankets. Jim accepted one gratefully, but yielded to the irrational surge of anger.

He had been one second away from learning the truth about Gorkon's assassination. No matter that he had been only two seconds away from death.

"Dammit! Dammit all to hell!" he snapped at Chekov and the Vulcan, both of whom seemed appalled by his and Bones's appearance. "If you had only waited two seconds . . ."

Spock seemed entirely unmoved by his captain's anger; if Jim hadn't known better, he would have thought the Vulcan seemed truly moved to see his friend again. Chekov fought a grin as he bent down to burn off Kirk's heavy leg irons with a laser tool.

"Captain . . . ?" Spock asked softly, as if he could not quite believe his friends stood before him.

Exasperated, Kirk said: "He was just about to explain the whole damn—"

"Who?" Uhura interrupted.

Chekov was smiling openly now. "You want to go back?"

"Absolutely not!" McCoy half shouted in the captain's ear. "What the hell's the matter with you, Jim? We were just rescued!"

Jim paused, forced himself to master the anger but not the intensity. He was grateful to Spock and the others for saving him, but the two lost seconds had cost them all.

Yet perhaps he had already discovered the thread

that would allow them to unravel the entire mystery. If they could only act in time . . .

He turned to Spock. "We have to find out where they're holding the peace conference. That will be the next target."

Spock nodded, serious. "Agreed. But how—"

"Come on," Jim urged, and headed for the bridge.

Chang sat in the command chair of the newest Klingon vessel in the fleet: the *Dakronh,* the only ship of her class, equipped with the latest in Klingon-Romulan technology as well as an innovative new device that enabled her to fire while cloaked. Chang was deeply proud of his new ship's capabilities; it had enabled him, after all, to successfully eliminate the Empire's two greatest enemies.

First, Gorkon, and now—James Kirk.

At the moment, however, Chang was experiencing something other than pride. He was staring at the cringing image of Rura Penthe's commandant on the main bridge viewscreen.

"Escaped?" Chang's pale brows rushed together in disbelief.

"They were beamed aboard a Federation starship!" the commandant cried desperately, no doubt aware of the effect his words would have on his—very short, Chang decided grimly—future. "I could trace—"

Chang struck a control with the outside of his

fist—he had the information he needed, and he had no desire to waste his time listening to the commandant plead for his life—and swiveled to face General Grokh.

"Escaped," he said flatly.

"It does not matter," Grokh reassured him. "Kirk cannot know the location. . . ."

Chang's good eye narrowed. "Are you sure?" he asked Grokh with deadly gentleness. "Are you willing to take that chance?"

He held Grokh's gaze for several seconds. Chang was very good at reading others' expressions, at gazing into their souls. He saw Grokh consider the possibilities, hesitate, waver, change his mind.

Chang smiled.

"Helmsman," Grokh called. "New course! Engage cloaking device."

*Dakronh* came around in a wide arc, then vanished into the void.

Kirk, Spock, and the others strode down the corridor toward the bridge turbolift. The warmth had revived Kirk's energy, as had the sense of urgency: something had to be done, and quickly, before more blood was shed. Azetbur's life and the lives of all of those attending the peace conference were in grave danger.

"The Klingons have a new weapon," Spock reported as he easily matched Jim's stride. "A Bird of Prey that can fire while cloaked. She torpedoed Gorkon's ship."

"So that's it," Kirk mused. The bridge visual had been tailored to make it seem that the torpedoes had been fired from *Enterprise*. . . .

"Not entirely," the Vulcan admitted. "I have reason to believe Gorkon's murderers are aboard this vessel."

Kirk nodded; he turned and searched Spock's expression carefully, but could find no sign that the Vulcan had come to the same conclusion as his captain concerning the guilty party. He looked away, wondering how to break the news. "They're the key to the whole conspiracy. Has the peace conference begun?"

"Who knows?" Chekov said behind them. "They're keeping the location secret."

Kirk sighed. "There's always something."

Scott ran toward them clutching a wadded uniform in his hands and kept pace alongside them.

"Captain!" he exclaimed, too agitated to smile in welcome. "Mr. Spock, I've found the missing uniforms with Klingon blood on them! They belong to—"

As they rounded the corner, Kirk came to an abrupt halt.

Before them, two crewmen lay sprawled on the floor.

McCoy knelt wearily and examined them; he glanced up at Kirk and shook his head.

Aghast, Scott stared down at them. "But—the uniforms . . ." He gestured helplessly with them. "They belong to these men! Burke and Samno!"

"Not anymore," McCoy said dully. "Phaser on

stun at close range, so it wouldn't set off any alarms. At the base of the skull, disrupting the nervous system and causing arrhythmia, and death."

"That would be the most efficient method," Spock agreed softly.

Kirk nodded. "First rule of assassination: always kill the assassins."

"Now we're back to square one." Scott's tone was resigned.

Kirk met Spock's gaze and held it, sure at last that the Vulcan did not know. "Can I talk to you?" He glanced meaningfully at the others. "In private?"

Spock tilted his head curiously, but he followed Kirk down the corridor and waited.

Reluctantly, gently, Jim drew a breath and explained who Burke and Samno's killer was.

Valeris had been on the last leg of the search and was very close to drowsing when the voice over the intercom made her jerk her head sharply.

"Attention: Court recorder to sickbay. Code Blue Urgent. Deposition required at once for Yeomen Burke and Samno. Court recorder to sickbay on the double."

Her pulse and breathing quickened; she applied herself immediately to eradicating such immediate emotional reactions and decided carefully what to do: she would abandon the search and go immediately to sickbay.

There was no other logical course of action.

\* \* \*

In sickbay Spock lay on the pallet surrounded by darkness and the soft sounds of breathing. He did not permit himself the luxury of thought. If he thought, he would not react quickly, and if he did not react quickly, he would die.

Besides, the captain's revelation had left him stunned, unwilling to indulge in thought.

The door to sickbay slid open. Spock remained motionless and listened to the muffled sounds of bootheels gently meeting the floor.

A silhouette traversed the darkness, approached the bed where Spock lay. He lay quietly, listening to the slow, measured footsteps until an overhead light flashed on, revealing killer and intended victim to each other. Spock blinked as his eyes adjusted to the light, then gazed without surprise into Valeris's face. He sat up.

He should have known; she had come to speak privately with him the first night out of spacedock.

*Sir, I speak to you as a kindred intellect. Do you not recognize that a turning point has been reached in the affairs of the Federation?*

*It is an old story, sir . . .*

Her dark eyes were wider than he had ever seen them. She started, gaped at him, then fought to regain her composure.

"You have to kill," Spock told her calmly. "If you are logical."

Internally he experienced a curiously sharp bitterness that verged on physical pain. He controlled it, but did not repress it. So this was betrayal.

"I don't want to," Valeris whispered.

244

"I believe you," Spock said. "But what you want is irrelevant. What you have chosen is at hand." He looked pointedly at the phaser.

She took aim. He could see that her hand trembled almost imperceptibly.

On the pallet nearby, the second body sat up. "I'd just as soon you didn't," Kirk said easily.

She recoiled, then started again as the doctor emerged, arms folded, from the shadows.

"The operation is over," McCoy said.

Spock struck out. The phaser arced into the air and clattered to the floor.

Valeris followed its trajectory with open surprise, then returned her gaze to Spock. He tensed; she might yet resist, might attempt escape—attempt to kill. He watched her keenly, saw the mercurial instant of hesitation on her face.

And then, slowly, she bowed her head, obscuring her features in shadow—yielding at last to logic? Spock wondered. Or emotion?


As the security escort led her to the bridge, Valeris experienced both a sense of failure and relief.

Failure because she had not accomplished her mission. She felt no shame for what she had done; she had arrived at her philosophy most logically. That her father had done the same had little influence on her, except that she had had access to his most private writings.

The universe tended toward consistency; that fact allowed the scientific prediction of patterns. It was logical to expect certain behavior of stars, planets, animals, and sentient beings, given certain parameters. One could reasonably expect a human to behave in a consistently emotional fashion, just as one might expect Klingons to behave in a consistently violent fashion.

She knew this with more than just intellect. She had lost her mother—and, to an extent, her father —to the Klingons; she had seen what they were capable of on Zorakis. Kudao and Themis were merely continuations of a pattern.

Given that, it was illogical to attempt to negotiate peace. The inherent warriorlike nature of the Klingon race made it possible to predict that, once the pacifist contingent fell from power, all treaties would be violated. Gorkon was dead; it seemed doubtful that Azetbur would survive much longer. And there were no apparent successors who embraced their peaceful philosophy. War with the Klingon Empire—now or a decade in the future— was inevitable.

Logic insisted that the Federation could best win such a war now, while the Klingons were most vulnerable.

She had wanted to discuss this with Spock. She wished sincerely to be Vulcan, logical—but she saw no logic in seeking peace when it meant death. She had been shamed by her father's descent into madness, by the family's censure. But the distance of time and her training on Vulcan had won her a measure of objectivity. She was no longer so concerned with family approval, and she had come to see that her father's philosophy, before illness claimed him, was far from mad.

She regretted having killed Burke and Samno, but logic again relieved her of any sense of having committed a crime. Three deaths, theirs and Gorkon's, scarcely outweighed the uncounted millions who had perished at Klingon hands since the Federation first encountered them.

Indeed, the loss of the entire *Enterprise* crew seemed an appropriate sacrifice.

She had failed in her mission, but in the midst of failure she had found relief. At last she was free to discuss this with Spock. When she had approached him, on her first night aboard *Enterprise,* she had not intended to reveal herself, merely to cautiously present, in the guise of devil's advocate, a different viewpoint concerning the Klingons.

She had hoped he would be proud that she had found her own path. Yet, when they arrived on the *Enterprise* bridge and Spock took his place beside his captain and Dr. McCoy, his demeanor was distant, far from proud. She imagined—surely it had not actually happened—that she saw a brief flicker of pain in his dark eyes.

The other crew members went to their stations: Uhura to Communications, Chekov to the helm, next to a vacant chair, Scott to Engineering. Valeris, flanked by guards, remained near the lift. Kirk approached and stopped an arm's length away.

"Anyone else aboard this ship?" His gaze was intense, unyielding, meant to indicate he would tolerate no refusal to answer.

Valeris hesitated. No harm could come from responding; aboard this vessel she was alone in her convictions. At the same time, what logic lay in cooperating?

She shifted, aware of Spock's eyes on her. Even now she wished to behave logically, unemotionally, so that she might not prove a disappointment to him.

The captain's expression hardened. "Let's not waste time, Lieutenant. Name your co-conspirators and give us the location of the peace conference. In exchange, I'll retain the murder charge and drop the rest of the specifications." He turned toward the communications officer. "Commander Uhura, make a record of everything said by the prisoner."

"Aye, sir." Uhura pressed a control on the console.

That he thought she would be concerned with such mercenary issues as her own well-being angered Valeris. She had committed extreme acts for the sake of logic, for her own beliefs, with no concern for personal consequences. Did Kirk think she would stoop to plea bargaining out of fear, because she had been discovered?

Killing had repulsed her, had been the most difficult act of her life. She was not like Burke and Samno. She did not kill out of hatred or desire for a thrill. She had taken no joy in it, had done it mercifully, swiftly, efficiently. And she had done it because she was convinced that the act was justified, necessary.

For Spock's sake she controlled her anger, but

her voice was cold as she spoke to Kirk. "You cannot prove anything."

He wheeled on her, showing the rage she could not. "Yes, I can. At my trial, my personal log was introduced as evidence against me."

She drew back, glanced quickly at Spock, and saw no reassurance there.

"How long did you stand outside my quarters before you coughed, Lieutenant?" Kirk asked.

She turned to Spock. "You knew?"

He did not answer.

"I tried to tell you the night *Enterprise* left spacedock," she said simply. "You would not listen."

He drew in a breath, and in that instant the pain of betrayal flickered in his eyes and was gone. "Neither of us was hearing very well that night, Lieutenant. There were things I tried to tell you . . . about faith."

So . . . he felt she had deceived him; the thought infuriated her. "You speak of logic—yet Surak would have the last of us bow before our killers before we take any action to protect ourselves. You contend you are Vulcan, that you seek peace at any cost—yet you serve in Starfleet, on a ship equipped with weapons capable of massive destruction. You and your crewmates have defended yourselves in the past, have destroyed other vessels and those aboard them. And now you would seek peace with the Klingons? Would trust them?"

Spock lowered his eyes and remained silent, unwilling or unable to reply.

Valeris turned toward the rest of the crew. "You have betrayed the Federation—all of you."

"What do you think *you've* been doing?" McCoy countered hotly.

"Saving Starfleet." She turned toward Kirk. "Can you honestly say that you disagree with me? Klingons cannot be trusted, sir. You said so yourself. They killed your son. They murdered countless settlers on Kudao in a pattern that has been repeated for centuries. You would make peace with them? Did you not wish Gorkon dead? 'Let them die,' you said. Did I misinterpret you?"

Kirk turned away, unable to meet her gaze. "I said that to Spock, after the briefing with Admiral Smillie. That room was supposed to be secure."

"You were right," Valeris continued. "They conspired with us to assassinate their own chancellor. How trustworthy can they be?"

He jerked his head around sharply to look at her. "Who is *us?*"

"Everyone who stands to lose from peace," Valeris said evenly. "The universe was a well-ordered place. We all knew our roles. Ours was to protect those within the Federation from the Klingon threat. Why change them?"

Kirk advanced threateningly. *"Names,* Lieutenant."

Uhura swiveled quickly from her board to face them. "We can send a message to Starfleet Command—"

"Unlikely," Valeris said. *"Enterprise* has disobeyed orders and harbors two escaped convicts. All your ship-to-shore transmissions will be jammed."

"Spock." His expression a mixture of sympathy and reluctance, Kirk faced his first officer.

Spock nodded, understanding without the need for words, but hesitated, his gaze seemingly fixed on a far-distant, painful scene.

His eyes focused suddenly. He stepped toward Valeris, hand extended to touch her face.

She drew her head away from him, resisting. His Vulcan training was superior; there was no question that he could extract whatever information he desired from her thoughts. But to force himself on her consciousness was the mental equivalent of rape—immoral by any standards, considered by the Vulcans to be as heinous a crime as murder.

His cool fingers brushed her cheek, her forehead, settled against her temples. She tensed, anticipating the agony of mental intrusion that would follow.

It did not. The mind-touch, gentle as a caress, merely asked permission, then lingered.

She closed her eyes, stunned almost to tears by this unexpected courtesy. For a long moment she wavered. Illogical, for Spock to grant her this dignity, to allow lives and the course of history to hinge upon a single act of kindness.

Rather than tear the information from her, he opened himself. She saw, through the mosaic of his memory, how he had once sacrificed himself for the *Enterprise*, believing the Vulcan maxim that the good of the many outweighed the good of the one or the few; how his friends had banded together and risked their lives to save him; how Jim Kirk had told him that in this instance the good of the one outweighed the good of the many.

Spock had learned that a single life was beyond value, beyond logic. To kill in the hope of saving future lives was unforgivable; mathematics did not apply.

He shared with her, then waited.

Hardest of all to bear was the realization that, on the very deepest level, he still trusted her to make the correct decision.

And she still wished to please him. Hesitantly she opened her mind to him. The effect was quite painless, and actually rather pleasurable. She felt herself drift, as if in a waking dream.

"Admiral Cartwright," Spock said softly, both aloud and in Valeris's mind.

She heard Chekov's voice, muted, as if in a dream: "From Starfleet?"

"Who else?" Kirk, far away but insistent.

Spock again, his voice low, hypnotic, as Valeris felt the name slip easily from her memory: "General Chang."

"Who else?"

"The Romulan ambassador, Nanclus."

Scott interrupted. "This is incredible!"

The doctor's voice now, angry: "Is she telling us Klingons and Federation members are conspiring *together?*"

"Where is the conference?" Kirk asked.

Spock searched, but there was nothing left for her to give him. He withdrew his hand slowly, gently; Valeris opened her eyes and stared into his.

Spock shook his head, still holding Valeris's gaze as he answered his captain: "She does not know."

"Then we're dead," Scott said.

"I have been dead before," Spock told Valeris knowingly, referring to the knowledge he had just shared with her. He forced his attention back to his crewmates. "Commander Uhura, raise the *Excelsior*. She ought to have the coordinates of the conference location."

The captain frowned. "Why would they give them to us?"

It seemed to Valeris that Spock smiled without smiling. "The commander *is* an old friend of yours."

"What was it like," McCoy asked softly, "being dead?"

Lost in thought, Spock faced the screen and did not answer.


"This is Captain Hikaru Sulu, USS *Excelsior*," Sulu said smoothly, ignoring the aghast expressions on the faces of his bridge crew as they gaped at Jim Kirk's grizzled visage on the main viewer. All except Rand, of course, who had probably guessed this was coming. She half swiveled from Communications to stare somberly at Kirk.

"Sulu!" Kirk, a frightening sight in filthy, ragged

furs and the untrimmed beginnings of a salt-and-pepper beard, broke into a grin as he recognized his former helmsman.

Despite the seriousness of the situation, Sulu could not resist returning the smile. More than three years had passed since he had last seen Kirk; except for the silver in his hair and the grime left by Rura Penthe, the captain had changed little. "Standing by, Captain Kirk."

Kirk's grin faded. "You understand that by even talking to us, you're violating regulations, Captain."

Not a single member of the *Excelsior* bridge crew stirred or glanced questioningly at their captain. Sulu felt a surge of pride. He leaned forward, squinted at the screen, shook his head. "I'm sorry, Captain. . . . Your message is breaking up."

"Bless you, Sulu," Kirk whispered. Then, louder: "Where's the peace conference? They're going to attempt another assassination."

Sulu did not hesitate for an instant, though his heart began to beat faster. He had made his decision some time ago. In the periphery of his vision, he saw his first officer, Valtane, stiffen. "The conference is at Khitomer, in Klingon space near the Romulan border. I'm sending the exact coordinates on a coded frequency."

"I'm afraid we may need more than that. There's a Bird of Prey on the lookout for us. And she can fire while cloaked."

Sulu did a double take. "Surely not."

"I'm telling you," Kirk insisted. "Hang on." He

turned to speak to a striking young Vulcan woman flanked by security guards. "How many of those things are there? Come on, Lieutenant. . . . You want any more of your brain drained?"

"Just the prototype," the Vulcan answered stonily.

Kirk turned back to the screen. "You hear that?"

"I'm getting under way now," Sulu promised. "But I'm now in Alpha quadrant. The chances of my reaching the conference in time are slim."

"When does this conference start?"

"According to my information, today."

"Thank you," Kirk said, but his gaze conveyed all the thanks Sulu needed. He smiled faintly.

"Don't mention it, Captain Kirk." Sulu closed the channel and swiveled to find Valtane at his elbow.

"Sir!" Valtane tried to keep his voice low, but he could not contain his agitation. "You realize you've just committed treason."

Slowly, serenely, Sulu stretched out his legs and rested his bootheels on the conn railing, and gazed up at his first officer. The years he had waited patiently for command of *Excelsior* faded in importance, as did the likelihood of having that command taken from him. More than that: by coming to Kirk's aid, he risked his own life and the lives of those aboard his ship. Whoever had arranged Gorkon's assassination would stop at nothing to disrupt the peace conference at Khitomer. "To be candid, I always hoped that if the choice ever came down to betraying my country or betraying my friend, I'd have the guts to betray my country."

He paused and studied his crew. "I realize I can't ask any of you to follow my orders. If you do so, you may face charges along with me. Those who wish may retire to their quarters."

Valtane touched his mustache once, nervously, then crossed back to his station; the helmsman, Lojur, fixed his captain with an expectant gaze. Rand nodded mutely, her eyes shining.

No one left the bridge.

Sulu found he could not smile. In a low voice he said to Lojur: "Warp nine, mister."

*Excelsior* hurtled toward Khitomer, and confrontation.

# Chapter Twelve

As ENTERPRISE SPED THROUGH Klingon space, Kirk sounded the chime at Spock's cabin door.

After the luxury of a shower, shave, fresh uniform, and a stop by sickbay, Kirk had yearned for sleep. There was still time for a brief rest before they arrived at Khitomer; there would be no time after. Even now it took conscious effort not to tremble with exhaustion.

But the look in Spock's eyes when he had learned of his protégée's treachery haunted Kirk.

The door opened onto darkness; Kirk expected to hear the Vulcan's voice bidding him enter, but he met only silence. He stepped hesitantly into the doorway. "Spock?"

No answer. Jim reached for the light panel.

"I prefer it dark." Spock's voice emanated from the shadows. Jim squinted in the dimness and saw the silhouette of Spock's form on the bunk. He lowered his hand and entered quietly, glad he had come. The door slid shut behind him.

"Are you dining on ashes?" Jim asked softly, his tone faintly tinged with disbelief. He had known Spock for decades now; he had never thought to see him depressed.

The Vulcan's eyes, narrowed thoughtfully, were focused on the ceiling; he did not rise, did not look at Jim. For a time he did not speak.

"You were correct," Spock said at last, his tone one of hard-won detachment. "It was my arrogant presumption that put us in this situation. I had no right to volunteer you for the mission."

"You did what you thought best," Jim soothed.

Spock shook his head. "Arrogance. I believed that allowing you to meet Gorkon would help alleviate some of your anger and pain over your son's death."

"It worked," Jim said.

"I should have anticipated intrigue. You might have died."

Jim shrugged. "The night is young. Anyway, you said it yourself: it was logical. Peace is worth a few personal risks. How could we have prevented what happened?"

He paused, waiting for a response; none came. He tried again, feeling his way, trying to think of words that would comfort as he paced slowly through the Vulcan's quarters. "You know, you're a great one for logic. I'm a great one for . . . rushing in where angels fear to tread. We're both extremists. Reality is probably somewhere in between us." He stopped to admire a Romulan sculpture, ran a finger over dust.

Spock did not answer.

"I couldn't see past the death of my son," Jim said. "I couldn't see beyond the past, beyond what the Klingons had done. In a way, it was frightening to actually believe that their policies might change, that they might stop waging war. Too frightening to trust them. Who will I be if I have no enemy?" He shrugged. "I couldn't trust."

"I trusted too much," Spock said finally. "I was prejudiced by her achievements as a Vulcan. I wished her to be my successor. I took great pride in her." His voice lowered abruptly. "I trusted her simply because she is a full Vulcan, though she received Vulcan training only recently and her mastery of the disciplines is far from complete. Yet I was so certain of her loyalties that I put her in charge of the search.

"Perhaps you are right that the answer lies somewhere in between logic and emotion. I am frightened to discover that logic, untempered by compassion, can be used so cold-bloodedly to justify war." He hesitated. "I had never experienced betrayal. Certainly I never expected to experience it at the hands of a Vulcan. I had been disturbed to see what I deemed prejudice among the crew. Now I see my own prejudice as well."

Kirk nodded as he moved closer. "Gorkon had to

die before I understood how prejudiced I was. I didn't really believe the Klingons could change."

For the first time Spock met his gaze. "Can we two have grown so old and inflexible that we have outlived our usefulness?" He paused, and for the first time, Jim saw a trace of warmth come into his eyes. "Would that constitute a joke?"

Jim smiled faintly. "Someone said the difference between 'comic' and 'cosmic' is the letter *s*. Spock, don't crucify yourself. It wasn't your fault. If I'd refused the assignment, the assassination would still have happened; someone else would have taken the blame."

Spock looked away. "I *was* responsible."

"Not for any actions but your own."

Spock turned his head and arched a skeptical brow. "That is not what you said at your trial. As I recall, you took responsibility for the actions of your entire crew."

Jim sighed. "As captain. That's different. Human beings—"

"But I am not human. I am only—"

"Spock," Jim interrupted impatiently, "you want to know something?"

Spock watched as Jim knelt beside him.

"Everyone's human," Jim said.

"You insult me." Spock turned away.

"Only human," Jim insisted gently.

"Racist," Spock murmured, his gaze fixed on the ceiling, but Jim saw the glimmer in his eye.

"Vulcan," Jim countered. He held out his hand. "Come on. I need you."

Spock hesitated, then, very deliberately, took Jim's hand.

Waiting with the Vulcan delegation outside the huge elaborate dome that housed the council chamber, Sarek stared up into Khitomer's sky and felt the wind ruffle his hair. It was agreeably warm on this sparsely populated agricultural world, though not as warm as Vulcan, and the lush green foliage reminded him more of Earth. He had often heard it said that many of the Klingon worlds were very beautiful, but he had never expected to have an opportunity to test the statement with his own eyes.

Once security was in place, the Vulcans would be ushered into the chamber, along with the Earth, Klingon, and Romulan delegations. Elaborate precautions were now necessary—according to the Romulans and Klingons, at least—to protect them all from the escaped prisoner Kirk.

Sarek believed increased caution was necessary, though for quite different reasons; Kirk had been as much a victim of intrigue as Gorkon. Because of the escape and the opportunity presented by the conference, the assassins were now forced to take action.

Sarek feared not for his own life but for that of the Klingon chancellor, Azetbur, and for the peace process itself. He doubted the conspirators had much to gain from murdering Vulcans.

Unless, of course, they had political use for another massacre like Kudao.

He did, however, feel an entirely logical concern

for Spock's sake. He knew that *Enterprise* had not yet obeyed the order to return home. Knowing Spock and Spock's friends, he surmised that *Enterprise* was probably en route to Khitomer now, but for reasons far different from those the Klingons suggested. Sarek suspected that "increased security" was merely a euphemism Ambassador Kamarag had invented for revenge on Kirk.

Of course, *Enterprise* had to negotiate its way safely through Klingon space first.

In recent years, Sarek thought he had come to understand his son quite well. Their past disagreement over Spock's choice of career had long ago been resolved—although Sarek still did not quite approve of Starfleet. At any rate, Spock's stubbornness—a legacy from his mother, Sarek knew, despite her claims to the contrary— precluded that option. Even as an infant, Spock could never be forced to do anything, only reasoned with.

Now Spock was preparing to retire from Starfleet. Sarek did not know if his son had made a firm decision as to an alternative career. But, much to his surprise, Spock had indicated an interest in pursuing diplomacy. Certainly Spock's achievements with Gorkon and the High Council had been most impressive. Perhaps he might even return home to Vulcan. That would please his mother, Amanda, greatly.

If he survived.

Sarek sighed inaudibly as he studied the pale,

cloud-studded sky and wondered whether *Enterprise* lay beyond.

On the *Enterprise* bridge, all members of the crew had assumed their stations—all, Pavel Chekov noted, except one. The chair beside him at the helm remained noticeably empty. Security had removed Valeris to the brig.

Chekov simply could not understand it. He had known Spock for more than two decades, and he could not imagine anyone more loyal—or more capable of inspiring loyalty. And now, for Spock's protégée to be a traitor . . .

He sighed and looked away from the vacant chair, feeling a surge of nostalgia as he remembered Sulu. Change was an inescapable law of the universe. Now that the senior *Enterprise* crew was retiring, Chekov faced one of the most difficult decisions of his life, assuming he survived this mission. He had no desire to serve aboard *Enterprise* without his friends; he had intended to retire early from Starfleet and return to Earth—and Irina Galliulin. Since their encounter aboard *Enterprise* some thirty years before, they had rekindled their romance; Chekov had spent every available moment of leave with her. He had thought Irina understood that when his last tour of duty aboard the *Enterprise* ended, he would return to her.

She had not understood. She had sent him a subspace message recently to let him know that she was currently involved in a serious relationship and was relocating to Rigel. She hoped they could remain friends.

Chekov struggled not to react with bitterness, but at the moment he found himself split into two halves, one of which did not give a damn whether he returned from Khitomer alive. After all, what was he surviving *for?*

He stared into the main viewer, into the star-strewn blackness of Klingon space, where unseen dangers lurked.

The part of him that still wanted to live broke the tense silence on the bridge. "Captain . . ." He glanced over his shoulder.

Gripping the arms of the conn chair, Kirk stared intently at the viewscreen, as if by looking hard enough he could see the invisible foe that awaited them. He remained perfectly motionless, but his gaze refocused on the helm.

"When we get to Khitomer, how will we defend ourselves?" Chekov asked. "If this new Bird of Prey can fire while she is invisible . . . ?"

"Now, there's a poser," McCoy said lightly, from his usual place at the captain's elbow, but his expression remained grim.

The captain and Mr. Spock exchanged hesitant glances. Chekov shifted nervously in his seat. If the captain was worried, then the situation was hope-less indeed. . . .

But the Vulcan said, "I do not believe anxiety is called for." He paused as the others reacted with hope. "According to my calculations, we have another five minutes and twenty-two seconds to resolve this dilemma."

"Hell of a time to develop a sense of humor," McCoy muttered under his breath, though Chekov seriously doubted that Spock had intended to be funny.

The captain reacted stoically, but uncertainty flickered in his eyes.

Wincing, Chekov turned back to the helm and decided that he really *did* want to live, after all.

Azetbur sat in the place of honor beside UFP President Ra-ghoratrei and watched the procession of red-sashed Klingon delegates, led by Ambassador Kamarag, file into the council chamber. Azetbur personally disliked Kamarag; he was little more than an actor, presenting the opinions of the High Council with dramatic flair, possessing none of his own. Yet he performed his job adequately, and his willingness to argue the case for peace as ably as that for war made him useful.

The Klingons took their places, followed closely by the Earth delegation. The profusion of banners and bright sashes, chosen by mutual agreement among the participants—yellow for the Vulcans, red for Klingons, blue for Romulans, green for Earth humans—reminded Azetbur more of a sporting event than a diplomatic conference. Perhaps the comparison was apt; she did not doubt there were those here in the crowd who had come to engage in the bloodiest of sports.

She shifted beside Ra-ghoratrei. She had heard of the legendary effect Deltan pheromones had on humans and other aliens, and was glad that Klingons were somewhat immune to their charms. She did not need such distraction now; she wished to remain alert in the event of an assassination attempt, and her mind was already dulled from two nights without sleep. She had spent the time preparing for the conference and contemplating her own mortality. After learning of Kirk's escape and the *Enterprise*'s disappearance, Kerla had surreptitiously arranged additional security. If he proved as untrustworthy as Chang contended, she had no hope of surviving.

The previous evening she had cautioned Ra-ghoratrei. The Deltan seemed aware that he might also be a target, but feigned confidence. The security was adequate, he insisted. If the chancellor was concerned, perhaps she should make private arrangements. . . .

Azetbur did not fear death. But she feared deeply what would happen to her people should she be killed and the peace conference fail. The knowledge that she might die at any moment induced an acute hypersensitivity of sight, hearing, touch. The music accompanying the parade of delegates seemed agonizingly loud, the yellow of the Vulcans' sashes painfully bright. The large metal circlet her father had worn hung so heavy against her neck that Azetbur struggled to hold herself upright beneath its weight.

The Romulan delegation entered, led by Ambassador Nanclus and his aide, Pardek. Azetbur let her gaze travel over the crowd: here was Sarek, father of Spock, whom she had trusted; here, Ambassador Kamarag; here, Colonel Worf, who had performed a distasteful task honorably; beside them, Kerla, whom she loved but did not trust.

She did not believe that Spock was capable of betraying her father. In her darkest moments, as she had sought sleep and failed to find it, the thought had come: What if Kirk was not guilty? What if the assassination was the result of a conspiracy rather than an act of personal revenge by a grief-stricken father?

If such was true, then Azetbur had more to fear than she had thought.

President Ra-ghoratrei had politely scoffed at the notion that James Kirk's escape presented any danger. He seemed to believe it, but if so, why did Azetbur now see a glimmer of fear in his eye?

The music swelled to a close. Ra-ghoratrei rose and took the lectern.

"Madam Chancellor, members of the diplomatic corps, honored guests: the United Federation of Planets welcomes you to Camp Khitomer. Now that we are assembled, I move we conclude these ceremonies and get down to business. Madam Chancellor?" He turned to her, smiling.

Azetbur rose with grace and a curious sense of finality. Human myths likened fate to a wheel; she imagined that she heard a faint groan as it turned.

"Agreed," she said, but she did not smile as the assembly applauded.

*Let it begin. . . .*

Admiral Cartwright took his seat along with the other Federation dignitaries and feigned an expression of polite interest as he peered out at the crowd.

Ra-ghoratrei began his speech. "We are gathered here today in high hopes, believing that differing civilizations of goodwill can work together to overcome intolerance. . . ."

Normally Cartwright would not have had the patience to listen to long-winded diplomatic patter, but today he was grateful for it; he had not yet seen the face he sought.

Concealing his agitation was not altogether easy. They had been dealt a blow when they learned of Kirk's escape and of *Enterprise*'s part in his rescue. The worst of it had come when they lost contact with Lieutenant Valeris aboard *Enterprise;* now Cartwright could only anticipate the worst—that Kirk and company had somehow managed to piece the puzzle together and were on their way.

He tried to convince himself that there was little reason for concern; Kirk and the *Enterprise* crew would be stopped before they ever made it to Khitomer—like those aboard *Kronos*, without knowing what had hit them.

"We believe that, with understanding and patience," Ra-ghoratrei continued, "it will be possible to resolve what separates us. Let us redefine progress to mean that just because we *can* do a thing, it does not necessarily follow that we *must* do that thing."

Admiral Cartwright joined in the applause, though he could not have disagreed more with the Federation president. He had been a starship captain once, long ago, before the time of the Organian Treaty. He had lost crew to the Klingons; he knew what they were capable of, then and now.

Gorkon had been a fool to think his people could change. He had only to look as far as his own chief of staff.

Ra-ghoratrei paused and stared meaningfully into the crowd. "We believe that the responsibility for destiny rests squarely on our own shoulders. . . ."

Cartwright started slightly as he glimpsed the face he sought: dark-skinned, heavy-browed, Klingon. He craned his neck and tried to establish eye contact, noting with relief that the Klingon had managed to get a small, unobtrusive valise past security.

The room thundered with applause once more as the president finished his speech. Chancellor Azetbur rose and approached the lectern; Cartwright did his best to repress a smile. The timing could not have been better.

The Klingon surreptitiously scanned the crowd; at last he stared in the admiral's direction.

Their gazes locked. Cartwright gave a slow, discreet nod and felt his pulse quicken as the Klingon, valise in hand, inched toward the lectern.

\* \* \*

*Enterprise* slowed to impulse as she neared Khitomer.

For Jim Kirk, time slowed as the tension, and the silence, on the bridge escalated to near-unendurable levels. On the main visual, the empty starfield revealed nothing of the danger awaiting them.

He rose and paced over to the science station, where Spock was bent over his scanners, his solemn features illuminated by reflected blue light.

Kirk peered over the Vulcan's shoulder and spoke, his voice hushed. "Are we close enough yet to beam down?"

The Vulcan shook his head. "Not yet. Scanning section four-two-three-six . . . section four-two-three-seven . . ."

"She's here . . . somewhere," Kirk said, impatient, glancing back at the screen as Khitomer came into view. Too bad the solution wasn't as easy as it had been before the Romulans improved the design of the cloaking device by eradicating the minute spatial displacement that had once marked the unseen vessel's location—and had led to the loss of more than one warbird.

Chekov turned from the helm, his movements taut with anticipation. "But if she's cloaked—"

"Then all we've got is a neutron radiation surge," Kirk finished. "And by the time we're close enough to record it, we're ashes." He looked back at his science officer, hoping impossibly for a solution.

Spock straightened, his expression thoughtful.

"Captain, perhaps we're going about this the wrong way. Our job is to get to the conference. Her job will be to stop us."

Kirk hesitated. "You mean . . . *make* ourselves a target?"

The Vulcan did not answer, merely gazed steadily at his captain.

Jim drew in a breath. Spock was right, as always: there was nothing else they *could* do, except hope for Sulu, and *Excelsior*'s hypersensitive scanners, to arrive in time.

In the meantime *Enterprise*'s chances of surviving an attack by the cloaked Bird of Prey were absurdly small; Jim knew Spock had done them all a favor by not stating the odds. In one sense, he felt a curious lightness, a relief: he had always feared he would die alone. The thought of dying here, on the *Enterprise* bridge, among his friends, held no terror for him. In fact, it was more appealing than the thought of retiring and going his separate way.

But the death of his friends was another matter. Jim could not make that decision for them.

The calm steadiness in Spock's eyes made it clear the Vulcan harbored no regrets. Jim turned and met Uhura's gaze, then Chekov's, and last of all McCoy's . . . and found loyalty and willingness there.

Jim looked away, moved, and hesitated only for a split second before finding his voice.

"Shields," he said firmly. "Battle stations." He touched a control on the conn arm.

"Shields up," Chekov replied. The Klaxon sounded an automatic red alert; the crew was bathed in pulsing bloodied light. "Battle stations."

"Mr. Chekov, take us forward. Thrusters only. One-half impulse power."

Chekov's fingers played the board with practiced ease; his eyes remained focused, as did those of the others, on the unrevealing visual. "Aye, sir. Thrusters . . ."

*Like walking on eggs,* Jim thought. Watching the board, he called softly: "Uhura?"

"Nothing, Captain," she answered quietly behind him. "If they're here, they're rigged for silent running and have engaged the cloaking device."

"If she fires," Spock stated, "she has a perfectly valid excuse. We are a renegade vessel coming dangerously close to two heads of state during a vital interstellar conference."

At Jim's elbow, McCoy grimaced. "Thanks for sharing that, Spock—"

He pitched forward as the ship heaved. The viewscreen flashed with blinding light from the explosion.

Jim clutched the arms of his chair and held on until, slowly, *Enterprise* righted herself.

McCoy pulled himself to his feet and said bitterly, "This is fun . . ."

"Captain." Chekov was back at his station. "Shall we attempt to return fire?"

"At what, Mr. Chekov?" Tracing the torpedo back to its launch site would require time. By then the Bird of Prey would have changed position, especially if her commander was as shrewd as Kirk suspected.

The force of the next hit threw him from his conn, against McCoy; he reached out blindly in an effort to catch hold of something, and stopped when he struck the back of Chekov's chair with his forehead.

He untangled himself from the doctor and, ignoring the bruise forming on his temple, scrambled back to the conn. He could do nothing, but he had to find a way to buy some time, to give *Excelsior* a chance to show.

Instinctively Kirk glanced at the main viewscreen: nothing. He struck the intercom control with the outside of his fist, unsure what he was going to say until he said it. "Scotty, reverse engines! All astern one-half impulse power. Back off. Back off!"

Bathed in the dim green light of *Dakronh*'s cramped bridge, Chang stood silently beside his gunner and watched the battered *Enterprise* retreat.

Earlier he had despised James Kirk because he believed the captain had surrendered to cowardice. He had heard many stories about Kirk; all of them had spoken of his courage. But the human Chang had met was no warrior; that Kirk had tried to swallow his hatred, had never even tried to seek revenge for his son's death.

A Klingon would have avenged a kinsman's death at any price. Failure to do so was the mark of a coward. Chang had hated Kirk for that failure—

and for his dishonesty during the dinner aboard *Enterprise*. Better for Kirk to state his hatred openly than hide behind false diplomacy.

Now Chang felt a grudging admiration. *Enterprise* could have lingered, cloaked and cowardly, but she arrived facing death openly, as a true warrior would.

And then this strange tactic.

Chang frowned and said, very softly, to his helmsman: "What's she doing?"

The helmsman shrugged. With a nudge and a gesture, Chang instructed him to follow.

And then smiled suddenly, understanding. *Enterprise* had reversed, drawn back, as if she had detected her enemy. Kirk was simply trying to befuddle him, to gain time.

But why? From whom did he await help? The crew of *Dakronh* had no need to fear anyone. . . .

Chang's smile widened. Let Kirk play his games, bid for time. Chang was in no hurry to destroy him; in fact, he regretted that they were not evenly matched. Destroying a helpless foe seemed somehow dishonorable. At the very least he felt he should allow Kirk the privilege of knowing his killer.

He signaled his helmsman as *Dakronh* closed in.

# Chapter Thirteen

"WHAT'S SHE WAITING FOR?" Kirk murmured, narrowing his eyes at the main visual, at what appeared to be empty space, straining with fading hope to see the sleek, familiar outline of *Excelsior*. The silence was more nerve-racking than the attack.

"No doubt attempting to ascertain why we have reversed course, wondering if we have detected her," Spock answered softly.

Kirk started as Chang's harsh voice reverberated over the intercom. "I see you, Kirk."

The captain glanced swiftly up at the useless visual. "Chang . . ."

The Klingon's tone grew mocking, ironic. "Be honest, Captain. Warrior to warrior: Don't you prefer it this way? As it was *meant* to be? No peace in *our* time. 'Once more unto the breach, dear friends. . . .'"

*Before Gorkon's death,* Jim thought, ashamed, *I might actually have agreed with you.* He glanced at Uhura, but she shook her head: no chance of a trace.

Kirk hit the intercom control. "Our time is over, Chang. History won't stand still for the likes of either of us."

The Klingon did not respond. Kirk tensed, ready for the next blast. "Chang . . . ?"

"'There's a divinity that shapes our ends,' Kirk, 'rough-hew them how we may . . .'"

A brilliant flare appeared on the viewscreen, and rocketed toward *Enterprise.*

"Incoming," Chekov reported tightly, a split second before the impact rocked the ship. Kirk held on.

Scott's plaintive voice filtered through the intercom grid on the console arm. "She canna take much more of *this,* Captain."

The engineer terminated the channel abruptly, apparently too busy at the moment to do more than register a complaint.

Between clenched teeth, Kirk said, too softly for Chang to hear: "Sulu, where the hell are you?"

"'And this above all,' Kirk," Chang intoned silkily. "'To thine own self be true.'"

*Enterprise* reeled again.

Well inside Klingon space, *Excelsior* shuddered as though trying to shake herself apart. Sulu relaxed his jaw as much as possible under the circumstances, to keep his teeth from chattering as the conn vibrated beneath him.

*Excelsior*'s engineer had just finished registering a complaint via the intercom, in a tone that—though she was half Ukrainian, half Bengali, with an accent that, to Sulu's ears, defied categorization and was the farthest possible from Scottish—reminded Sulu strongly of Montgomery Scott and his poor bairns.

Sulu thanked her, then terminated the conversation and turned to his helmsman.

"In range?"

"Not yet, Captain," Lojur replied, his dark eyes focused on the screen.

"Come on, come on!" Sulu cried. Kirk and the others had made it to Khitomer minutes before; every second of delay made it more likely that *Excelsior* would arrive to find *Enterprise* a smoking burned-out hull and the peace conference in shambles. "Increase speed to—"

Lojur swiveled in alarm. "She'll fly apart!"

"Fly her apart, then!" Sulu ordered.

Lojur's eyes widened with fear as he complied.

Doing his best to appear impassive and calm, Admiral Cartwright watched as the Klingon assassin moved skillfully through the crowd. The audience listened politely as Chancellor Azetbur spoke.

". . . Many people speculated about my father's motives." Azetbur laid a strong, delicate hand on the lectern. "There were those who said he was an idealist, driven by visionary notions. Others said he had no choice, that he was a pragmatic technocrat, making the best of a devastating situation."

She paused to raise her eyes and look beyond the crowd at some far distant, invisible sight. "Great men are seldom good men. The truth is, my father was both: a pragmatist and an idealist. If Praxis had not exploded, quite possibly his idealism would not have found expression. Nor would mine.

"We are a proud race. We are here because we intend to go on being proud." Her expression grew grim. "If we cannot make war . . . we will make peace. . . ."

Cartwright listened, as enthralled as the rest of the crowd by Azetbur's charismatic presence. He had nothing against her personally; in fact, she was actually quite attractive, in a vulgar Klingon sort of way. Certainly she possessed a certain dignity—a regalness—that most of them lacked.

It was almost a pity to have to watch her die; but then, it was all for the best.

Cartwright shifted in his chair to watch as the Klingon moved into position.

Jim Kirk watched as, on the bridge viewscreen, another photon torpedo arced toward them.

"Ahead full impulse!" he shouted at Chekov.

*Enterprise* sailed out of the torpedo's range with less than a millisecond to spare.

Kirk allowed himself a rueful smile, but did not relax. Still no sign of *Excelsior;* maybe Sulu's vessel had been sighted and destroyed once it arrived inside Klingon space—but, knowing the ship and her captain, Jim doubted it.

Chang's voice seemed to echo off the bulkheads; Jim could hear the sardonic smile in it. "'After her . . . poor thing. If you have tears, prepare to shed them now.'"

His tactic of leading the Klingon ship on a chase had bought them a little time—but only a little. Chang's vessel was no doubt in full pursuit, and they had only seconds. Desperate, Kirk turned to Uhura as Chang declaimed on the intercom: "How long will a man lie in space ere he rot?"

"Keep him talking," Spock murmured.

But Uhura shook her head. "They're moving too much to get a fix on."

"'Our revels are now ended,' Kirk."

Kirk frowned up at his invisible enemy.

"What about heat?" Uhura asked, still trying.

"Not from any real distance," the captain said. "She won't show up on *any* type of scan."

"Too bad we can't smell her," McCoy sighed.

Chekov half swiveled to join the conversation, his expression one of glum resignation. "In space, no one can hear you sweat."

Chang's dramatic delivery continued to filter through the main intercom. As aggravating as it was, Kirk decided the Klingon would have made a passable Shakespearean actor.

"'Whether 'tis nobler in the mind to suffer the slings and arrows of outrageous fortune, or to take up arms against a sea of troubles . . .'"

"A pity starships were never equipped with

bloodhounds," Kirk muttered—then grabbed the conn arm as another torpedo slammed into *Enterprise*.

Steam hissed from the ceiling as the ventilation and humidifier sealants gave way. The captain glanced up at them as he pulled himself back up into his chair, knowing that the life-support systems would be next.

Spock continued the conversation without missing a beat. "I do not believe Starfleet could have envisioned our current predicament."

Uhura twisted her lip skeptically at him. "Maybe we should write them a letter?"

"Better postdate it," Scott said from Engineering, his voice filtering through Uhura's board.

The ship reeled again, harder hit.

Kirk managed to stay in his seat this time. Through it all, he watched Spock. Bent over his viewer, the Vulcan frowned, narrowing his eyes in a thoughtful expression the captain knew very well.

Inspiration. Perhaps Spock had stumbled on an answer. . . .

"'Hath not a Klingon hands, organs . . . affections, passions?'" Chang intoned. "'Tickle us, do we not laugh; prick us, do we not bleed—and wrong us, shall we not revenge?'"

"Captain," Spock said. "Sensors reveal faint traces of plasma."

Kirk turned toward his first officer; Bones caught the Vulcan's expression as well, and leaned forward to listen hopefully.

"Under impulse power," Spock told them

quietly—too quietly for those aboard the Klingon vessel to hear, "she expends fuel like any other ship. We call it plasma. I do not know its Klingon name, but by any designation, it is merely ionized gas. The tremendous power drain caused by simultaneous use of the cloaking device and the weapons systems cannot be without cost. Perhaps they must reduce cloaking power shortly before firing—"

"Which would explain the traces of plasma," Kirk finished.

"Precisely. They may be unable to completely cloak the exhaust products of their impulse engines. But accurate targeting will prove difficult."

Kirk did not quite smile. "The portable equipment in the science lab, for atmospheric analysis . . ."

Spock nodded. The doctor's eyes widened as he looked from the Vulcan to the captain and back.

"That's it, then," McCoy said cheerfully. "Pretty delicate work, though, and Scotty's tied up in Engineering right now." He started for the lift. "I'm going to perform surgery on a torpedo. You never know . . ."

Spock glanced at the captain and, after receiving a nod, accompanied McCoy. "You may need assistance, Doctor."

As the lift doors snapped open, McCoy gave the Vulcan a sly glance. "Fascinating . . ."

They entered the lift just as the ship shuddered, struck again.

Kirk stared at the viewscreen with renewed hope. If *Enterprise* could only withstand the pounding, there was a chance . . . "Mr. Chekov, slow down. Take us forward, thrusters only, one-quarter impulse power."

"Aye, sir," Chekov replied. "Thrusters . . ."

For the first time in his life, as he raced alongside Spock toward the science lab, McCoy was beginning to understand the exhilaration Jim Kirk felt in life-threatening circumstances.

Normally the doctor would have been flat-out terrified—too much so to have been of much use—despite the number of times he'd faced death. But now he found himself invigorated, actually looking forward to the chance to beat the odds, to have a hand in saving the ship.

Maybe, he decided, it was because this was his last chance.

Ridiculous, of course. He'd been looking forward to retirement, to all that free time to use as *he* pleased. On Rura Penthe, where he had thought himself a goner for sure, the thought of all the time lost with Joanna and his grandchildren had brought tears to his eyes. He was tired of warping around the galaxy, risking his life at Starfleet's whim. . . .

But now, as he looked at Spock beside him, McCoy's eyes stung once again. He and the Vulcan had been through life . . . and death . . . together. They had shared consciousness, and it occurred to the doctor that there was no one else in the universe who knew him so well—not Jim, not even his own daughter.

McCoy blinked and cleared his throat as they entered the science lab. He let the Vulcan locate the equipment. Spock's memory was better, his movements faster; over the years he'd known Spock, the Vulcan had scarcely aged, had not a single silver hair, though McCoy—and even Jim, now—had a respectable amount of gray.

What would it be like for Spock a century from now, dealing with the loss of all of his friends?

*Well, dammit,* McCoy thought as he misted up again, *that's what he gets for hanging around us humans . . .*

Spock found one of the heavy sensors and hoisted it as though it were feather-light, but its bulk made it unwieldy; McCoy took an end and helped balance it, but Spock supported its entire weight.

The doctor's heart pounded with excitement, but he felt no fear at all, only an intense, glad awareness that he was with Spock, aboard the *Enterprise,* making a difference in the universe. He wanted the moment never to end—yet, at the same time, if it ended abruptly in death, then that would somehow be all right, too.

No wonder Jim had once sworn never to give up his ship. . . .

"Spock," McCoy gasped as they half staggered, half ran down the trembling corridor with the bulky sensor, "I know you won't believe this, but . . . in a way, I'm gonna miss this."

The Vulcan glanced at him; for an instant McCoy fancied he perceived something very like nostalgia in Spock's eyes. Then Spock lifted a brow. "I suspect you do not refer to this *specific* situation."

McCoy groaned with fond aggravation. "Bet you wish you'd stood in bed."

The brow arched even higher. "I see no profit in standing in bed, Doctor. Vulcans sleep lying down."

For a moment McCoy didn't follow; and then he realized that the stress had caused him to use an ungrammatical colloquialism, one he hadn't heard since he was a boy. All the kids in his neighborhood had used "stood" to mean "stayed."

*Okay,* he almost snapped, *so I goofed. Do you have to be so damned lit—*

And then he saw the glint in the Vulcan's eye.

"Spock," he said, with dawning amazement, "that was actually *funny.*"

"We *do* sleep lying down," Spock admitted, his expression perfectly deadpan, but the glimmer of humor was unmistakable.

The corridor pitched wildly to one side. The sensor's weight suddenly shifted toward McCoy, nearly knocking him off his feet.

Chang's voice thundered over the central intercom: "'I am constant as the northern star . . .'"

"I'd give real money," McCoy said bitterly, as Spock adjusted the sensor, allowing him to regain his balance, "if he'd shut up."

\* \* \*

Kirk listened grimly as Scott's voice filtered through the intercom: "Captain, she's packing quite a wallop. Shields weakening."

"Damage report," Kirk said, keeping his eyes on the viewscreen.

"Primary hull scarred," Uhura reported, her voice even. "Hull breach likely if—"

She broke off suddenly; Kirk heard the broad smile in her voice without seeing it. He was too busy smiling himself at the sight on the screen.

"Captain, message from Captain Sulu: 'The cavalry's here!'"

As *Excelsior,* sleek and beautiful, loomed on the bridge viewscreen, Chang's voice filtered through the intercom once more: "So . . . 'The game's afoot.'"

On the visual, a torpedo streaked toward *Excelsior* and exploded harmlessly against her shields.

"'Cry havoc! and let slip the dogs of war.'"

Kirk said a silent prayer of thanks to Sulu; aloud he ordered: "Hold us steady, Mr. Scott. Ready to fire . . ." He punched another control. "Bones . . . ?"

As the torpedo bay trembled with the impact of the last hit, Spock calibrated the ionic sensor while McCoy frantically drilled an opening in a torpedo's nose.

"Bones . . ." Kirk's voice filtered overhead. "Where's my torpedo?"

"Me and my big mouth," McCoy muttered.

Spock completed his work and looked up, noting

that the doctor's initial steadiness had deserted him; McCoy was on the verge of producing a hole capable of accommodating the sensor, but anxiety made him fumble.

Spock addressed him in what he hoped was a reassuring tone. "Calm yourself, Doctor. The operation is almost complete."

McCoy glanced up, almost smiled, nodded. Within seconds he had produced an adequate opening. Spock lifted the sensor and allowed the doctor to guide it into the opening.

Curious, that he worked so well with this human, understood him better than he had another Vulcan.

In one sense, Valeris's twisted philosophy had been logical. He, Spock, was working now to destroy a Klingon, just as Valeris had done. He was killing in order to bring about peace.

But he was destroying the destroyers. She had killed in order to perpetuate war; he would kill in order to perpetuate peace.

He did not need to ask himself which was the more logical.

McCoy tightened the sensor into place with a final twist and looked up, radiant with accomplishment. "Thank you, nurse. Jim, she's ready! Lock and load!"

He and Spock leapt out of the way as the torpedo started forward down the lift. McCoy sighed. "Pity we're retiring just as I was starting to understand you, Spock."

Spock allowed himself a small internal smile. "We *were* beginning to hit our . . ."

The impact of the next explosion hurled them both to the deck.

On the bridge, Jim Kirk was flung from his chair. He scrambled back to his feet, not feeling the bruises, knowing only that this hit had been the worst—which meant *Enterprise*'s shields had collapsed.

And if that had happened . . .

"Uhura—" he gasped, steadying himself against the conn as he turned toward Communications.

For a moment her chair remained empty. And then he saw a slender dark hand reach up and grip the edge of the seat.

Kirk stumbled past recovering crew members and pulled her up into the chair. She took in a deep breath and nodded her thanks.

"Captain . . ." Chekov said, as Kirk hurried back to the conn. The helmsman was already back at his station, answering the question on Kirk's lips. His tone held an air of doom. "Shields have buckled, sir."

Kirk didn't waste a second. "Fire!"

Chekov pressed the control before the captain finished forming the word.

On the visual before them, a torpedo—this one truly from the *Enterprise*—flared. Kirk held his breath and watched as it took a looping, hesitant trajectory. No way to know until the very last second if the damn thing worked. . . .

\* \* \*

Aboard *Dakronh,* Chang smiled at the *Enterprise*'s feeble attempt to fire blindly. She was no threat. Indeed, he saw no reason to waste the power necessary to raise *Dakronh*'s shields. If he had any concerns at all, they related to this new vessel, the *Excelsior,* which had come to aid Kirk. *Excelsior* might be faster, her shields stronger, but Chang knew she could never outlast *Dakronh.* All that was needed was patience, and a modicum of cunning.

Chang had both.

He also felt a growing admiration for these humans who banded together against hopeless odds. Certainly he could not fault the captain of *Excelsior* for coming to a former commander's aid, especially in such dangerous circumstances. Nor could he fault Kirk for his tenacity, his little tricks to buy time—like this misguided torpedo launch. These acts were worthy of Klingon warriors.

And so Chang did not hurry to destroy them; instead, he allowed them to savor the battle, as he did. And when the torpedo began its circling pyrotechnic antics, Chang chuckled low under his breath. Kirk was a most entertaining adversary.

The torpedo executed a final loop, then steadied itself and headed in *Dakronh*'s direction.

Chang raised a brow and gave a short bray of disbelief. Mere chance, that it came this way; *Dakronh* was undetectable. Soon the weapon would go back to its erratic circling. . . .

The gunner turned excitedly to his commander. "General, it's headed straight for us!"

"Then move out of its way," Chang ordered with

an air of impatience, though his heartbeat quickened. "Impulse power."

The helmsman complied; the gunner sighed with audible relief as *Dakronh* neatly sidestepped the oncoming warhead.

The torpedo paused. Circled once more. Then slowly turned and pursued *Dakronh.*

Chang stared in disbelief.

"General, it follows!" the gunner cried.

"'. . . or *not* to be,'" Chang whispered, fascinated, his monocular gaze focused on the impossible sight on the viewscreen.

The words sealed his death warrant. By the time he opened his mouth to issue the command to raise shields, it was too late.

With exultation, Sulu watched as *Enterprise* scored a direct hit. On *Excelsior*'s bridge visual, the Bird of Prey spun, illuminated by firelight, spewing debris as she struggled to regain her position.

"Aim for the center of that explosion and fire!" Sulu ordered. In the back of his mind, he was stunned by the Klingon commander's hubris; the Bird had never even attempted to raise shields.

"Shields up!" Chang screamed, as *Dakronh* reeled from a second crippling blow. The helmsman cried out, raising his hands as his console rained sparks; acrid, throat-closing smoke filled the bridge.

"Shields critically damaged!" the gunner shouted above the chaos. "They won't hold."

"Are we still cloaked? Can we move?"

"Yes. We have some impulse power."

Chang squinted a tearing eye at the viewer just in time to see *Enterprise* and *Excelsior* move into position, with *Dakronh* completing the fatal triangle.

He saw no point in railing at fate; and there was no dishonor in being bested by the likes of Kirk. He closed his eye and smiled as the two ships opened fire.

Around him the bridge dissolved into screams and fiery fragments.

Admiral Cartwright's Klingon found his way easily up a back lift to a deserted alcove overlooking the speakers' dais; here, for all except the critical second, he could remain sheltered from the spectators' view.

He sat, opened his valise, and began assembling the weapon that had been designed especially for this event. Security scanners had mistaken its disassembled components for an innocuous datapad; only a visual inspection might prove otherwise. He had passed through the sensors with ease.

Assembled, the phaser was quite lethal, with four times the range and double the accuracy of its standard Fleet-issue counterpart.

The assassin completed his task and lifted the weapon, taking aim at the far wall, then lowered it.

He had never killed before—not one-on-one, where he saw his victims—but he knew the discipline of the service and had served as weapons officer near the Federation-Klingon border. His hands did not tremble even slightly. He had seen friends killed at the enemy's hand, and that was enough.

Below, the audience applauded the end of Azetbur's speech. The assassin stood, raised his weapon, and held the chancellor lingeringly in his sights, then smiled as President Ra-ghoratrei moved into the frame.

When Rear Admiral Smillie joined the two, the assassin slid his finger onto the trigger. Only the slightest pressure was necessary. . . .

Jim Kirk materialized into the Khitomer throng and broke into a dead run toward the central dais where Azetbur, Ra-ghoratrei, and Admiral Smillie stood.

He pushed through the crowd, his back totally vulnerable, half expecting at any second to feel a phaser blast, whether a conspirator's or a security guard's or an outraged Klingon's . . . but there was no time to feel fear, no time to do anything but trust those of his crew who followed.

"Mr. President!" Kirk shouted.

President Ra-ghoratrei started, and stared at him in utter shock—a perfect target, Jim thought. Three powerful people, all at once . . .

He burst past the guards, onto the dais, and knocked Ra-ghoratrei squarely off his feet, aware in the midst of the confusion of two things: the alarm on Azetbur's face, and the searing heat of the phaser blast millimeters above his back.

The room rumbled with sounds of panic and outrage as the spectators tried to flee to safety. Jim looked up at the sound of Admiral Cartwright's outraged voice.

"Arrest those men!"

The crowd thinned to reveal Spock, stepping forward to confront Cartwright. In a tone as icy as Jim had ever heard him use, the Vulcan said, "Arrest yourself, Admiral."

He stood aside to reveal Valeris, pale but composed, hands cuffed together.

McCoy joined the Vulcans to glare angrily at Cartwright. "We've got a full confession."

They started at the sound of phaserfire. Kirk followed the direction of Scott's blast, upward, to a glass-enclosed alcove where a Klingon assassin had apparently been hiding. The assassin cried out, clutching his face, where Scott's fire had caught him, and fell through the glass into the scattering crowd below.

Cartwright, Ambassador Nanclus, and a handful of officers broke into a run, scattering in different directions. Sulu materialized, phaser in hand, in time to head some off. At the other end of the room Bones did his part to stop some—with, Jim noted delightedly, the enthusiastic if overly physical help of Brigadier Kerla.

Ra-ghoratrei and Azetbur were on their feet and flanked by guards. The Federation president still gaped at Kirk with disbelief.

Azetbur's stare was icy. "What is the meaning of this?"

Kirk held out his hands to show he meant no harm, and smiled faintly at the less-than-trustful guards. "It's about the future, Madam Chancellor. Some people think the future means the end of history."

He paused to make eye contact with the Romulan ambassador, Nanclus, now flanked by Federation security personnel. "But we haven't run out of history just yet."

He turned back to Azetbur. "Your father quoted *Hamlet*. He called the future 'the undiscovered country.'" He paused as Spock, with Valeris in tow, joined him.

"I always assumed Hamlet was speaking of death," Spock offered.

Kirk nodded. "Gorkon thought 'the undiscovered country' might mean something else— another kind of life. People can be very frightened of change." He hesitated. "I know I was." He swiveled his head to meet Valeris's gaze. "There's an Old Earth expression: it takes one to know one."

The Vulcan lowered her eyes, unable to look at him; at first Jim thought—though he felt he must be mistaken—there were tears in them.

He faced the chancellor again. "It took your father's death to make me see I was wrong. I came because I wanted to bring his killers to justice . . . and to be sure that his death was not wasted, that the peace conference continue." He lowered his voice. "The Vulcans have an expression: I grieve with you. . . ."

For an instant Azetbur's expression was dark,

unreadable . . . and then it brightened with a slow-dawning radiance. Jim felt he had never seen a face more beautiful—be it Klingon, Vulcan, Romulan, human.

"You've restored my father's faith," Azetbur said softly.

Jim struggled to keep his voice from breaking. "You've restored my son's."

He was not sure who reached out first, Klingon or human. In the end it did not matter. He and Azetbur embraced each other in shared grief and joy, and for a time neither heard the resounding applause.

# Epilogue

AT THE END OF a day's successful negotiations on Khitomer, Azetbur slipped away from her guards, relieved to be rid of them, to fear no longer for her life.

As she hoped, Kerla was in his guest room. He stepped back as she entered, his expression polite; she sensed wariness but no anger in him. He remained by the door as she turned to speak.

"General Chang is dead," she said. "Raghoratrei and I met with Kirk. As best we can determine, Chang conspired with Admiral Cartwright and Ambassador Nanclus, among others, to keep us at war."

"Chang," Kerla repeated softly, staring beyond her as he tried to absorb it. "But he was a warrior, sworn to protect your father. And you."

"He was a liar," Azetbur said. "Not all warriors

are so honorable, Brigadier." At last she understood why she had not been killed: Chang and his conspirators deemed it necessary for her to live long enough to attend the conference. "He arranged for my security, so that the negotiations could continue—and Ra-ghoratrei could be assassinated as well. With both the Federation and the Klingon Empire blaming each other for their leaders' death, war would be inevitable."

Kerla shook his head in disbelief. "Then conspirators aboard *Enterprise* arranged the attack on *Kronos One?*"

"No. Chang arranged the attack, using a new vessel designed to fire when cloaked. He was aboard the vessel, attacking *Enterprise,* when his ship was destroyed along with him." Azetbur paused. "My father's death can be blamed as much on the Empire as on the Romulans and the Federation. We are as much at fault as the others.

"And I am to blame." She lowered her voice. "I listened to Chang. I believed him when he said you were plotting against my father."

Kerla stiffened angrily. "Chang told you—"

She did not let him finish. "When Gorkon died, I feared you were using me as a means of obtaining power—that you wanted me only because you wanted to be the consort of the chancellor. I was wrong." She stepped toward him, placed a hand on his chest, and felt relief when he did not recoil from her. "I should have trusted you. You were right: I regret sending you away."

She felt his hesitation as his relief warred with

anger; and then he spoke softly, his deep voice resonating beneath her fingers.

"Now you know. I hope there can no longer be any question in your heart, Zeta."

In reply, she clasped his wrist and pulled his hand to her face. He smiled, teeth white against his bronze skin, then hesitated.

Azetbur frowned. "What is wrong?"

Kerla released a wistful sigh. "Did you say there was only one of those vessels? What an incredible weapon it would make for the Empire."

She started, indignant, and dropped his hand, on the verge of scolding him before his laughter stopped her.

"For the sake of negotiating, of course. You can trust me, Zeta. But do not ever make the mistake of trusting the Federation or the Romulans."

"I suppose," Azetbur told him, "I need a warrior to advise me."

"I can advise you, my lady, in far more interesting things besides politics." Smiling, he drew her to him.

Safe and unchallenged, *Enterprise* hovered above Khitomer.

On the bridge, Jim Kirk could not bring himself to give the order to return home—not quite yet, not when all his friends were here, together. He gazed in turn at each one—Spock, McCoy, Uhura, Chekov, Scotty—trying to commit the scene to memory.

Only one seat remained inappropriately vacant

—the one at the helm, where Sulu and, later, Valeris had sat.

Uhura sat with her back to her station, facing the empty chair next to Chekov. Its most recent occupant was now cooling her heels down in the brig; when they arrived back on Earth, Valeris would be tried and court-martialed along with her co-conspirators.

In consideration of the help the *Enterprise* had provided in exposing the scheme, the charges against Spock and the crew for refusing to obey direct orders and for violating Klingon space had been dropped, as had the charges against *Excelsior*'s captain and crew.

The same subspace message had relayed news of Carol Marcus's recovery. The distance between Khitomer and Starbase Twenty-three was too great to permit direct communication, but in a matter of hours, Jim knew he would speak to Carol again.

Behind him, Uhura sighed gustily. Jim swiveled in his chair to see her sitting, one arm propped against her console.

"They might as well arrest me, too," she said glumly. "I felt like Lieutenant Valeris."

*We all did,* Kirk thought, *except Spock.* He looked over at his first officer, keenly aware of the hurt the Vulcan must have experienced. But Spock's expression remained impassive; he arched a slanted brow in Uhura's direction. "But *you* did not join a conspiracy," Spock told her.

From his traditional spot at the captain's left,

McCoy joined the exchange. "They don't arrest people for having feelings."

"If they did," Chekov said, swiveling toward them, "we'd all have to turn ourselves in." He paused to eye Kirk meaningfully. "How *can* we rely on them?"

A difficult question. Who could say, Kirk wondered, how many more Changs existed within the Klingon Empire and whether the Gorkons and Azetburs could subdue them?

At the same time, Jim saw what Spock had known all along: peace was the only logical choice.

"All I can say, Mr. Chekov, is"—Kirk hesitated long enough to catch Spock's gaze—"the only way to find out if a man is trustworthy—"

". . . is to trust him," Spock finished, and suddenly, amazingly, graced Jim with the faintest ghost of a smile.

"Captain Kirk?" Sulu's image appeared on the main visual.

Kirk turned toward it, a grin still on his lips. "Kirk here." He studied Sulu fondly; at last he was surrounded by all of his dearest friends. "As much as to the crew of *Enterprise*, I owe you my thanks, Captain Sulu."

Sulu's broad, placid features brightened in a smile. "Nice to see you in action one more time, Captain Kirk. Take care."

On the viewscreen, his image faded into that of *Excelsior*, sleek and stunning as she hurtled into warp speed and out of sight.

With affection and more than a little sense of loss, Jim watched him go.

"By God," McCoy breathed, staring transfixed at the screen, "that's a *big* ship."

Nearby, at his station, Scott—who in years past had ribbed Sulu mercilessly about *Excelsior* being a collection of useless gadgetry—wore an expression of frank admiration. "Not so big as her captain, I think."

"Time we got under way ourselves, gentlemen." Kirk stretched his sore muscles casually, as if the thought of returning home was not a painful one for him. As desperately as he wanted to see Carol again, he suddenly found it impossible to imagine life without this ship, this crew. "Once again we've saved civilization as we know it."

McCoy released a small, sarcastic sound. "And the good news is, they're not going to prosecute."

"Captain . . ."

The note of alarm in Uhura's voice made him turn around to face her.

"I'm receiving a message from Starfleet Command." She frowned; her tone grew indignant. "We're to return to headquarters at once—to be decommissioned."

Jim stared at her, unwilling to issue the order, aware of the sudden, tense silence, of the eyes focused on him.

At last Spock spoke—clearly, precisely. "Were I fully human . . . I would tell them to go to hell."

McCoy jerked his head sharply in the Vulcan's direction to favor him with an amazed but grateful grin; like the others, Jim found it impossible not to smile.

In a tone that unmistakably reflected Spock's sentiment, Chekov turned to Kirk and asked: "Course heading, Captain?"

Jim gazed at the viewscreen, into starry space. "Second star to the right and straight on till morning."

Serene and unchallenged, *Enterprise* set sail through Klingon space.

Captain's log, USS *Enterprise,* Stardate 9529.1:
This is the final cruise of the Starship *Enterprise* under my command. This ship and her history will shortly become the care of a new generation. To them and their posterity will we commit our future. They will continue the voyages we have begun and journey to all the undiscovered countries, boldly going where no man . . . where no one has gone before.

J. M. Dillard is the author of the Pocket STAR TREK novels *Mindshadow, Demons, Bloodthirst* and *The Lost Years*, as well as the novelizations of *War of the Worlds: The Resurrection* and *Star Trek V: The Final Frontier*. She has also written a psychological thriller, *Specters*.

The First Star Trek: The Next Generation
Hardcover Novel!

# STAR TREK®
## THE NEXT GENERATION™

# REUNION

## Michael Jan Friedman

Captain Pickard's
past and present
collide on board the
U.S.S. *Enterprise*™

POCKET
BOOKS

Available in Hardcover
from Pocket Books

444-01